MONTANA NOIR

EDITED BY
JAMES GRADY & KEIR GRAFF

BROOKLYN, NEW YORK, USA
BALLYDEHOB, CO. CORK, IRELAND

This collection comprises works of fiction. All names, characters, places, and incidents are the product of the authors' imaginations. Any resemblance to real events or persons, living or dead, is entirely coincidental.

Published by Akashic Books
©2017 Akashic Books

"Motherlode" by Thomas McGuane originally appeared in the September 8, 2014 issue of the *New Yorker*. ©2014 Thomas McGuane. Reprinted by permission of the author.

Series concept by Tim McLoughlin and Johnny Temple
Montana map by Sohrab Habibion

ISBN: 978-1-61775-579-8
Library of Congress Control Number: 2017936114

All rights reserved
First printing

Akashic Books
Brooklyn, New York, USA
Ballydehob, Co. Cork, Ireland
Twitter: @AkashicBooks
Facebook: AkashicBooks
E-mail: info@akashicbooks.com
Website: www.akashicbooks.com

ALSO IN THE AKASHIC NOIR SERIES

ATLANTA NOIR, edited by TAYARI JONES
BALTIMORE NOIR, edited by LAURA LIPPMAN
BARCELONA NOIR (SPAIN), edited by ADRIANA V. LÓPEZ & CARMEN OSPINA
BEIRUT NOIR (LEBANON), edited by IMAN HUMAYDAN
BELFAST NOIR (NORTHERN IRELAND), edited by ADRIAN McKINTY & STUART NEVILLE
BOSTON NOIR, edited by DENNIS LEHANE
BOSTON NOIR 2: THE CLASSICS, edited by DENNIS LEHANE, JAIME CLARKE & MARY COTTON
BRONX NOIR, edited by S.J. ROZAN
BROOKLYN NOIR, edited by TIM McLOUGHLIN
BROOKLYN NOIR 2: THE CLASSICS, edited by TIM McLOUGHLIN
BROOKLYN NOIR 3: NOTHING BUT THE TRUTH, edited by TIM McLOUGHLIN & THOMAS ADCOCK
BRUSSELS NOIR (BELGIUM), edited by MICHEL DUFRANNE
BUFFALO NOIR, edited by ED PARK & BRIGID HUGHES
CAPE COD NOIR, edited by DAVID L. ULIN
CHICAGO NOIR, edited by NEAL POLLACK
CHICAGO NOIR: THE CLASSICS, edited by JOE MENO
COPENHAGEN NOIR (DENMARK), edited by BO TAO MICHAËLIS
DALLAS NOIR, edited by DAVID HALE SMITH
D.C. NOIR, edited by GEORGE PELECANOS
D.C. NOIR 2: THE CLASSICS, edited by GEORGE PELECANOS
DELHI NOIR (INDIA), edited by HIRSH SAWHNEY
DETROIT NOIR, edited by E.J. OLSEN & JOHN C. HOCKING
DUBLIN NOIR (IRELAND), edited by KEN BRUEN
HAITI NOIR, edited by EDWIDGE DANTICAT
HAITI NOIR 2: THE CLASSICS, edited by EDWIDGE DANTICAT
HAVANA NOIR (CUBA), edited by ACHY OBEJAS
HELSINKI NOIR (FINLAND), edited by JAMES THOMPSON
INDIAN COUNTRY NOIR, edited by SARAH CORTEZ & LIZ MARTÍNEZ
ISTANBUL NOIR (TURKEY), edited by MUSTAFA ZIYALAN & AMY SPANGLER
KANSAS CITY NOIR, edited by STEVE PAUL
KINGSTON NOIR (JAMAICA), edited by COLIN CHANNER
LAS VEGAS NOIR, edited by JARRET KEENE & TODD JAMES PIERCE
LONDON NOIR (ENGLAND), edited by CATHI UNSWORTH
LONE STAR NOIR, edited by BOBBY BYRD & JOHNNY BYRD
LONG ISLAND NOIR, edited by KAYLIE JONES
LOS ANGELES NOIR, edited by DENISE HAMILTON
LOS ANGELES NOIR 2: THE CLASSICS, edited by DENISE HAMILTON
MANHATTAN NOIR, edited by LAWRENCE BLOCK
MANHATTAN NOIR 2: THE CLASSICS, edited by LAWRENCE BLOCK
MANILA NOIR (PHILIPPINES), edited by JESSICA HAGEDORN
MARSEILLE NOIR (FRANCE), edited by CÉDRIC FABRE
MEMPHIS NOIR, edited by LAUREEN P. CANTWELL & LEONARD GILL
MEXICO CITY NOIR (MEXICO), edited by PACO I. TAIBO II
MIAMI NOIR, edited by LES STANDIFORD
MISSISSIPPI NOIR, edited by TOM FRANKLIN
MOSCOW NOIR (RUSSIA), edited by NATALIA SMIRNOVA & JULIA GOUMEN
MUMBAI NOIR (INDIA), edited by ALTAF TYREWALA
NEW HAVEN NOIR, edited by AMY BLOOM
NEW JERSEY NOIR, edited by JOYCE CAROL OATES
NEW ORLEANS NOIR, edited by JULIE SMITH
NEW ORLEANS NOIR: THE CLASSICS, edited by JULIE SMITH

OAKLAND NOIR, edited by JERRY THOMPSON & EDDIE MULLER
ORANGE COUNTY NOIR, edited by GARY PHILLIPS
PARIS NOIR (FRANCE), edited by AURÉLIEN MASSON
PHILADELPHIA NOIR, edited by CARLIN ROMANO
PHOENIX NOIR, edited by PATRICK MILLIKIN
PITTSBURGH NOIR, edited by KATHLEEN GEORGE
PORTLAND NOIR, edited by KEVIN SAMPSELL
PRISON NOIR, edited by JOYCE CAROL OATES
PROVIDENCE NOIR, edited by ANN HOOD
QUEENS NOIR, edited by ROBERT KNIGHTLY
RICHMOND NOIR, edited by ANDREW BLOSSOM, BRIAN CASTLEBERRY & TOM DE HAVEN
RIO NOIR (BRAZIL), edited by TONY BELLOTTO
ROME NOIR (ITALY), edited by CHIARA STANGALINO & MAXIM JAKUBOWSKI
SAN DIEGO NOIR, edited by MARYELIZABETH HART
SAN FRANCISCO NOIR, edited by PETER MARAVELIS
SAN FRANCISCO NOIR 2: THE CLASSICS, edited by PETER MARAVELIS
SAN JUAN NOIR (PUERTO RICO), edited by MAYRA SANTOS-FEBRES
SEATTLE NOIR, edited by CURT COLBERT
SINGAPORE NOIR, edited by CHERYL LU-LIEN TAN
STATEN ISLAND NOIR, edited by PATRICIA SMITH
ST. LOUIS NOIR, edited by SCOTT PHILLIPS
STOCKHOLM NOIR (SWEDEN), edited by NATHAN LARSON & CARL-MICHAEL EDENBORG
ST. PETERSBURG NOIR (RUSSIA), edited by NATALIA SMIRNOVA & JULIA GOUMEN
TEHRAN NOIR (IRAN), edited by SALAR ABDOH
TEL AVIV NOIR (ISRAEL), edited by ETGAR KERET & ASSAF GAVRON
TORONTO NOIR (CANADA), edited by JANINE ARMIN & NATHANIEL G. MOORE
TRINIDAD NOIR (TRINIDAD & TOBAGO), edited by LISA ALLEN-AGOSTINI & JEANNE MASON
TRINIDAD NOIR: THE CLASSICS (TRINIDAD & TOBAGO), edited by EARL LOVELACE & ROBERT ANTONI
TWIN CITIES NOIR, edited by JULIE SCHAPER & STEVEN HORWITZ
USA NOIR, edited by JOHNNY TEMPLE
VENICE NOIR (ITALY), edited by MAXIM JAKUBOWSKI
WALL STREET NOIR, edited by PETER SPIEGELMAN
ZAGREB NOIR (CROATIA), edited by IVAN SRŠEN

FORTHCOMING

ACCRA NOIR (GHANA), edited by NANA-AMA DANQUAH
ADDIS ABABA NOIR (ETHIOPIA), edited by MAAZA MENGISTE
AMSTERDAM NOIR (HOLLAND), edited by RENÉ APPEL & JOSH PACHTER
BAGHDAD NOIR (IRAQ), edited by SAMUEL SHIMON
BERLIN NOIR (GERMANY), edited by THOMAS WOERTCHE
BOGOTÁ NOIR (COLOMBIA), edited by ANDREA MONTEJO
BUENOS AIRES NOIR (ARGENTINA), edited by ERNESTO MALLO
HOUSTON NOIR, edited by GWENDOLYN ZEPEDA
JERUSALEM NOIR, edited by DROR MISHANI
LAGOS NOIR (NIGERIA), edited by CHRIS ABANI
MARRAKECH NOIR (MOROCCO), edited by YASSIN ADNAN
MONTREAL NOIR (CANADA), edited by JOHN McFETRIDGE & JACQUES FILIPPI
PRAGUE NOIR (CZECH REPUBLIC), edited by PAVEL MANDYS
SANTA CRUZ NOIR, edited by SUSIE BRIGHT
SÃO PAULO NOIR (BRAZIL), edited by TONY BELLOTTO
SYDNEY NOIR (AUSTRALIA), edited by JOHN DALE
VANCOUVER NOIR (CANADA), edited by SAM WIEBE

ALBERTA, CANADA

GLACIER NATIONAL PARK

SHELBY

FARM COUNTRY

FLATHEAD NATIONAL FOREST

POLSON

GREAT FALLS

MISSOULA

LEWIS & CLARK NATIONAL FOREST

LOLO

HELENA

BUTTE

IDAHO

YELLOWSTONE NATIONAL PARK

SASKATCHEWAN, CANADA

HAVRE

MONTANA

GLASGOW

JORDAN

GLENDIVE

NORTH DAKOTA

BILLINGS HEIGHTS

DOWNTOWN BILLINGS

SOUTH DAKOTA

WYOMING

BIGHORN NATIONAL FOREST

TABLE OF CONTENTS

INTRODUCTION
NOIR'S LAST BEST PLACE

When people learn we're from Montana, we can almost predict what they'll say: *I've heard it's so beautiful. Why would you ever want to leave?*

One stock reply, always good for a laugh at a party, is, *You can't eat the scenery.* Which also saves us from having to admit that, as young men, neither of us could wait to get out.

With some very notable exceptions, most of the Montana writers we've known came there from some other place. Those of us who were born there often leave. We leave for the same reasons people leave their hometowns all over the world—to see what else is out there. For both of us, leaving was the very thing that made it possible to have careers in writing and publishing.

Of course, having left, all we ever do is think about going back. Editing this anthology has been a wonderful way to return to our home state, with everything that's good and bad about it.

Montana is indeed beautiful. It can be as picture-postcard perfect as you imagine, with the grandeur of legendary mountains rising in the famously clean and blue Big Sky, rivers crashing through piney canyons, and prairies rolling like a golden sea.

It's the kind of beauty that makes us think, when we're visiting, like every other tourist: *I should live here.*

But living in beautiful places can be just as hard as living in the most soul-crushing cities.

Nobody—well, almost nobody—lives in Glacier Park. Or the Bob Marshall Wilderness. They live in the towns nearby, trying to figure out how to afford all that beauty. Even those who live to paddle, fish, and hunt spend far more hours at work, whether their incomes derive from seasonal trade, state jobs, the Internet-gig economy, or what remains of the extractive industries. Some of them are noble cowboys who'd give you the shirt off their backs. Others work and worry, scheme and dream, drink and take drugs, and sometimes lie, cheat, and steal. Or kill.

Just like everywhere else.

For those of us who have its soil in our blood and its sky in our soul, Montana is more than its clichés. For us, Montana is as real as our true loves, and under its sky are human sagas in a brutal noir world where easy choices are hard to come by.

This has long been reflected in the fiction of Montana, which runs like a river through the culture of America.

Dashiell Hammett, the global dark knight of noir, worked as a Pinkerton detective in Butte during the copper king and union wars that rocked the mining city with the "richest hill on earth," and fictionalized it as "Personville" for his revolutionary first novel, *Red Harvest*.

Feisty Montana newspaper reporter Dorothy Johnson channeled noir in her fiction to produce award-winning novels and stories whose Hollywood adaptations brought realism to the same screens that shaped our cowboys-and-Indians clichés: *The Hanging Tree*, *A Man Called Horse*, *The Man Who Shot Liberty Valance*.

The great A.B. Guthrie, a Pulitzer Prize winner and an Academy Award–nominated screenwriter for *Shane*, captured Montana's small-town, cowboy-era culture with a perfect noir lens in his classic novel *These Thousand Hills*.

Starting in the early 1970s, the University of Montana in Missoula incubated a crew of noir prose-slingers, including internationally acclaimed authors James Lee Burke, a quiet and kind man who gave the world the introspective private eye Dave Robicheaux, and legendary wild man James Crumley, whose *The Last Good Kiss* boasts as fine an opening page for a novel as you'll find. That landmark novel drew on the life and works of Crumley and Burke's UM colleague, the wonderful poet Richard Hugo, for its title and central character. Hugo also wrote a crime novel, *Death and the Good Life*, and his poetry protégé, James Welch, who grew up in the Blackfeet and Gros Ventre Indian tribes' cultures of his parents, let noir swirl through novels like *Winter in the Blood* and *The Indian Lawyer*.

Norman Maclean, perhaps Montana's most acclaimed twentieth-century author, used fine nonfiction prose to reveal the beauty and tragedy of Montana's noir world with two unforgettable works: *Young Men and Fire* and *A River Runs Through It*.

Now you hold this, the first-ever anthology of Montana noir short stories.

Howdy.

This anthology is a road trip through the dreams and disasters of the true Montana, stories written by authors with Montana in their blood, tales that circle you around the state through its cities and small towns. These are twenty-first-century authors writing timeless sagas of choice, crime, and consequences. Besides traveling back in time to the birth of Montana's modern era in 1972, your trip will include stops on the state's concrete and forest floors. You'll meet students and strippers, cops and cons, druggies and dreamers, cold-eyed killers and caught-in-their-gunsights screwed-up souls.

But mostly, through all our fiction here, you'll meet quiet

heroes and see the noir side of life that makes our Montana as real as it is mythic.

No doubt the state's beauty will still make the very idea of *Montana Noir* seem incongruous to some. Noir is black-and-white. Streets and alleys. Flashing neon lighting a rain-streaked window. But while noir was definitely an urban invention, it knows no boundaries. Noir is struggle. It's doing the wrong thing for the right reasons. It's being trapped. It's hubris. It's being defeated yet going on. Sometimes it's being defeated and not going on.

That's life everywhere.

This is our Montana.

James Grady & Keir Graff
June 2017

Acknowledgments

Our posse of authors couldn't have come together without dozens of helpful people, chief among them François Guérif, the French literary icon, and Kim Anderson, the former director of the Montana Festival of the Book (now the Montana Book Festival), without whom key contributors would not have signed on to this project.

Early support from Barbara Theroux, Ariana Paliobagis, and Bob Harrison was instrumental in ensuring you could hold this book in your hands.

Lisa Cordingley, Bill Johnston, Lois Welch, Amy Guthrie Sakariassen, Martha Elizabeth, Neil McMahon, and Deirdre McNamer deserve special mention for advice, encouragement, and behind-the-scenes assistance.

Keir would like to thank Bill Ott, whose definition of noir is hard and true (if not always easy for authors to live up to).

We're indebted to Bonnie Goldstein and Marya Graff, our eternally patient better halves, for their support during this sometimes challenging journey.

Especially deserving of our gratitude is Akashic's brilliant publisher Johnny Temple, whose vision for a literary franchise of noir anthologies revolutionized publishing with nearly a hundred volumes and counting. We're honored and proud to be part of that great cultural triumph.

But mostly, thank *you* for coming on this ride with us.

PART I

COPPER POWER

RED, WHITE, AND BUTTE
BY DAVID ABRAMS
Butte

Marlowe was dead and that was fine by me. The two of us had gone off to war together, but only one had returned with his jaw still attached to his face, able to describe what he'd seen. Which was also fine by me since I was the one telling the war stories.

Marlowe lay in pieces in a coffin at Duggan-Dolan Mortuary in Butte, waiting for the official start of his hero's welcome: a parade, lying in state for two days under the courthouse rotunda, and a picnic complete with a huckleberry pie bake-off, a three-legged race, and earnest old men in combat ball caps passing around a boot to raise money for a new veterans home. Next to Evel Knievel Days, everyone said it would be the highlight of Butte's summer.

The rest of us got a limp salute from our commander and a three-inch stack of discharge paperwork, but Marlowe would have a big to-do—the kind of fuss showered on the dead after they can no longer appreciate it: red-white-and-blue bunting along Granite Street, his widow the grand marshal of the parade, Republican senators inserting Marlowe into their campaign speeches, and Democrats a little more reservedly acknowledging the Butte native's service and the terrible cost of war.

Montanans love their hometown heroes. Dead or living, soldiers like Marlowe are praised with words that bloom like fireworks and boom like parade drums from their speakers' throats.

But I knew the truth: Private Chandler Marlowe had died a coward in Iraq. Just before the bomb did its work, Rayburn told me, he'd seen the damp piss stain on Marlowe's BDUs and the terrified crumple on his face when he heard the click under the sole of his boot. Those are Rayburn's words—*terrified crumple*—not mine.

Rayburn and the rest of the squad were just back from Salman Pak, still juiced up by all they'd seen: the blood-scorched crater, the three Iraqis zip-tied and facedown on the sidewalk, Marlowe's lone boot in the middle of the street. Rayburn and the others were upset. Where we came from, Marlowe had the reputation of being as tough as the hard rock walls of a mine. He'd quarterbacked Butte Central all the way to State, despite his daddy's drinking and his uncle's notorious stint at Deer Lodge that ended with the upthrust of a shiv.

That afternoon in Iraq, Rayburn and company punched the marble walls in the old palace where we'd set up our barracks. "One more week!" they cried. "There's one more week left on the clock and then we're out of here. Why wasn't the dumbass more careful and watching where he walked?"

They paced and growled and yelled. "Stupid Marlowe! What was he doing out there anyway? Wasn't this supposed to be his day off?"

Me, I just lay on my cot with the latest issue of *Maxim*—I'd been fondling the Girl Next Door's boobs with my thumb before the interruption—and let the news settle in. Marlowe dead. Me still alive. Funny how it all worked out.

None of the others asked why I'd been back here while Marlowe had been out there on that street and I didn't volunteer an explanation.

After our National Guard unit got to Iraq eleven months earlier, we'd quickly learned that luck, not muscle or willpower, would be what got us through to the other side of the deployment. That "Butte Tough" mentality Marlowe and a few others from the Mining City carried around like a chip on their shoulders lasted two weeks, until the first car bomb took one of us—Noonan, I think it was. After that, none of us were tougher than any other.

Jesus, the things we saw. Wounds the length of a body that blackened the skin. Children flung to the sky by bombs. Men turned inside out. Sights we couldn't unsee. Blood pictures stuck in our heads. The things we'd carry forever.

Now, two weeks after putting the war in my rearview mirror, I was still dealing with it, but at least I had a distraction, a new mission. I was returning to my hometown to get a woman.

A decade before Iraq, I'd left Butte after saying good riddance to a needy, clingy girl who thought three fucks and a wake-up were grounds for marriage. For a few years, I drifted here and there around the state picking up odd jobs before deciding to join the Montana National Guard. I'd been putting it off since 9/11, but after I got fired from a hateful job I was about to quit anyway, I figured it was time to grab patriotism by the balls. I landed in a unit full of computer nerds, gun enthusiasts, overweight fathers too devoted to their daughters, and a boisterous cluster of Butte natives, Marlowe the loudest of them all.

I didn't recognize the younger ones—I was well out of high school before they got their first pimples—but Marlowe and I had some history. I had a year and thirty pounds on him, but that skinny little bitch had still managed to kick my ass on the football field. Every practice we came at each other like rutting bull elk. I hit hard and broke his nose—head-butting all the way through his helmet—but a month later, he dislocated my jaw. Ever since that day, when I'm really pissed off, I click when I talk, thanks to Marlowe.

Our state championship year, when the whole city was painted Bulldog purple, Marlowe had his photo on the front of the sports section four times, while I only got two mentions on C3. Butte lifted Marlowe to its shoulders and carried him all the way to a banquet at the Civic Center—a softer prelude to what he was about to get this red-white-and-blue week in June. He was no genius, but he got a full-ride scholarship to Montana State, while I was voted Most Likely to Succeed.

Success to me was getting the hell out of the Mining City three months after graduation. I left it and that whiny cheerleader behind me for good. Or so I thought. Butte, pitted and tunneled to within an inch of its life, was dead to me. But then I joined the Guard and had to deal with Butte Rats like Marlowe, Noonan, and Rayburn, and I realized, with a sinking heart, the gutted city would always be with me.

I kept a low profile, did my work, and weaseled out of invitations for Sunday-night drinks with the other NCOs. I couldn't give two shits about the boys from Butte.

And then came the day in Baghdad when Marlowe got that letter from home and started passing around the photo of his wife.

As I drove down off Homestake Pass at sunset, Butte drowsed under a bloodpool sky. The uptown streets, soaked in red evening light, were empty. I was unsurprised to see little had changed. There were a few more casinos and a new Walgreens, but other than that it was still the same sleepy place. I'd lived here long enough to know that, apart from the nightly drunk-stumble and vomit-cough at the Party Palace, nothing much happened around the old mining town. It was always naptime in Butte.

I came around a downhill bend in the interstate, the view of the city opened up, and there it was: the Berkeley Pit. The gouge of earth glowed orange in the late light. It was the oozing wound of the city, both its pride and shame. Work at the open-pit mine had stopped decades ago when the owners moved on to more mineral-rich pastures down in Chile. Once the underground pumps were shut off at the Butte mine, the pit began to fill with water laced with arsenic, sulfuric acid, and eleven other essential vitamins and minerals. One day, the water would reach the lip of the pit and breech the banks, flooding the downslope homes, drowning them in poison. Until then, the people of Butte went about their business, trying to pretend the pit wasn't there—like a man with an eye patch insisting he could see just fine.

I was back in town for an undetermined amount of time. My job, if I could get it, was Widow Comforter. The usual: nods of sympathetic grief, hand pats, lies about the deceased, a suggestion of drinks at the Silver Dollar, a little snuggle later on. If I could get it.

I planned to get it.

She sat on a rock beside Georgetown Lake: arms behind her, head tilted, breasts tickling the sky, sun washing all the color from her hair. Right away I could tell two things: she wasn't wearing a bra, and it was cold outside when the photo was taken. At first I thought Marlowe had snipped a photo from a magazine and was trying to pass a supermodel off as his girlfriend—or wife, if he was to be believed.

But then I recognized the waterline of the lake, just downslope from a tavern on the way to Phillipsburg where

I'd had more than a few drinks on more than one occasion. I might have even sat on that same rock myself once, beer-stunned and singing ballads to the wheeling stars.

I didn't get a good look the first time Marlowe passed her around, but when the photo came to me again, I held it longer and gave it a good stare. She was vaguely familiar, but I couldn't place her until Marlowe said, "You don't recognize her, Franklin?"

"I do, but I don't."

"That's Chloe."

"Chloe?"

"Lockmer. Remember?"

Now I did. I grinned and shook my head. Chloe Lockmer, the titless wisp of a girl who ghosted through the halls of Butte Central—a freshman when I was a senior. How had she turned into *this*? This was a grown woman full of sugar and spice and everything vice.

The way she had her head tipped back, sitting on that rock, I took it as an invitation.

I pulled off the interstate at the first Butte exit, drove up Harrison Avenue, and headed straight for the Finlen where I booked a room for a week. I figured I'd get the job done in seven days. If God could do it, why couldn't I? Then again, He never had to deal with zippers on grieving widows' blue jeans.

I needed a little alcohol to loosen the rust on my gears, so I asked the desk clerk for the best place.

"You might try the distillery."

"Distillery? Butte has one of those now?"

"Had it for a couple of years. Their booze is smooth and gets the job done quick."

He wasn't kidding. Two minutes after taking a stool at the

Headframe, I was halfway to numb. Go a year without booze in a combat zone and your tolerance gets pretty low.

I held up my tumbler, looked through the generous two fingers of amber, and ordered another. I asked the girl behind the bar, "What do you put in this?"

"The Neversweat? The blood of virgins and a few drops of Novocaine."

"Funny lady. Don't quit your day job."

"I don't plan on it. Where else could I meet fascinating people like you?" She was wiping the bar with a rag and when she leaned over, there was plenty of agreeable movement inside her T-shirt. I could see all the way to Thursday from where I sat.

"You lived in Butte long?"

"Long enough," she said. "I'm about ready to leave this dump."

"I hear you."

"What about you? Just passing through?"

"Sort of." I was still reluctant to show my Butte roots. Five hours in town and I hadn't seen any familiar faces. Fine by me. "I'm here for the Marlowe Memorial Madness, or whatever the hell they're calling it."

The girl snorted. "Red, White, and Butte Days."

I made a gagging sound.

"Exactly," she said with a laugh. She'd finished wiping, but still hung around at my end of the bar.

"You knew him?"

"Who, the war hero? Never met him. What about you? You a friend of his, or are you just one of those whaddayacallits—Rolling Thunder guys who go around protecting military funerals with baseball bats?"

"Do I look like one of those kind of guys?"

"I guess not," she said. "So, friend of the family?"

"Not really. Like I said, just passing through." I wondered if she noticed how I tap-danced my way around her questions.

A guy with a heavy, skunk-smelling coat came in and planted himself at the other end of the bar. My girl moved away to help him, leaving me to wonder what kind of weirdo wears a parka in June.

I finished my whiskey and called her back for another.

"Rules of the house—I can only give you two drinks per visit."

"Oh," I said. "What if I was to step outside for a minute, then come back in?"

She looked to her left. She looked to her right. Then she smiled. "I'd say I never met you before in my life."

I went out and came back and she set up another pour.

She was nice, so I figured I'd proceed with my fishing expedition: "You know the widow?"

"Whose widow?"

"The war hero. Marlowe. He left a girl back home, didn't he?"

"Sure, Chloe. I know *of* her, but I don't *know her* know her. Rumor has it she runs with a different crowd."

"What kind of crowd?"

"Funny you should ask. See that guy down there?" She tipped her head toward Mr. Skunk Parka.

"Yeah."

"*That* kind of crowd."

"Who is he?"

The barmaid leaned closer. Now I could see all the way to Sunday. "I forget his name. Brian something. But I know what he does."

"And what's that?"

"He deals."

"Blackjack? Texas Hold'em?"

"Funny man. You should hold onto your day job."

"I plan on it." *Widow Specialist*, I thought to myself. "Never mind. I knew what you meant." I leaned in and whispered, "He's into methametics."

"One plus two equals *you're right*."

"Interesting," I said. "I'll bet Marlowe had no idea he was going to come home to a skinny skank covered in sores."

"I thought you said you didn't know him."

"I never said that. I said I wasn't a friend of the family." *Not yet*, I thought.

"But you knew him?"

I grinned. "In bits and pieces."

"Well, the dude sure has a reputation around here."

"Like what?"

"To hear folks talk, that guy is everything right about the war. He could do no wrong. Cut him, he bleeds stars and stripes. That kind of thing."

"Hoopla-worthy."

"Apparently."

"And now his wife is mayor of Skankville."

"Well, I don't know." She scrunched her face. "I'm just repeating what I've heard here and there. You know how the truth gets watered down the more it's repeated."

"Yeah. So they say."

"One thing's for sure. If she *is* using, she hasn't lost her looks. I mean, she was good enough to be on the front page of the paper yesterday. Smiling and shit. What kind of widow goes around smiling?"

Maybe the kind with insurance money. My plan was looking better and better by the minute.

I was about to say something else—better yet, I was about to drop something on the floor she'd have to pick up—but Mr. Skunk Parka interrupted by calling her down to his end again. Not to get another drink, but to pay his bill.

What kind of man walks away before his limit of whiskey smooth as this? The kind who has other people to deal with. Literally.

I finished my drink because I had another idea percolating. With regret, I'd have to leave the barmaid and her fabulous T-shirt, but I knew my thirst would bring me back to the Headframe before too long.

Marlowe and I had chased the terrorist into an abandoned warehouse and now I stood over him with my rifle. Its muzzle pressed against his forehead like a cold kiss. Rules of engagement said this guy was a *suspected* terrorist, but I had no doubt in my mind.

Marlowe wore out the warehouse floor with his pacing.

"This is wrong," he said. "This is wrong, Franklin."

"Shut up, Marlowe. We got him dead to rights. Nobody goes around with a washing-machine timer in one hand and a Nokia in their other when they're just out for an evening stroll."

"We should wait for the MPs. ISP at the very least." There was something in Marlowe's voice that almost sounded like a sob.

"Shit, Marlowe. Our MPs couldn't navigate their way out of their own mother's cunt even if they had a compass and a flashlight *and* a GPS. As for the Iraqi police—"

At my feet, the guy was waving his hands and starting to make too much noise. Like screaming and begging-for-mercy kind of noise.

I made sure he got quieter before he could get louder.

"Shit, shit, SHIT! Look what you did, Franklin! Look at what you went and did."

"I'm looking, Marlowe, and it looks okay to me. But if you don't shut up, I'll be forced to make it a two-fer tonight. And I don't really want to do that, my friend."

In response, Marlowe went fifty shades of pale, then brought up that afternoon's MRE all over the warehouse floor.

When he had coughed his way out of it, I said, "If you're through, hand me that washing-machine timer so I can put it back in this butt-fuck's hand."

"You're a goddamn criminal, Franklin. Before long, you'll be a regular butt-fucker yourself at Leavenworth. That's what I think."

It didn't matter what Marlowe thought or who he tattled to because two days later he'd been divided a dozen different ways into the wind.

Now everyone wanted their own piece of Marlowe: claiming his legacy, his fortune—his sun-washed blond wife with legs up to *here* and breasts out to *there*, according to the photo Marlowe had tucked inside his helmet. The helmet and the snapshot of Chloe sitting leg-cocked on a lakeside boulder were the only things to survive the bomb blast intact. I carried that picture in my pocket now. The left edge was charred, burning away the tips of her bare feet, but the rest of the girl still had all that glorious flesh packed around her bones. Her head was tipped back—any farther and her hair would take a dip in the lake—and she looked through the camera as if to say, *Come get me.*

I followed the skunky smell up Montana Street. It was full

dark now and Butte's old headframes, the hundred-foot iron skeletons that had once lowered miners into the earth on cables, glowed red against the sky. Civic-minded do-gooders installed lights on the headframes years ago as a way to remind the city of its heritage—even if the past was not just dead but rotting in this place. What was once Butte's pride now stunk like Brian's coat.

Someone had to stop this guy from spreading his stink all over town and onto nice, pretty girls like Chloe.

As I walked, leaning into the slope of the Richest Hill on Earth, I kept thinking about how the army's engineers swept Baghdad's streets with heavy machinery—armored vehicles they called "Buffaloes." They rode their Buffaloes, sniffed out bombs buried by the side of the road, and disarmed the explosives before we followed in our thinner-skinned Humvees.

That's what I'd be doing now here in Butte. Making life easier for Chloe. Clearing the obstacles off her highway to happiness.

When Brian wobbled into the Party Palace, I hesitated. The Neversweat whiskey had me pretty loose already. I didn't want to go any further and have my limbs fall out of my joints.

I found a patio table on the sidewalk with an empty beer bottle. I sat and pretended I was nursing that bottle back to health.

Thirty minutes passed. A group of bikers came out for a cigarette, telling jokes punctuated by smoker's coughs. They were too into themselves, preening with their bandannas and leather chaps, to pay any attention to me.

Another hour passed.

A dog trotted past and lifted his leg on the table next to me. The man and woman sitting there did not appreciate that.

A fire truck, followed by a police car, screamed down Park Street.

I had time to examine the sidewalk in front of the Party Palace. I'm no engineer, but I determined the pavement there was a good inch higher than the surrounding concrete, built up by a decade's worth of vomit from drunk miners and bikers with smoker's coughs.

A woman with a ruined face and too-short shorts came out, put her arm around me, and slurred her undying, unconditional love. I led her over to the nearest lamppost where she professed the same type of affection.

Another twenty minutes passed.

My man finally came out of the swinging door, stumbled, and ran to catch up with his body before he fell onto the vomit-paved sidewalk. He pivoted and announced to the now-closed door, "I'mallright."

As he walked past me, he weaved off course and bumped into my table. I was there to catch him by the elbow and said, "Whoa there, Brian."

He raised his head and looked at me with alarm and puzzlement, then said, "Byron, I'mmmByron."

"That's what I said, Byron."

"Allright then."

"You should be more careful."

He took back his elbow and said, with sudden clarity, "Thank you, I will." He bowed, turned, and continued to walk up the sidewalk toward the dark mouth of an alley. He lowered his zipper as he walked—clearly a man on a mission.

"Yo, Byron. Wait up."

He swivel-wobbled again. "Whut?"

"I want to have a little talk with you."

"Whutabout?"

"Chloe."

"Who?"

"You know a girl by the name of Chloe, right?"

"Whut of it?" His hand was still down his pants.

"You know where I can find her?"

"Mebbe I do, mebbe I don't." He turned and resumed his stutter-walk to the alley.

"Maybe you'll tell me now, huh?" I called after him.

"Mebbe I will, mebbe I won't." He went around the corner and less than ten seconds later, a trickle of piss carrying a load of alley-dust reached the sidewalk.

I picked up my empty beer bottle by the neck and followed him into the alley to get some information. I was betting mebbe he'd tell me.

Two minutes later, I was back out of the alley with no beer bottle. But I had an address.

Behind me, a trickle of blood joined its fluid brothers Piss and Puke on the sidewalk.

Before I removed his teeth, Byron had given me an address that sent me north, up the hill to Walkerville. He said Chloe's sister Jacinda lived up there and maybe she'd know where to find the girl—a girl, by the way, he swears he never did meth-ametics with. I didn't believe him when he said this, and I only half-believed him when he gave me the sister's address.

There was a good chance I'd find plenty of wild geese but no Chloe. After all, this was the city's rough neighborhood, the kind of place where good intentions go bad. I went anyway—drawn by the beacon of sun-washed hair.

The hair and the breasts and the legs were just part of it, though. This girl was starting to get under my skin. I needed to see her in person to find out a few things for myself. Like, if

I pressed a gun barrel to her forehead, would she beg for her life, or would she tell me to go fuck myself?

After two hours of wandering Walkerville's maze of streets and asking three guys in wifebeaters working on a gutted Ford in their front yard if they knew someone named Chloe—or Jacinda or Byron, even—and getting a wrench thrown in the general direction of my head, and deciding retreat was the better part of valor, and rib-kicking a dog who got in my way, and wandering in the dark, and squinting at unlit porches, and not finding even one goddamn trace of 1321 Transit Street, I turned back.

Ask anyone in Bravo Company and they'll tell you I don't even know how to spell the word *surrender*, but I'll admit Walkerville defeated me that night.

I made my way back down the hill to the Finlen, consoling myself with one thought: Marlowe's welcome-home parade was tomorrow and I was sure to find Chloe riding in the grand marshal's car. I would catch her as she floated like a blond goddess, waving to all the little people who lined the streets cheering for her dead husband. I would grab her, pull her to me, and find my future somewhere in her eyes. Yes, that was my plan.

I woke to the sound of a firing squad.

Rifle shots cracked the air and brought me out of a swamp of bad dreams. I lifted my head and looked at the clock beside my bed at the Finlen. 10:32.

Another round of gunshots echoed through the empty brick canyons of the city. I tumbled from bed and crouched on the floor, panting. Then I remembered I was in Butte, not Baghdad, and I had a mission this morning.

I dressed quickly, sloppily, and raced down the Finlen's

stairwell. When I came out onto the street, I heard the ampli-
fied voices of city officials, one after the other stepping to the
microphone and extolling the virtues of the brave and selfless
Chandler Marlowe. Those lies only made me run faster up
East Broadway.

I followed the off-key blats of the high school band warming up and, turning onto Granite Street, found myself sur-
rounded by big men zipping around in tiny cars. They wore
maroon fezzes on top of their heads and big Shriner grins on
their faces. Cowboys on horses clopped up the street behind
me. I stepped to the side, walking in the gutter as stooped
veterans marched past, struggling to stay in step as they recalled their drill-and-ceremony training from fifty years ago.
Four of those wrinkled warriors had buckets of candy. Every
half block, they reached in and tossed taffy to the kids along
the parade route.

I dashed alongside the parade until I saw it gleaming
ahead of me: a white 1960 Cadillac convertible, the fins above
its taillights sharp and polished. It crawled along the stained
and potholed street like it was visiting from another world,
carrying a diplomat from a faraway planet.

She sat on top of the car's trunk, slender legs dangling into
the backseat. She had one hand propped behind her while the
other cut the air with nonstop waves. The hand gently turned
back and forth to the crowd with just the right balance of grief
and greeting: *Yes, I'm a widow, but I thank you for this honor.*

I stopped to catch my breath, hands on my knees. The
Richest Hill on Earth was proving hard to climb.

"There she goes."

"She can keep on going and not stop until she gets to
Missoula for all I care."

I half-turned to my right. Two women who looked like

they lived on a daily diet of Pork Chop John's watched the Caddy roll down the street.

"Poor gal," the first woman said. "All that trouble with her sister and that drug money."

"Poor nothing," the second lady said. "That family made their bed."

"Well . . . that one there's got a nice bed now." She snorted a laugh. "Mattress stuffed with all that insurance money from the army. I say good for her, shaking loose of her druggy sister."

The second lady looked sharp in my direction. "Do I know you?"

"No, I guess you don't," I said. Answering the beckon of Chloe's cupped palm, I started forward. I could almost hear the crisp scrunch of all those hundred-dollar bills as the two of us rolled across that mattress—a clean Chloe, not a vacant-eyed skank like I'd been led to believe. Things just kept getting better and better.

But then three men stepped from the crowd and blocked my way: Byron and two guys who looked like they got their full money's worth from their gym memberships. Byron's head was swaddled in a bandage. It clamped his head together and would have been perfectly white if it weren't for three brownish-red stains that bloomed like flowers along his jawline.

I heard Byron mumble-yell something approximating, "That's him!" and then they were rushing me.

Once upon a time, I'd soared down the field at Naranche Stadium to cheers of hundreds, carrying the ball to victory. I was older and a little slower now, but I gave it my all, dancing and dodging those three dudes on Granite Street.

I had a convertible to catch and when I reached it, I would touch Chloe on the elbow and make her turn to face me. I wasn't sure what I would say, but I knew what I *wouldn't* say. I wouldn't tell Chloe the truth of what went down in Baghdad that day, how her husband was supposed to be off-duty that afternoon, how I hadn't gotten much sleep the night before, how I made a deal with Marlowe to take my shift on that patrol, and how he looked at me dead in the eye and said, "Sure, I'll swap with you. But it'll cost you."

I knew what his price was: a demand that I confess to the MPs I'd shot an unarmed civilian the day before. If I could just get Marlowe out of the way for a little bit, off the base and out on patrol for one afternoon, maybe I'd have some time to think this situation through and see my way clear to the end.

So I begged him to swap with me.

No, I wouldn't tell Chloe all this. I'd just let her go on thinking her husband died a hero's death, earning his medals without so much as a piss stain on his pants. I'd let Chloe enjoy this parade and cheer this evening's fireworks because after this, she'd have a new man to think about, and she would be worth my coming back to Butte.

As three men roared at my back, I ran to catch the white convertible. I was almost there. I reached out to touch the taillight.

Then the driver stepped on the gas, the white convertible pulled away with my Chloe, my waving Chloe, as the parade crowd cheered and clapped, and I heard footsteps charging closer behind me.

CONSTELLATIONS

BY CAROLINE PATTERSON

Helena

"I'm sure she's a lovely girl," Mrs. Neal said as she peered over the scarred wooden desk at Peg Thompson. Mrs. Neal's face was lined, her bosom wrinkled with cleavage that dove into folds of gray flesh and undergarments, the thought of which made Elizabeth vaguely sick. She wondered why Mrs. Neal held her playing cards fanned out in front of her, why the lights weren't turned on, why the halls of the Helena YWCA were empty. Addressing the shriveled woman next to her, Mrs. Neal added, "Lillian and I just love the young ladies, don't we?"

Peg studied the two women. "Elizabeth gets straight A's. Her father's a lawyer in Missoula, her mother's on the symphony committee, and Elizabeth plays the piano. Mozart."

Moe-zart? Elizabeth winced.

Mrs. Neal set down her cards and struggled to her feet. "All the way from *Missoula*," she told Lillian. "A college town."

Peg lifted her chin and straightened her shoulders. "I was elected delegate to the constitutional convention. Elizabeth is my page."

"How educational." The YWCA director studied Elizabeth's shirtdress as it rode up her thighs.

"We're making a new constitution," Peg continued. "And this one is going to be written by the people, not the Anaconda Company."

"*We the people*," Mrs. Neal said. "Indeed."

"Elizabeth will be working hard and her mother wants her in bed by ten."

"I can put myself to bed," Elizabeth said. "I *am* sixteen."

"We understand about young ladies." Mrs. Neal looked from Peg to Elizabeth to Lillian. "I've been in charge here for thirty years, and Lillian's been here for seventeen. We can just tell by looking at this young lady that she is simply a lovely girl."

Elizabeth was sure she'd be murdered there.

"This will be the experience of a lifetime," Peg had said as they drove to Helena through a canyon lined with cottonwoods and threaded by the Little Blackfoot River. She glanced over at Elizabeth in the passenger seat. "You'll see how a constitution is built."

Elizabeth studied Peg's red hair, pug nose, and cat's-eye glasses. She didn't approve of Peg. Even though Elizabeth was a tomboy, she had strict standards for grown-up women: they should clean house, bake delicious meals, tuck their feet in at their ankles, and be quiet. Peg's house was a jumble of political posters and wobbly stacks of magazines and newspapers. Her standard contribution to the Methodist Church potluck was beans and weenies. When she and her husband played bridge with Elizabeth's parents, Peg ignored Elizabeth's mother's attempts to discuss hairstyles and hemlines, turning the conversation to the Domino Theory. Nevertheless, when Peg said she was abandoning her son and husband to six weeks of hot dogs and dirty laundry to "cook up a constitution," and asked Elizabeth to be a page, Elizabeth was thrilled.

She would be 114 miles away from her parents. She would be on her own for an entire week. And she planned to have sex.

It was 1972. It was time.

Everyone who was anyone was doing it. There was woozy, sex-oiled music on the radio with lyrics about kissing and free love and opening your mind. She didn't have a partner, but that was irrelevant. Sex was the key that would unlock the door between her and the great throng of human life. She'd had the standard boyfriend experiences: going-steady rings wrapped in yarn, movie theater make-out sessions. She'd even examined her vagina with a hand mirror as *Our Bodies, Our Selves* instructed, but she thought it was a hideous, drippy piece of flesh, disfigured by masturbation. This was different.

She wanted shock, a bolt of pure pleasure to blast her out of her paralysis. Paralysis stemming from bridge nights, when the Thompsons came over and as the adults studied their cards, Peg's son crept upstairs, opened the door, unzipped his pants, and shoved her hand onto the thick, knobbed head of his penis, the bumpy swollen shaft, moving it up and down until he ran to the bathroom next door where she could hear his grunting release.

"We're making history, Elizabeth!" Peg said as they drove past beaver slides, large contraptions farmers used to stack hay, and pastures of dreamy cattle with newborn calves curled in small bundles of black or brown, their mothers licking their coats. "Aren't you excited?"

"I can't wait," Elizabeth replied, thinking of an empty room and some boy she would meet, the image of his face blurred and indistinct. She looked out the windshield at the larch logs, round and raw, on the truck ahead of them as it roared through a mud puddle and fanned dirty water over the side of the road.

The room at the Y was the color of canned salmon. The bed

frame was iron. There was a window, a rickety chest of drawers, and a closet with a pipe to hang clothes on. Elizabeth stacked her underwear in a drawer lined with newspaper and set her patent-leather loafers on the closet floor. She hung her dresses hemmed to *four inches above the knee*—as specified by the *Dress Code for Pages*—on the pipe, grimacing at the scratchy *ping!* of wire hangers against the metal. She set her cherished Yardley Slicker lipstick, paid for with weeks of babysitting, on the dresser.

She stood at the window and looked out past the filmy curtains, the kind her father called *Band-Aids,* as the cathedral tower in the distance rang the hours with slow, dolorous chimes. Behind that was another sound: skittering footsteps somewhere in the YWCA.

She opened the door to walk to the bathroom and in the dim hall came face to face with Lillian dressed in a nubby, stained robe, holding a dented pie tin.

"My God!" Elizabeth's heart banged against her chest. "You scared me. I didn't realize you were here."

Lillian looked at Elizabeth like she'd never seen her before and hurried down the hall as if she were being chased.

From the direction of the old woman's room, Elizabeth smelled the tang of cat piss. She put her coat on and locked the door behind her. As she walked down the hallway, she heard tinny music from a distant radio and the thud of her footsteps on the floorboards.

Outside, she took gulps of cool air until her heart settled, until she felt the quiet of the streets enter her. She felt close to the great, mummified heart of Helena. There was something ghostlike about the town, with echoes of its former glory days when rich people built mansions here to have a presence in state government. She imagined parties spilling onto elegant porches, waiting carriages, women in muffs, piano music slicing the frosty night. Her parents, who loved turn-of-the-century novels, longed for that world, not the one her father cursed each night on television.

She felt lonely as she walked, but lonely in a new way; not the weak, piercing abandonment of the playground, but the loneliness of dark streets, of looking in at lighted windows, of watching trees toss their armloads of leaves in the wind, a loneliness pure and singular and strong.

As she headed down the hill into the Gulch, she walked past bars named the Gold Dust, the Claim Jumper, and the Mint, where men peered at her through open doors with vague curiosity. She saw herself through their eyes: an unaccompanied girl walking the street at dusk, no doubt on her way to ballet or piano lessons, a girl with family connections, a girl who meant trouble.

How would she make this happen? She wasn't old enough to walk into a bar. Would she stand at the door until someone suitable came out, and then just ask him point blank, *Hey, mister, want to have sex?*

The thought was erotic and terrifying.

When she imagined having sex, she pictured herself and her lover wearing wool sweaters and making snowmen, walking in leaves and crying a lot because they were so in love.

She headed back to the Y, down sidewalks lined with dirt-crusted snow. As she pushed open the heavy door, a voice said: "Where have you been?"

When her eyes adjusted to the dark, she saw the large shoulders of Mrs. Neal rising above the sofa.

"For a walk," Elizabeth said.

With a grunt, Mrs. Neal heaved herself up. "Let's keep our

breaths of fresh air to the daytime, shall we, dear? Walking at night is not something ladies do."

At the Hen Haus, Peg gave her name to the receptionist and steered Elizabeth to a flank of green leather chairs. The beauty parlor was a riot of pink sinks and blue and green curlers, the air an overripe tang of hairspray, shampoo, and perming solution.

Peg patted Elizabeth's knee. "This is nice. It's like having a pretend daughter."

Her ears buzzing with the patter and slice of women's voices and scissors, Elizabeth didn't know how to respond. She felt suddenly superior to Peg, with her creepy son and her husband who hid behind a newspaper wall. Maybe Peg was lonely. Maybe her politicking was just a way to escape.

Elizabeth startled herself by asking, "Did you want a daughter?"

"I lost twin girls." Peg flipped the pages of *Screen Star* then turned a pained smile on Elizabeth, leaning in so close that Elizabeth could see the large pores on her nose and the reddened tear duct in her left eye. "Some things just aren't meant to be."

The words were right there on Elizabeth's lips: *Your son. Made me. Touch him.* She saw him standing by her bedside, pants pooling at his knees. "Did you know?" she blurted.

"Know what?" Peg asked.

Elizabeth's face felt numb. The room receded.

"What?"

"I want to go on a protest march." Those words seemed to arrive in her mouth on their own. *The creak of his foot on the stairs, the triangle of light widening across her bed.*

"Against the war?" Peg stiffened. "With hippies? Honey, they're killing Communists over there."

"I don't believe in the war." Elizabeth hated Peg's glasses, the cat's-eye shape, the thick lenses, the way her eyes seemed magnified and blind at the same time. She thought of telling those glasses about the boy and how they'd shatter, shards flying in a million directions.

Peg stood when the hairdresser called her name. She patted Elizabeth's leg. "Don't worry, I won't tell your parents."

A thin blade of nervousness propelled Elizabeth through the Capitol rotunda where, as people moved about, talking, their voices grew whispery and ancient. She met the other pages—she and the boy from Dawson County were the only ones who didn't live on a ranch. The pages tried not to stare at one another as the legislative coordinator explained their duties: fetching newspapers, copies of amendments, cigarettes, and coffee, gallons of coffee.

In the assembly hall, pages sat in black mahogany chairs facing the one hundred delegates, who were seated alphabetically to encourage fraternization. A lighted board featured their names. When a delegate pushed a button at his or her desk, the corresponding number lit up on the board, and the pages went quickly to help.

There was a comfortable, early morning ease about the room. Aides handed out papers while the delegates milled about, chatting, drinking coffee, smoking cigarettes, or tipping back in their chairs behind newspapers. Elizabeth only half-listened, absorbed in the smell of cigarette smoke, the red swirled carpeting, the long windows, and the huge painting by Charles Russell of Lewis and Clark meeting the Flathead Indians.

There was a dark, Serbian delegate from Anaconda with slicked-back hair and a pinstriped suit. The oldest delegate was an elfin librarian from the University of Montana who was rumored to have an encyclopedic memory; the youngest was a graduate student with frosted hair and a Southern accent. Peg was an anomaly: the housewife with shooting-star veins was a Missoula Republican who hailed from Butte and hated the company. Handsome research analysts scurried about, with their array of sideburns—neat college-boy sideburns, curly mutton-chop sideburns, and narrow Elvis Presley sideburns— handing out research ranging from Supreme Court rulings to Montana statutes to copies of Plato's *Republic*.

President Graybill pounded his gavel to open the session and announced the date: Tuesday, February 29, 1972. The members of the Natural Resource Committee walked to the podium, where they stood and congratulated one another on having created one of the strongest environmental-resources amendments ever written.

The delegate from Glendive, the committee chair, tapped the microphone. She had a mane of wild black hair held back from her drawn-in face with barrettes. "We have failed this state," she said. "The amendment that this committee is so busy congratulating themselves about is weak, watered down, and basically useless."

The other committee members looked shocked.

"We are facing a future of strip-mining. This committee has failed to defend Montana's right to a *clean and healthful environment*. They voted it down in committee, folks. And now they are congratulating themselves on what a fine job they've done. Let me ask you this: Will you be proud that you failed to support Montana's right to a clean and healthful environment? Will we still be congratulating ourselves after we've destroyed our land and air and rivers?"

She started crying. The room erupted. President Graybill

pounded his gavel and shouted for order. Peg and several others rushed over to comfort her.

The page next to Elizabeth handed her a note that read:

You have red hair.
I think I'm in love with you.
Patrick

That night, as they ate cabbage and corned beef in Dorothy's Cafe, Peg told Elizabeth that her father left the house each morning before dawn to work in Butte's Alice Mine.

"He took an elevator 5,000 feet into the earth," she said. "Can you imagine? Rock walls, just a candle for light, coming up once a day for lunch, and then going back into the dirt and the dark again? The horses that worked down there went blind. That's what that woman is fighting against with *clean and healthful*."

Elizabeth looked at her stringy corned beef. If horses went blind, wouldn't people, too? "It seems like they would have just killed themselves."

"I can't believe you said that." There was an edge to Peg's voice. "They didn't kill themselves because it was a sin. They had families and they were tough."

"I didn't mean it like that," Elizabeth said, stung.

Peg's smile looked like a grimace. "I know you didn't, honey. But think about what you say."

As they walked outside, Elizabeth wished she were anywhere but here, on this brick sidewalk, making torturous small talk. She thought about Patrick and the way his hair curled over his collar, the way his nose tipped up slightly at the end.

"My father was killed in a mine explosion," Peg said as they continued down the deserted street. "He left my mother to raise seven children. That's why, when Mr. Thompson asked me to marry him, I told him, *I'll marry you if you don't work for the Anaconda Company!* You know what he said?"

"What?" Elizabeth couldn't imagine Mr. Thompson having the nerve to ask Peg out for coffee.

"He said: *Let's take the next bus to Missoula!* And we did!" She held her arms open, her purse hanging from one of them like an ornament.

"That's a nice story," Elizabeth said, wondering why grown-ups assumed younger people were interested in old folks' origin stories. She followed Peg down the narrow streets of Last Chance Gulch. They stopped in front of a store called Mr. Dash's Haberdashery, looking in at the window display.

"Funny beings, men are," said Peg.

Hilarious, Elizabeth thought, wondering exactly how many steps lay between her and the Y.

Four mannequins stood in a shaft of light from the streetlamps, dressed in suit coats and sweater vests, in dress shirts and ties, headless and waiting.

The next day, the Anaconda delegate tried modifying the natural resources amendment so the state of Montana could preserve a *clean and healthful environment* as a *public trust.*

The delegate spoke for an hour about *trusts* and how environmentalists were trying to take over public lands for the government. This was socialism, he explained.

The room grew hot.

Peg stood up and turned to the delegates. "We all know who this delegate is really representing—right, folks? It's a company named for a snake. The company created our first constitution, and if you wonder how people felt about it, think about what they called it: the copper collar."

Her opposing delegate rose and began reading the Magna Carta.

Elizabeth jumped up to answer bell number 46.

This delegate was from Poplar. "Jesus H. Christ," he said. "Nobody told us the Anaconda Company was going to filibuster this. We're gonna be here till next goddamn Christmas." He told her the last page he had was from Missoula. "Kid was a hippie, but you know what? He was the smartest page I ever had."

Elizabeth resolved to be smarter. "What can I get you?"

"The paper," he said, and handed her a dime.

She headed down to the newspaper machines in the basement. She put in the dime, pulled up the glass box, and took out a newspaper.

When she returned, the same delegate was talking about how his grandfather had taken the train to Yellowstone and toured the park in a buckboard and how, with these socialist ideas of a clean and healthful environment, everybody would be suing the state.

She handed the newspaper to the Poplar delegate and he scowled at her. "Oh for God's sake, girl. This is yesterday's."

Elizabeth's eyes teared.

"Forget it," he said.

Peg stood up. "Delegate Burns, is it in the public trust for the company not to pay taxes?"

"That *is* public trust," Burns said. "And my grandfather, when he came to homestead—"

A Billings delegate interrupted him: "I'm a simple man, but I know this. We've got the Beartooth Mountains over there, highest in Montana, and I've been in them many times. We've got five mining companies that want to take those mountains, rip them wide open, and dig a pit five miles long and three miles wide. And once they've dug that pit and taken the soil out of there and polluted the river down below it, it's not going to be there anymore. And we won't be able to put it back."

The amendment failed, 58 to 36.

The graduate student in a lime-green miniskirt shot up, her eyes blazing. "Mr. Chairman, I'd like to introduce a new amendment, guaranteeing Montanans' right to a high-quality environment which is clean, healthful, and pleasant, for the protection and enjoyment of its people and the protection of its natural beauty and natural resources, including wildlife and vegetation."

The Anaconda delegate shook his head. "Those words— *healthful, high-quality, pleasant,* and *reasonable*—are too metaphysical."

"I'd like to point out that in the Bill of Rights, we have metaphysical terms such as *liberty, freedom,* and *inalienable rights.*" Her voice was as direct as a bullet. "But we have no trouble determining what they mean."

The amendment was defeated, 51 to 43.

As Elizabeth walked from the Capitol down Montana Avenue, white clouds moved across the blue highway of sky and shadows pooled under the ash trees. She liked the momentum of moving downhill with the sun on her face and the snow-covered Sleeping Giant Mountain dozing on the horizon in front of her.

A pickup truck pulled up next to her. The driver leaned over and rolled down the passenger window. "Wanna ride?"

Patrick, wearing mirrored aviator sunglasses. Her breath caught in her throat as she stepped up into the cab.

At a drive-in, they ordered root beers and hamburgers

from a carhop in a short skirt and ski parka, who skated with their orders back to the window, past heaps of sooty snow.

Patrick pushed his sunglasses up on top of his head and looked over at Elizabeth. His eyes were green flecked with brown.

The cab felt very close.

They talked. Patrick explained that he was a junior at Dawson County High School. He ran track, played trumpet, and had collected the autographs of almost all one hundred delegates. He had an older brother who was serving in an artillery unit in Vietnam. Then he leaned over and sang, badly: "*Do you want to go to San Francisco?*"

She almost laughed.

"I want to get out of here so bad," he said, his eyes shining. "I need to see something besides goddamn cowboys. Rolling Stones. Cream. Jimi Hendrix. How 'bout you?"

"'Frisco for sure," Elizabeth replied, though in truth that city's flower-child scene scared her. "I want a yellow Karmann Ghia and a dog named Spud." She paused, tilted her head, and looked at him. "And I want to have sex."

He flushed and reared back. "You want to what?"

When she didn't answer, he reached out for her.

She pressed herself against the door. "No! Not like that. This is a project."

"What do you mean, *a project?*" He settled back behind the steering wheel.

"Eat your cheeseburger," she said.

He studied Elizabeth, his hair falling across his face. "You're an odd one."

The two of them sat in a companionable silence, watching cars spin down the highway, drinking the sweet root beer and eating greasy hamburgers, watching a dog pick its way across the parking lot, nose down and looking for scraps.

As she crumpled up their hamburger wrappers, Patrick put his hand over hers and asked, "Are you serious?"

"About what?" she said, although she knew fully well what he was asking about.

He shook his head and started the pickup. Seeing her squinting in the light, he took off his sunglasses and handed them to her. "You can have these if you want."

She took them, glimpsing her oblong reflection in the mirrored lenses, the way her face looked wide and egg-like, pink and contorted, all eyes and nose, and wavering.

During the afternoon break in the next day's session, Elizabeth was getting a drink at the water fountain when she felt a tap on her shoulder.

"Follow me," Patrick said.

They walked to the base of the rotunda. When Patrick was sure no one was looking, he grabbed her hand and led her to a small door. He opened it and led her inside. A sudden dusty quiet enveloped them.

They stood in a tiny closet where a narrow iron ladder rose up into the shadows.

"What are we doing?" Elizabeth was afraid a bat would fly out from somewhere and tangle itself in her hair.

Patrick began to climb the metal rungs. "Trust me."

Elizabeth followed him, hand over hand, foot over foot. Her dress ballooned out and she worried that if someone opened the door they'd see her underwear.

As they climbed up into the shadows, shoes scraping iron, she stopped caring. In the cool, quiet shaft, Elizabeth thought she heard the flutter of birds. Finally, the curved underside of the rotunda appeared.

"Where are we?" Her voice sounded hollow.

"You'll see."

"It's cold."

When Patrick reached the top rung, he took a flashlight out of his pocket. He shined the circle of light on the wall. "Look."

Above his head, on the narrow curved ceiling of the rotunda, were hundreds of signatures scrawled in marker, charcoal, and what looked like candle smoke. Some were large and loopy, some small and precise, some blurred, some feathery, others delicate as lace. The two of them clung there, sheltered by the names' ghostly constellation.

Patrick climbed down over the top of her, pressing her into the iron ladder. She turned her head to him. They kissed. His lips were cool and soft.

Molly Stensrud, 1895. Joseph McKinsey, 1923. Hope Smith, 1911. Kilroy Was Here, 1941. Class of 1964 Rules.

That night, Patrick scaled the porch support to the balcony as Elizabeth waited in her room with the lights off.

She eased open the window, holding her breath at the scrape of wood against wood. "Hey, Romeo," she whispered.

He crept under Elizabeth's window, balanced himself on the clinker brick, and put his hands on the windowsill. Then he was inside. He seemed so tall in the cramped room.

Patrick looked at the rickety dresser and the iron bed. "So this is where you stay? What a dump."

"It's *my* dump," Elizabeth said, irritated. "And keep your voice down. There's someone next door."

Patrick's hands dangled at his sides like rope. His face was smudged. "What do we do now?"

"We kiss."

He grabbed her waist. They sat on the bed and kissed.

They lay on the bed and kissed. Each time they shifted position, the bed creaked. The walls and door were so thin they barely seemed to exist. In the hall, a door opened and footsteps shuffled down the threadbare carpet runner. Elizabeth and Patrick kissed as pipes groaned and water turned on and off.

Maybe she didn't want to join the big chorus. She glimpsed the two of them in the speckled mirror over the dresser, tangled together on the lime-green bed: his brown hair, her red hair, his arms, her arms. She felt his smooth stomach and muscled shoulders and she felt her breasts swell and heard the women in her head saying, *Chippie, slut, whore.*

Patrick slipped his hands under her shirt. He unsnapped her bra and cupped her breasts in his hands. Electricity shot through her.

Hmmmm, the voices said.

"You're lovely," Patrick said.

Elizabeth took off her shirt and bra. In the mirror, she saw her pink-nippled breasts, her long hair and round face, Patrick sitting next to her with his long legs dangling. Her stomach grew cold.

"Are you still okay with this?" he said.

"Yes," Elizabeth whispered.

"What about . . . ?"

Reaching under the pillow, she pulled out the rubber she'd stolen from her father.

Patrick took off his shirt and she ran her hand through his chest hair. His nipples were brown, his chest lightly freckled. He had a scar on his abdomen.

"Appendicitis," he said when she touched it. "I was ten."

You will always regret it, said the voices in her head.

She put her hand on his stomach. His finger teased her nipple until it was hard.

"What are you smiling about?" he said, pulling her down on his chest. Their skin warmed together.

She shook her head. "Nothing."

There was the awkwardness of Patrick turning away from her, struggling with the condom.

He stroked Elizabeth's back, pulled her to him, and mounted her, and the aunts and mothers in her head resumed that odd, *Hmmm.*

Then Elizabeth split in two: the Elizabeth on the bed who felt the lushness of Patrick entering her, slowly, the slight pain, then the warmth of him filling her; and the Elizabeth who hovered above herself, watching, listening to her murmurs in counterpoint to the rattle of the bed.

They woke up in a tangle of covers, sheets, and clothes. The window was still dark.

"Oh my God," Patrick said, "are you all right?"

"I'm fine." She wasn't. She was shaky and upset. She wanted to be alone.

She got up to wash the blood from between her legs. As she crossed the room, she caught sight of herself in the mirror and stopped to see if she looked different. She didn't, but she *felt* different, like one of those pod people who hatched into perfect but emotionless replicas of themselves.

It was the new version of her that slipped on Patrick's shirt, buttoning it halfway. She opened the door, stepped out into the hall, and came face to face with Lillian.

The old woman was returning from the bathroom with her bent aluminum pie pan dripping with water, trembling in her unsteady hands. Her eyes registered the man's shirt and glanced through the doorway before Elizabeth could pull it shut.

"You scared me," said Elizabeth. "Are you feeding your cat?"

"I have no cat," Lillian nearly spit. In her worn-thin nightgown, Lillian appeared even older, her back humped, her hair hanging in white wisps about her shoulders. Looking into her dark, empty eyes, Elizabeth wondered if she was demented.

"I guess we both have secrets," Elizabeth said.

The woman's mouth cracked open but no sound came out—a thin line of spittle stretched from one lip to the next. She pressed her lips back together and hurried down the hall, her footsteps scratching like paws.

Shit, thought Elizabeth.

She used the bathroom and returned to bed, trying to concentrate on Patrick's smooth skin, the brush of his hair across her face, his smell of sweat and soap. The words *fouled this earth* flashed across her brain and then she was lost, remembering the warmth of him entering her. She wanted to stay inside herself, on this bed, in this room, but she rose up and out of herself. Hearing the voices and their deep, guttural *Hmmmmm,* she imagined the mouths of mothers and grandmothers opening and closing like fish out of water until they lost the ability to breathe. Elizabeth imagined the sound of a clear, single note that seemed to arrive from a distant galaxy.

Blood dripped into a pad between Elizabeth's legs as she sat with the other pages at the front of the room. Patrick was just three seats away from her, his hair brushing his collar.

The delegates were discussing wording for *a clean and healthful environment,* which had come up for a third and final vote. It was late in the day, late in the convention. Everyone was rushed and frenzied by the sense that this moment in history was winding down. The air was thick with cigarette smoke.

A Missoula delegate with sideburns stood to read his revision of the amendment: "*The state of Montana and each person must maintain and enhance a clean and healthful environment in the state for the enjoyment and protection of present and future generations.*"

"Oh Lord," another delegate sighed. "Haven't we been through this?"

A buzzer buzzed. Elizabeth got up to answer it.

"Coffee," Peg said. "We're gonna be here awhile. You all right? You look tired."

"Just that time of the month," Elizabeth lied, her stomach knotting.

Peg patted her hand. "Oh, hon, I'm so sorry."

The click of Elizabeth's shoes on black-and-white tiles hammered into her brain as she walked to the coffee stand. Through an opened window in the rotunda, she saw wet snow falling and smelled the sweetness of budding cottonwoods. It surprised her that outside the riot of her body and the chaos in the rotunda, there were still seasons.

She delivered the coffee and returned to her black mahogany chair.

After hours of wrangling, a young delegate rose, cleared his throat, and said to the assembly: "When you go home, and a voter asks you what you did for the environment, what are you going to say? That we're all for *clean and healthful,* but we don't want to use the words in our constitution?"

The amendment passed, 68 to 26.

The next day was Saturday, her day to ride home with Peg. When Elizabeth walked downstairs to go to breakfast, Mrs.

Neal and Lillian were waiting at the desk like clerks at a hotel. Lillian had taken some care with her appearance and was wearing a blue polka-dotted dress.

"Why, you are *just* the person we're looking for," said Mrs. Neal in a saccharine voice.

Elizabeth went numb.

"Why don't you sit down?"

It wasn't a question. She lowered herself on the doily-covered chair in the front room.

A door opened and Peg walked in. She nodded curtly at the two older women, two small red circles burning in her cheeks.

Elizabeth began to shake.

"Let's leave these Missoula people alone, Lillian," Mrs. Neal said.

The woman in the polka-dotted dress seemed reluctant to leave. She opened her mouth and Elizabeth pictured the thin strand of saliva that had spanned her lips that night in the hall.

Lillian said: "Some people seem to just think they're above the rules. Awful high and mighty."

Mrs. Neal shut the door behind them before Elizabeth could respond.

Peg turned on her. "I'm so mad I could spit. How could you do this to yourself? To your parents? To me?"

Elizabeth stared at her hands. She tested the nubby brown brocade fabric of the chair. She would forever think of shame as having exactly this texture.

"Why would you, a good girl, a straight-A student with everything to lose, risk it all for a night in the sack?"

Elizabeth lifted her head and stared at Peg. Over the noise in her head—*chippie, slut, whore*—and despite the way her face seemed frozen, she forced the words out: "Because I chose to."

"You chose to?"

She nodded, gripping the armrest to keep from shaking.

"For the love of God, why?"

"Your son."

"My son?" Peg was genuinely puzzled. Elizabeth saw where the woman's lipstick was smeared, the gray roots at her scalp, and the white hairs Elizabeth's mother called *goat hairs* growing from her chin. "Why are you bringing my son into this?"

"Your son made me touch him. While you and my parents played bridge, he snuck upstairs and unzipped his pants. He made me touch him. Over and over. And I hated it. Hated it. Hated it!"

Peg crumpled in the chair, her head in her hands, her back heaving.

When Peg came back a few hours later, she was wearing sunglasses that didn't hide how much she'd been crying. Elizabeth felt strangely dry-eyed, but she slipped on the sunglasses Patrick had given her before she got into the car. They muted the day's brightness but brought out other colors, subtle greens and browns.

The only sound on the ride back to Missoula was the tires crackling across the pavement as Peg piloted the car. Elizabeth saw that they were both driving away from who they had been, driving away from what the state had been, toward what it could become.

At MacDonald Pass, both of them were silent as the road snaked down through the mountains to the wide oxbows of the Clark Fork River. As the old car wound through the valley, the Garnet Mountains folded in on themselves like the Y of a woman's body, their round flanks split by a coulee—a French word meaning *to flow*—the land bending toward water. Years later, Elizabeth would learn to love those broad flanks, the undulating plains of flesh, and the Y of a woman's body, her body, with its mysteries, its givings and takings, but on that drive, she had to content herself with a weak spring sunlight warming her face and hands and the knowledge that, at least for now, they had crossed the Continental Divide and she was halfway home.

ACE IN THE HOLE
BY ERIC HEIDLE
Great Falls

Civic-pride billboards and the drab county jail swept past the chilly Greyhound's windows as it dropped down the hill into the night of Great Falls. Through frosted glass, Chance watched the town pull him in as the Missouri passed below, the bus thrumming over dark water and skiffs of ice. Beyond the bridge he saw the OK *Tire* sign was gone; its cinder-block building was now something new.

The bus pulled a lazy turn toward downtown, rolling through blocks of low brick warehouses before banking hard into the alley behind the depot. It settled with a hiss in the garage as the passengers roused and began filing off.

The snap of deep cold hit him at the door. The driver's breath huffed with each suitcase he tossed from the coach's gut. Chance only had his green duffel. He split off from the line shuffling into the warmly lit lobby. Ducking under the half-open bay door at the front of the garage, he stepped onto the street and walked toward Central Avenue.

He went into the first bar he found, easing past a gleaming line of poker machines gaily draining the life from their patrons. Finding a stool, Chance slid a twenty across the bar. The man behind it inclined his chin and Chance replied, "Whatever ditch." When the drink came he held the brimming glass of whiskey and "ditch" water to his lips, toasted his reflection and a town he'd found a little less OK, and enjoyed a first delicious violation of parole.

Chance and his father leaned against opposite sides of the truck bed, resting on grimy forearms. The shop was quiet. It was Sunday and the town was in church.

"Battery's fucked," his father said. "Put the trickle charger on it but in this cold it probably won't hold."

The pickup, a great square International, had been Chance's since high school. It was brutish and lovely and filled with garbage from the glory days. The engine idled, exhaling a fragrant plume of exhaust.

"I'd have picked you up at the station. Or Deer Lodge, for that matter."

"I know. Thanks."

"You ever hear from your mom over there?"

"Not once."

"Too bad. So you know, I put the place up last fall. Sold it to Charlie Carter."

Chance looked up, surprised for the first time. "Why?"

His dad glanced off toward the light. "No point keeping it since your grandma died. Charlie could use the pasture and I could use the pocket money. Kept the buildings, though. House is yours to stay in if you like."

"Thanks. I might, for a bit."

"Good. I threw something in the cab for you. Your grand-dad's wool coat. Winter's been a bitch." He gave the truck an approving nod. "Come see me about a job in a couple days."

"Sounds good."

His dad drummed the heel of his hand against a rusty quarter panel. "Well. Let 'er rip."

* * *

Chance drove the rifle-shot length of Tenth Avenue South under a cold overcast sky. The engine pulled grandly and he allowed himself a vision of swerving the steering wheel, plowing through burger chains and payday loan shacks, feeling their matchstick frames explode against the truck's hungry grille. Goodbye, strip mall. Goodbye, Target. Sayonara, Tokyo Massage. He pulled off when he reached the east end of town with nothing but icy stubble fields and the towers of the air base beyond. The truck idled and the cab heater muttered its low sigh. He reached across the bench seat to a buffalo-plaid Pendleton he recalled his grandfather wearing at the ranch. He pulled it on and it fit, a bit snug but warm.

Sitting back, he felt a lump against his spine. Reaching into the coat's rear game pocket, he found an envelope with CHANCE scrawled in pencil by his father's crude hand. Inside was three thousand dollars.

The mermaid traced a slow, liquid curl through the turquoise pane of water, revealing a pleasantly bare midriff as she rolled into a sinewy loop. Her metallic tail chased behind, drawing gorgeous curlicues with each wondrous pelvic kick.

Chance lifted his drink and followed her silvery shape as she swam to the glass separating the bar back from the motel's indoor pool. She gave him a bubbly grin from behind blue swim goggles.

"She'll do," said the big Indian sitting next to him at the bar, swiping the screen of his phone and sipping a High Life.

"But will she do me?" Chance added, just to be polite.

"Only if you're lucky." He offered a paw. "Amos."

"Chance." They shook.

"Lucky Chance. How could you lose?" Amos fished some

bills from his Seahawks jacket and waved the barmaid over. "Another one for my lucky friend. Me too."

Chance thanked him and they sat in blue vinyl chairs watching the mermaid flit in and out of view. Behind them a crowd of college kids and ranchers sipped Windex-tinted drinks beneath the bamboo-thatched ceiling as a small old woman at the organ crooned a gravelly "Mack the Knife." Amos took a pull from his beer and stood, waggling the phone. "Have to check my stock portfolio." He clapped Chance on the back and faded into the crowd.

Chance sampled his drink. A second mermaid had entered the pool and she entwined with the first, forging a heavenly double helix suspended in chlorine. He ran his eyes along her shape and realized that he knew her. Amy. They'd dated in school. He raised his drink, tilted the glass in a toast.

From behind the glass she threw a sidelong smirk, cocked a finger at him, and fired. Then she went up for air.

Chance grinned and watched her tail slip up out of sight.

"She's easy on the eyes."

Chance turned to find Amos's chair filled by a fit-looking man his own age wearing a bright yellow down jacket. His short black hair had a touch of gray at the temples.

"Hello, Matt."

"Hello, Chance . . . Out already. Good behavior?"

"Good enough."

"Glad to have you back." Matt set his whiskey on the bar.

"You follow me from my dad's?"

"More or less. Thought we should chat, since you're a free man."

"I'm not sure how free, but okay."

Matt centered his drink between index fingers. "Lots of

free time, at any rate. Enough time to work off some debt." Matt looked at him for the first time.

"Sure," Chance said from behind his glass. "Just not sure how."

"I have a few ideas."

"I can't make any runs into Canada, if that's what you have in mind."

"Fucking A, you can't. Legal or otherwise."

"Well?"

Matt drained his drink. "Be creative. Rob a bank."

"Great." Chance turned in his chair. "I'll sling all the weed you can give me but I need to keep a low profile."

"That's not going to work. Town's too small. And it would take a lifetime to earn off that much." Matt stood. "Walk me out."

They came out into the second-floor parking lot, ringed by motel rooms on all sides. The moon was up and gleaming through an iridescent layer of cloud. Matt fumbled with his keychain and a red Suburban yawned to life in the parking lot.

"Matt, I don't have that kind of money, and I'm never going to have it without selling dope. Plain and simple."

"Join the club. I'm already losing my ass to medical marijuana. Anyone with a card can run out to a trailer house in Vaughn and buy in broad daylight. I need to be retired in five years. I need that money."

"What can I do? I got caught."

"Not my problem. You gave a hundred thousand dollars' worth of weed swimming lessons, not me. Fuck you. Find it."

"Fuck you, too. Maybe I can ask your mom the fucking cash fairy for it."

If it hadn't been for the drinks, he might have caught Matt swinging. The punch hit his gut through the heavy coat and he was going backward and Matt was on top of him, throwing right after right into Chance's nose. Matt was still fond of his class ring. The sound of Matt yelling, getting fainter. Something red going all over Matt's bright yellow jacket.

"Lucky."

There was a circle of light but a shape loomed in and eclipsed it. Something was spinning and he discovered it was the world.

"Hey, Lucky. You still alive?"

"Amos," he croaked, remembering. He sort of sat up.

"Easy, Lucky." Amos helped him stand, then held his arm while Chance leaned over to vomit. When he was finished he tried to lay down for a nap, but Amos pulled him upright. "Not a good idea. You look like you got beat up by five Indians, and three of them was my cousins."

"Oh my God!" Behind them the door to the motel held the silhouette of a woman, a hand to her mouth. "I'm calling the cops."

Amos let go of Chance's arm and raised his palms. "No, no. I just found him."

From the ground, Chance put up a hand. "He's okay. He's Amos. Amos, Amy."

Amy held her phone, ready to dial. Her hair wasn't quite dry from the pool. A halo of steam framed her face in the yellow courtyard light. Chance thought she looked pretty good, but he could really use a nap.

Amos and Amy each took an arm and lifted Chance to his feet. He pointed toward the International and they dragged him over, sitting him in the passenger side. Amy probed his nose with a finger and winced. "You need to go to the ER."

"No ER. No police. Just give me a second."

Amos and Amy shared a glance. Amos shrugged. "Your call, Lucky."

Chance tried to fish the keys from his jeans but razors shaved his fingertips. "I think my hands are frostbit."

Amos shook his head. "I'm not gettin' 'em."

Amy shot him a look and sighed. She reached in Chance's pocket, pulled out the keys, then walked around to the driver's side. "Guess I'm driving."

She got in and turned the key: nothing. "It's dead. When was the last time you drove this thing much?"

"Five years," Chance groaned.

"That sounds about right." She slid the vehicle into neutral. "Amos, can you help me push it?"

Amos and Amy leaned into the front grille and got the truck backed into the center of the courtyard.

Amos touched her arm. "You get in and I'll push you down the ramp. Get him to the ER. Nice to meet you, Amy."

"You too. Take care." She hopped in and slammed the door. From the far edge of the cab Chance mumbled, "It's a stick."

"I know, genius. That's why this shit will work." Amos put his shoulder against the tailgate and the truck inched forward, tires crunching in dry snow. The wheels cleared the edge of the parking ramp and took off.

Amy waited till the bottom of the ramp before popping the clutch. The engine caught and roared to life.

Chance sat up as she turned onto the street. "Really. I'm okay. Not my first fight."

"Sure looks like it was. Did you even land a punch?" She pulled over and let the truck idle.

"Don't recall. But, hey. Amy, how you been? You still married?"

"I'm going to make a judgment call here. You probably aren't going to die at this point, and I'm guessing this has something to do with your time in prison. So I'm going to let you drive yourself home if you can. I'm not going to be involved in whatever this is. But you have to call me when you get there, so I know you made it."

She scribbled a number on a card from her wallet and tucked it into the dash. "Can you drive home?"

He slid over as she stepped out onto the street. "I'll be fine. But can we go for a beer sometime?"

"A convicted felon with shitty friends, a shitty truck, and a broken nose," she purred. "Mmm . . . tell me more." But she pecked his bruised cheek before closing the door.

He awoke the next afternoon in the farmhouse's back bedroom. His nose had bled through the sheets, but he could smell the sawdust-and-baby-powder scent of the house. He got up and made coffee to the ticking of the old mantel clock in the front room. The house was cool but not cold and it looked like his father had left everything in place. Hopefully.

Back in his room, he reached under the bed: the box was still there. He tipped it open and drew out the .357, worn but clean. He broke it open and loaded five rounds, leaving the one on the chamber empty. The gun barely fit in the inside pocket of the Pendleton coat.

Driving out from the old place, he topped the rise leading to the county road.

A tan military-spec Humvee sat parked at the pullout along the square chain-link enclosure where giant signs read, *WARNING: USE OF DEADLY FORCE AUTHORIZED,* in red. The missile silo had been on their ground since his grandfather's time. Joking about the sale, Chance's dad had called it a pot-sweetener for Charlie Carter: "Property includes one Minuteman III missile, well-maintained, never fired." Now Chance drove past the Humvee and lifted a few fingers off the wheel. The nineteen-year-old airman in the rig gave a curt nod from behind wraparound shades.

Chance drove around town. He had a pint of Jim Beam from the state liquor store between his legs. He let the truck take him wherever. He rolled to a stop in front of the high school, then eased out the clutch and pulled away. He turned onto Central headed for downtown.

The line of stone storefronts leered from either side, the pulled-molar gaps where businesses used to be. It was nearing five o'clock and the cold blue light of evening was settling in. Passing the burned-out drugstore he saw a friendly shape at the curb: Amos. Catching sight of the International, a big grin spread over the Indian's face and he put up a burly set of dukes. Chance slowed to lift the pint in salute, but Amos crossed behind him with a wave and was gone.

The engine coughed. He'd go for a new Diehard in the morning and firm up an exit strategy while bolting it in. He saw the card wedged in the seam of the dash and ran his thumb across Amy's delicate number before flicking it over. The front read, *BLACK EAGLE COMMUNITY CENTER,* above a dated line cut of the building. Chance tucked it back in the dash and spun the wheel with his palm.

He passed along the riverfront park and its hollow band shell covered in snow. He'd kissed a girl there once, in summertime. A thin sheen of ice lay over the duck pond and the truck guided him under the low rail bridge onto the drive along the river. On the far shore rose the great chrome mass of the refinery, a glittering cathedral of plumbing and sodium light. He should've turned at 9th Street but he knew he'd have to do it sometime. The truck knew it too, and slowly it pulled him back to the scene of the crime.

It had been this time of day but with the balm of a fine June evening. He'd dropped into town on the far side of the river, coming from Havre and Canada beyond. Having walked a heavy backpack through a sympathetic farmer's field, he'd passed a concrete pylon marking the border and over to his waiting rental. The drive was a couple hours. The slopes of the Bears Paws waxed and waned as he sipped a Coke behind the wheel, one arm propped on the open window.

Something went haywire at the edge of Great Falls. Whether he'd been informed on, he still didn't know. But down the hill toward the river a deputy's lights were in his mirror and the backpack was propped against the passenger seat.

He'd pulled over, counting the officer's steps toward his window. He saw the man unsnap his holster. That was enough for Chance. He stood on the accelerator, watching the scrambling deputy recede in his mirror as the rental shot through the night.

Chance pushed the engine hard but the traffic light was red on the 15th Street bridge. He saw another sheriff's rig coming at him.

Braking to a halt, he'd run the pack to the bridge's east rail. He tore open its flap and hurled compact green bales over the side. The last had taken flight before the deputy's brakes howled. Chance watched the bundles tumble toward the water below. They smacked into the face of the Missouri, rolling off toward the hungry turbines at the dam.

All but one. The last bale, thrown just a little short, landed with a dusty puff atop a piling below his feet and settled to rest. Another three inches and it would have floated to Fort Benton. Three inches short and he'd gone to jail.

Now Chance crossed the bridge slowly, easing past the point where the chase and life had stopped. Ice jammed up against the Black Eagle Dam. He turned off the bridge at the south end of Black Eagle, toward the absence in the sky where the giant smelter stack should be. His grandfather had worked in its furnace as a blacksmith in the war, forging one link in a great chain bringing bright nuggets of copper from the bleeding earth of Butte to Nazi brainpans in France.

At the edge of the hill, the community center lay squat above a mostly empty lot overlooking the river and lights of Great Falls. Chance goosed the throttle to give the battery some juice, then switched it off.

Double doors opened on a hall lined with faces of men his granddad had known. Built by the Anaconda Company as a place these boys could drink and fight respectably, it opened on one side to a bowling alley. Chance peered through the door and saw knots of rowdy, pretty women whooping it up on the lanes. League night. He went the other way into the bar and pulled out some money. The place was vacant except for the haggard gamblers growing roots at their machines. Amy was tending bar.

She sidled toward him, drawing a pilsner glass from the rack and filling it with beer. She wore jeans and a black T-shirt and arrived with a quiet grace to set the glass by his hand.

"Joe Frazier. Still alive?"

"More or less." He hoisted the glass. "Thanks for helping me out."

Her naked left hand rested on the flat bar. "You see the doctor yet?"

"I'll be fine. You work here too, huh?"

"Mermaiding doesn't pay the bills."

"Yeah. So what happened to Billy?"

"He went to drill for oil in North Dakota. Wasn't all he wound up drilling." She threw a wan grin and looked him up and down. Her gaze stopped at his side. "Naughty, naughty."

Chance touched the pistol's checkered grip and realized the gun was peeking out of his coat pocket. "Yeah, well. I'm not going another round like last night."

Amy shrugged and shied away from the bar, sweeping its top with a rag. Chance sipped his beer and slid off the stool to find a poker machine. He fed a twenty into the slot and got three of a kind his first hand. He fooled with the notion of going on a run, cashing out at eight hundred to parlay into a big stake to pay off the debt. Maybe go to Vegas and hit a streak. Maybe just go.

He tapped the buttons for a while, earning a few dollars in the pale glow of the machine. He reached for his beer and found a fresh glass in its place, turned to see Amy retreating to greet new arrivals. The place was starting to fill. He settled back in to earn his way to freedom.

Chance sat in the truck, his breath frosting the glass. The outside of the windshield was layered with a rime of ice. He dug the pint from below the seat. Took a shallow pull. Tried the key. Nothing.

He opened the door to go back in and saw Matt standing there with his hands in the pockets of his yellow jacket. "Hello, Chance."

"Matt."

"Sit back and take it easy. I just want to talk." Matt glanced toward the community center. "Mermaid hunting again?"

"Gambling my way to glory." Chance felt his pistol against his ribs and wondered if there was one in Matt's hand.

"Two days, Chance. Whatever you're drinking on now, you're going to piss it away. The sooner you sober up and get me my money, the sooner I won't have to come back."

"It's a down economy, Matt. Smelter's a bit slow." Thumbing the air behind him where the stack used to be, he took a pull from the bottle.

"I'm done threatening you, Chance. I won't do it again." Matt turned toward his running rig. "Two days."

Chance toasted him with the pint as he left. He sat back and stared at the bar's fuzzy light leaking through the windshield. Dropped the bottle and went back in.

He worked through the buzz of the crowd to the bar and propped himself against it. The whiskey was taking hold and the throb in his nose faded out. Amy appeared from the back and placed a coaster in front of him.

"I thought you took off."

"Battery shit itself again."

"Bummer. You just can't seem to catch a break, now, can you, cowboy?"

"Not so far."

She glanced at the clock. "I get off in half an hour. Sit right here and when I'm done, I'll be happy to jump you."

"What's wrong with your face?"

Chance opened his eyes. A small boy stood in front of him, staring. Chance sat up on the couch. "Hi."

"Hi." The boy didn't blink. "Did you get hit?"

"Did I ever." He stretched and looked around. It was a tiny

living room, blank except for photos on the wall. He caught his reflection in the TV's curved screen.

"Did you hit him back?"

"Not yet. Where's your mom?"

The boy pointed at the closed bedroom door.

"Gotcha." Chance stood, wobbling a bit. He'd slept in his clothes. "What's your name?"

"Alex."

"Chance." He put out his hand. The boy shook it solemnly.

They sat at the kitchen counter eating Cap'n Crunch. The boy watched him and didn't say anything. Chance heard the bedroom door open and Amy say, "Good morning."

"We're just having some chow here. Need a bowl?"

Amy was dressed in a long T-shirt and shorts. She stood with a hand on the counter, regarding the two boys. She glanced out the window. "You remember getting here? You were pretty drunk."

"Yeah. Sorry about that." Chance stole a look at Alex, who grinned through a mouthful of Crunch.

"I just didn't want you leaving town like that." She folded her arms and stared into the sunlight.

She drove him to Black Eagle to pick up his truck. They put jumper cables on it and sat in her idling car. Snow fell against the windshield.

"So what's your plan?" She fiddled with a loose bit of trim on the dash.

"I don't know. I can't stay here if I want to keep breathing."

"What's your dad say?"

"As little as possible. Wants me to work for him at the shop."

"I always liked him."

"Swing by and say hello. I'm heading there now."

"Nah, I have to pick up Alex in a bit. Say hi, though."

"I will. He's a cute kid."

"Yeah."

Chance stepped into the snow and fired up the truck. He pulled off the cables and leaned into her window. "Well, I guess that's it."

She stared. "Yeah, that's it." Then her hand was around his neck, pulling his mouth to hers. It was the first warmth he'd felt since he'd been home.

Chance pulled up on the office side of the shop. The *Open* sign wasn't on yet, so he unlocked the door. He flicked on lights as he worked his way into the shop.

His father lay facedown on the floor in a mirror-dark pool that wasn't oil. Chance knelt and felt his father's neck: cold. His eyes were half open and the wound at the temple had congealed to the concrete. Chance sat down, and then eased onto his side to gaze into his father's eyes. The dead man's mouth looked like it was preparing to say something.

Chance kept his fingers on the wheel as he drove past the missile silo. The gun was in his hand when he reached the farmhouse. He parked in the yard and slid out of the truck, the pistol hanging at his side. Chance walked the perimeter of the house before going in.

No one was there. He set the .357 by the sink. A blinking light caught the corner of his eye: the ancient answering machine his grandmother would not give up. He walked over and pressed *Play*.

"*Chance, it's your dad. You remember that spot at the farm you used to hide as a kid? I put something in there for safekeeping.*

If you don't hear from me for a few days, go check on it. No big deal but I thought you should know just in case. Talk to you soon, pard."

He rewound the tape and pressed *Play* again, hearing his father's voice. He rewound it again and understood—why his dad had sold the ground around him, and what was now hidden in the secret place.

He slid to the floor against the pine paneling. Some time went by. The mantel clock ticked. And he remembered hiding in the little place his dad had built for Ranger.

Chance walked to the side of the barn and it was there in an overgrowth of weeds. The little swinging door was rotting at the bottom, but painted red it blended with the shape of the barn. He pushed the door open and crawled inside.

Ranger had loved this spot in winter, and in the remains of the straw Chance's father had put there he could still see where the dog had dug in against the cold. In the farthest corner sat a five-gallon bucket of feed.

Chance dragged it out by its handle and pried off the lid. The bucket was full of money.

He sat drinking coffee at the kitchen table that night with the pistol near his hand and a single small light that would not be seen from the road. He wrote slowly on a yellow pad, working on a draft he'd started several times.

When dawn came, he sealed the pages in two envelopes. Then he took the gun and walked to the barn.

The truck started grudgingly, warmed in the sheltered space. He drove it onto the road. More snow would soon fall under the gray pall of sky. At the county road ran a line of mailboxes. He placed the letters in his grandfather's and put up its flag.

The town wavered on the horizon, a gray line in the air. Great Falls, his town, the place he was from. He'd never left here, really, and now he never would. The five-gallon bucket guaranteed that. He took another look and got back in the truck.

Matt's phone buzzed and he glanced at the number. "Hello, Chance."

"I have your money. You can come get it. You know where I'm at."

"Better if I pick the spot, Chance."

"We're doing this now or I'm gone. Come get your money."

"Okay." Matt ended the call and turned to his brother. "Let's go get him."

On the far end of the line, Chance opened the pistol and loaded the sixth round.

The red Suburban cut through a light snow. Matt and his brother Donnie rode in front, two men with rifles behind them. Matt's yellow jacket was stained with Chance's blood despite a hard cleaning. He drove calmly, gazing ahead. The day had turned warmer despite the snow; a Chinook wind was on the way.

They turned off the county road toward the farmhouse. Matt spotted the truck parked in the yard by the house. He stopped at the cattle guard and took a hard look. Nothing moving.

They drove in and parked. The four men got out and walked toward the house. Matt called Chance's name.

"I'm here," he said from behind them. He stood in the barn door and they saw his leveled pistol.

Matt stopped. "I just want the money, Chance. Then we're square."

"Is that what you told my dad?" He walked forward.

Matt hesitated. "He offered to pay me a couple months ago. When I went to collect he flew off the handle. That wasn't part of the plan."

"You forgot to mention that tidbit to me."

"It happened after I saw you last night. I figured you'd disappear."

"I'm here."

Chance cocked the pistol and watched the men slowly spread out in front of him.

Two days later, after she'd seen the news, a hand-addressed letter arrived.

Amy, I'm sorry to send you this, but you probably understand by now. I fucked things up bad but you deserve to have something good. Wait till things quiet down then come out to the farm. The address will be in the news. On the south side of the barn you'll see a little door. There's something in it for you in a big white bucket. Don't worry, it's not stolen. It was my dad's and he'd want you to have it. I also sent a letter to my lawyer. It's a will and I'm leaving you the place. I don't know if that will hold up but we'll see. Obviously my lawyer sucks. But this will help you out. There's a small chance you may hear from me again and if so I might need some of it to pay him. Thanks for everything. Chance

Matt spoke: "Chance, put that money in my hands right now or I swear I'll blow your new girlfriend's brains out."

Chance aimed the muzzle of the gun at Matt's chest. "I'm not fucking around."

Matt grinned and Chance caught Donnie opening his coat. Chance fired in warning but the back of Donnie's head came open and dusted the snow red. The other men scattered as Donnie fell. Chance backpedaled across the yard, putting the Suburban between him and them. He fired two rounds into the tires on his side, then ran straight for his truck.

He reached the cab and turned the key without hope, but the engine caught, and he hit the gas. One of Matt's men raised his weapon and fired, putting a line of holes in the International's side. Chance shot his gun dry through the side window as he tore out of the yard.

If they killed him, she was dead. If they got past him, she was dead. He had to stop them. But the pain in his ribs was suddenly very sharp and he felt a smear of blood spreading from his side.

The truck lurched and a plume of dark smoke boiled from the hood. Neither of them had long. In the mirror, the hobbled Suburban rolled slowly toward him. They couldn't get far—but far enough to reach him. He had to stop them here.

Chance played his last card. He put the wheel hard over and the International roared off the road and toward the silo's fence. It struck the chain link and went through, dragging fence and *DEADLY FORCE* signs and tumbleweeds through the gravel compound. He pulled a tight turn, mowing through antennas and sensors before the truck rocked to a stop against the squat blast door.

Chance coughed up some blood. He upended the pistol and thumbed the cylinder release. The spent casings dropped in slow motion, the last, the empty cartridge pinging off the wheel as it fell. He fished live rounds from the coat's pocket and reloaded with a shaky hand.

He leaned against the door and fell to the earth. Rolling onto his front, he saw the Suburban stop below, tires gone on his side. He crawled beneath the truck and set the pistol in both hands.

The men in the rig paused, deciding. In minutes helicopters would appear over the rise. Men in Humvees with guns drawn would sweep in to kill anything that moved. They were caught one way or another. They might as well shoot Chance first.

He saw them coming now. Eighty feet maybe, yellow jacket in the middle. He thought he heard the thump of rotors. He could feel his heart beating against the earth his grandfather had once run through with steel blades. The men were coming as three. Chance just needed to kill one.

PART II

THE HI-LINE

FIREWEED

BY JANET SKESLIEN CHARLES

Farm Country

It was Jim who found the body. Ten miles off the highway. In the middle of Sigurd Sorenson's summer fallow. Fireweed had taken root, its dull green leaves nearly concealing the blond stubble—stubborn, rigid—that stuck out of the gray dirt. In a fifty-mile radius, no other farmer let weeds onto his fields. Slumped in the passenger seat of the Ford, the dead man was not wearing a seat belt. His body leaned toward the glove compartment. A line of blood had dried on his cheek. *Like a tear*, someone insisted the deputy said, though that didn't sound like her. The gun sat in the driver's seat. The bullet had gone clean through his skull and even the roof of the car. As always, the sky was blue, but anyone who knew anything knew that snow was on its way.

I squeeze behind the counter and grab the coffee pot while Flo waits for her order to come up. I'm waitressing for one last year before I go away to college. As she serves their breakfast, four farmers huddle around the table and talk about the stranger—*Who was he? How the hell'd he get out there?*—at the Town Dump. That's what we call the Town Pump—the only café in town. The only gas station too. Like a boxing ring, it has corners: one for the Ladies' Auxiliary, one for the farmers, one for county workers, one for the hot shit posse. No one likes the posse, a handful of businessmen who act better than everyone else. "If you think you're such hot shit, why don't you get out of this pissant town?" Uncle Jarl responded when John Junior called him a hick, and the name stuck. The posse are good tippers, though, always making a point of contributing to my college fund.

The posse lawyer likes to give me advice while I pour his coffee. *Don't take too many credits your first semester, College Girl. You don't want to be overwhelmed. Take the billiards class, College Girl. When you start work and beat the good ol' boys at pool, they'll respect you. You should wear your hair down like that more often, College Girl. It looks nice.*

I smile. Flo frowns. Though nearing retirement, she's as nimble as the roller-skating teen she used to be. Truckers of all ages flirt with her. When she crosses her arms like that, she has the intimidating presence of a bouncer.

I move on to the farm table.

"Sorenson's is a hell of a place to die," Uncle Jarl says as I refill his coffee.

He's right. Now that Sig's in the nursing home, his farm is downright dismal.

Talk shifts to Sig. The first farmer to pull his tractor out of the Quonset to plow in the spring, the one with the highest yield. He lived on crackers and sardines washed down with vodka, and remained a bachelor until the age of fifty. Most people thought he was too smart to get hitched. He surprised everyone by marrying the Widow Crawford, who was half his age, and even adopted her son Billy. She'd been pretty then. How was anyone to know she wasn't just a drunk, but a mean drunk? Once she hit Sig with a skillet and fractured his cheekbone. Not that he ever pressed charges.

"Phyllis," the men say, remembering the dead.

"Her boy's not much better."

"Billy's all grown up, turned thirty-one this fall."

They nod.

Then my uncle says the worst thing you can about a man: "He has no ambition."

"Did you see Billy's summer fallow? I heard the damn car was half-hidden by fireweed."

We live in constant drought. Weeds show apathy. Weeds take what wheat needs. And like gossip, weeds spread. If a farmer doesn't take care of the problem, they become someone else's problem.

The conversation swings back to the stranger. He's been dead for five days, maybe more. "Of course it wasn't Billy who discovered the body. He hasn't spent a minute on the farm since harvest."

"Heard he's hiring custom cutters next year. Custom cutters! Do you know what that costs?"

"If only Sig had sold me the land, dumb bastard."

"I heard the Ford in the field had New York plates."

"I heard New Mexico."

Either is suspicious.

"Maybe it was a suicide," John Junior, the posse banker, says.

"I tell you right now," Uncle Jarl says, "he didn't kill himself. And the killer didn't walk ten miles back into town. So there's an accomplice. Someone who knows Billy Sorenson doesn't look after his land. Someone who knows *us*."

My uncle has birthed colts and babies. He's roped calves as well as his share of thieves who think that if no one lives on an old family homestead, everything from the light fixtures to the wood-burning stove is theirs to steal. An ambulance-crew beeper squats on his buckskin belt. He skinned the deer himself. Uncle Jarl dresses like a hillbilly and blows his nose with a big red handkerchief, but everyone listens to him because he's usually right.

According to the stranger's driver's license, Randall Sullivan was forty-two and had green eyes. No one could recall seeing him when he was alive. Not at church. Not at the grocery store. Not at the Town Dump. Anyone could have killed him. In a farming community, there is no shortage of guns. You never know when you'll come across a badger or a rattlesnake. My whole life, my uncle's had his rifle tucked in the gun rack of his truck. (Ford, Chevy, Ford, Chevy—never new, always alternating between dealers in Good Hope or south of here in Chaplain, so no one's nose gets bent out of joint. We spend a great deal of time making sure all noses stay straight.) Though Uncle Jarl's pickup changes every few years, the rifle doesn't. We don't lock our doors. The gun cabinet is only locked in December, to keep prying eyes away from the gifts stashed inside.

Children talk about the stranger and worry about dying. At the grocery store, they see dead bodies hidden behind quarts of Neapolitan ice cream. On the farm, the creak of the Quonset door sets my cousin Mindy on edge. Suddenly she wants to live in town like her friends. She hates the haunted howl of the wind, the desolate whistle of the train. She never gave much thought to the bogeyman but now believes he's taken up residence in the barn and won't tend her steer. She's half my age but tougher than I am. For the last three years, she's raised a bull to auction off at each county fair, earning a 4-H Best in Show ribbon and enough money to pay for a year of college. Four years ago, when I first moved to the farm, Uncle Jarl bought me a calf. The whole school year I babied Brutus, so much so that when the time came to sell him off for organic hamburger, I couldn't do it. He spends his time in the pasture, an obese bull who hobbles over when he sees me.

Tonight, Mindy wants me to go feed Theodore with her. I tell her I'm too tired after my shift. I don't tell her John Junior got in a fight with his wife at dinner. Or she got in a fight with him. Flo was out back having a smoke, so I was the one who had to break it up. I could smell the beer on his breath when he grabbed me. It was only when Flo stepped toward him that he backed away.

"Coward," his wife said.

After he paid, Flo said, "We see a lot of things we shouldn't have to in this job," before letting me off fifteen minutes early. I want to be like Flo, wise and tough, and fear I'll end up like her.

My arm is still tender. Bruises have formed. I just want to sit with my feet up. I tell Mindy not to worry, the killer isn't going to hunt her down on the farm.

"A man died in a field just like ours," she says.

I pull myself off the couch. When I pry open the barn door, she peeks her head in and looks both ways like she's crossing a busy street.

The next morning, Mindy tells us she wants to see where the stranger was found. My aunt—a hospice nurse used to dealing with death—says it's weird, and that no good can come of it, but my uncle tells me to take her, so we climb into the old Ford and crawl down the bumpy back roads. I don't know why she wants to go. I don't think she knows why. I suppose that for her, murder used to be something on TV, something far away. Now it's in our county.

At Sig's, all that are left are the indentation marks from

the cars. The field is a field. It's lonesome, but not sinister. The fireweeds are a foot high. Once I told my uncle they looked like Christmas trees and got the lecture of my life: *Do you know this "Christmas tree" is toxic to cattle? Do you know a single plant can produce 50,000 seeds? Do you know it'll break off at the base and travel for miles?* Looking over the long strip of summer fallow, I see the lines that tumbleweeds have drawn, sowing Russian thistle or fireweed on their journey. It drives Uncle Jarl crazy to see land abandoned like this. I understand why he asked me to bring Mindy. I glance over at her. Her blond hair is in a ponytail, and she has that look on her face, the one she gets when folks start bidding on her steer. Sad but stoic. She starts pulling up stalks of fireweed, ripping the roots from the soil. I wish I could remove the angst she feels as easily.

"Poor man," she says. "I feel bad for his family."

When she's ready to go, I tell her to take the wheel. We roll down the windows and turn up the volume. Maybe singing Dolly Parton at the top of our lungs will exorcise Mindy's feelings of fear. I learned to drive when I was ten, too. She hits the gas and the truck flies down roads that run parallel to the big sky.

We survey your land, we survey your life. We hear what you won't say. Nothing escapes us. Nothing escapes. If you were born here, you will die here. I think of the stranger. Even if you weren't born here, you'll die here. We know everything. We know that Nancy Mallard loves her horses more than her husband John Junior. We figure her brother Davey might be gay. We know the hospital administrator resigned because he got caught embezzling. (He's not from here.) Knowledge moves through us, around us, with us, against us. So why don't we know who killed the stranger?

* * *

Rob Skelton, the posse lawyer, starts coming into the café earlier. *Choose your friends wisely, College Girl. Partiers might be fun, but you'll end up bailing them out for the rest of your life. Do you know how many times I had to go get John Junior from the drunk tank this summer? Nancy won't pick him up anymore. You sure do look good, College Girl.* I begin to think of him as apart from the posse. Rob. In crisp suits that still smell of dry-cleaning chemicals, he makes me think of life in New York City. Talking to him lets me dream of other worlds. It doesn't feel like he's almost twenty years older than me.

When John Junior and Brad Halsted join Rob, I move on to the Ladies' Auxiliary table. At my graduation party, Hazel Murphy gave me a homemade laundry bag embroidered with my initials. It'll come in handy in the dorm. Betty Davis gave me twenty-five dollars in quarters. "For warsh," she said loudly. But in my ear, she whispered, "Play the slots. I hope you win big."

People are still talking about the stranger. "What drove him to come here, of all places?" Brad asks as I pour his coffee.

"A Ford!" my uncle shouts out for a laugh. The Town Dump is a boxing ring after all, full of fights, jabs coming from all corners. It's a place we see everything, we hear everything.

Who killed Sullivan? Why here? Why now? Speculation continues all week though there's an hour intermission for church. After Pastor Joe frees us, we lumber over to the church hall for donuts. At the pulpit of the percolator, the sheriff tells us what he knows: "The stranger was"—a pause as he sips his coffee—"here undercover."

Like heavy heads of wheat whispering to each other right before harvest, murmurs ripple through the room.

"FBI?"

"Border patrol?"

"Workers' Comp?"

"PETA?" They were here last year, nosing around the Bar None feedlot, just out of sight of the highway, where 1,700 horses were crammed together in two corrals completely unprotected from the elements.

"I knew it," Uncle Jarl says. "He was investigating someone."

This is the thing: we're used to watching. But we had no idea we were being watched. That an outsider was interested in us.

"An investigator?" I ask my uncle. "What was he doing here?"

Was he after Jim Ballestreri? Jim said he injured his left shoulder plumbing underneath Blanche Hellinger's sink. He's been on disability for years. He's also the town's best southpaw bowler, playing in weekly winter tournaments.

Was the investigator targeting Meg Walker? She said she'd hurt her back hoisting bags of flour at her job in Albertson's bakery. In front of God and Great Falls, the doctor (her brother-in-law) swore that she could barely lift a bar of soap. Yet who hadn't seen her picking up fifty-pound bags of Purina for those pit bulls of hers?

Or maybe it isn't about disability at all. Maybe it's about fraud. Several tavern owners pay barmaids under the table. That's how farmers, even my uncle, pay summer help.

The possibilities are as endless as our horizon.

At noon, the Starks, who own the Breeze Inn, sit in one of Flo's booths. They answer our questions tersely. Mrs. Stark admits they talked to the stranger when he checked in. He kept to himself. Had been here two days. Hadn't ordered any of those extra TV channels. The Starks didn't know if he had any visitors. They didn't find any binoculars among his belongings, no camcorder either, just an empty Minolta and a metal briefcase they hadn't tried to open. There was a copy of *The Grapes of Wrath* on the nightstand.

No, they didn't know when he was at the motel or when he was out in the field, so to speak. They had twelve rooms and prided themselves on the privacy reserved for their guests. No, they didn't think he was having an affair. He was a middle-aged man, just like you see in the background of movies or at the mall.

The sheriff, who wears his holster strapped underneath that reassuring gut, is tight-lipped as he and Deputy Dina examine the dead man, his motel room, our faces. They find fingerprints on the gun, alibis in the bar. If they have a suspect, we don't know about it. And a suspect would be reassuring. Someone to blame. Someone to target. Someone who would let us relax, knowing the killer and his accomplice are locked away.

With no suspect, everyone is suspect. People start asking what Jim was doing on Sig's land. It was hunting season, but Billy insisted Jim hadn't asked permission to be there. Maybe Jim murdered the investigator and couldn't stand to wait till Billy got around to finding the body. And then there's Meg Walker, who has a permit to carry a concealed weapon. "So she carries a gun," Flo says. "How would she ever find it in that purse of hers?"

"Laugh all you want," John Junior says. "I'm telling you, she gets a look in her eye."

"So does every woman who sees you," my uncle says. "You ask me, Duke Miller has the most to lose. What if Uncle

Sam makes Duke reimburse all the workers' comp payments? There goes his bar. His house. His wife."

"That bar's his life."

"Some life."

A man is dead. There has to be a reason.

The sheriff and the deputy drive to the funeral in Helena, where there is already said to be talk of naming something after the inspector. The Sullivan Building. Or maybe Sullivan Street.

The widow comes up a week later. The sheriff's wife offers to let her stay with them, but Mrs. Sullivan wants to stay where her husband did. She reserved his room for a week. She walks around town in a daze. We don't know what to do. Meet her eye and nod? Give her privacy to grieve by glancing away and pretending we don't know who she is?

The Ladies' Auxiliary takes over homemade buns and salads. Mr. Stark puts his daughter's old dorm refrigerator in the room so the food will keep. In the end, Mrs. Sullivan stays just two nights before quietly bundling her husband's things into the trunk of her Chevy. Folks in town take care of her bill.

Late fall, it already feels like winter with flurries of snow swirling along the Hi-Line. Farmers feed their animals, then come in. Harvest long over, they have time. All morning, they sit in one of my booths. They talk taxes. Politics. Murder. I like the cadence of their voices, smooth as the cream they pour in their decaf.

"Remember the Johnson case?" one asks.

"It's been what, twenty years now?" my uncle responds.

"No, thirty."

It's hard to understand how they let an entire decade slip

from their grasp. The minutes of my life tick by so slowly.

The Johnsons were accountants, from Arizona originally. After a forty-year career here on the plains, he wanted to return there for good. The cold had seeped into his bones and maybe even a part of his brain. She wanted to stay in the home where she'd raised her kids and now spent time decorating with her son's old wrestling trophies and her daughter's photography. But Old Man Johnson wasn't sentimental. To get her around to his way of thinking, he doused the house and burned it down. She retaliated the only way she knew how: she grabbed her daddy's rifle and shot him. The judge, who we call "Catch-and-Release," was understanding. She'd been provoked. Still, he said, she couldn't stay in Montana. And that was her sentence.

"Duncan McKenzie," my uncle says.

The men look deep into their cups.

I wasn't alive when he raped, tortured, and strangled Lana Harding, a young teacher. Years of legal pirouettes keeping him on death row have not kept McKenzie slim. Most people want him to hang, but he's so fat that a noose would rip his head clean off his body. Frankly, no one sees a problem with this.

That murder happened not far from a one-room schoolhouse in another Montana field. Years later, my uncle still tears up when he thinks of Lana and her parents.

But these cases are different. The Johnsons were from Arizona. McKenzie was born in Chicago. We could console ourselves that these killers were not from here. But whoever killed Sullivan is.

Snow continues to come down, flakes glint on the garden and whisper along the sidewalk, the first of the season that stick.

When I come back from feeding the steers in the barn, Mindy is thrilled because KSEN announced that today is a snow day. For one day, no blaring bells, no soggy fare in the lunchroom. It is the middle of the week and her time is her own.

While she puts her pajamas back on, I get ready for work, tying my brown apron over my uniform, a sherbet-orange dress.

"Do you have to go?" asks Mindy, holding up the *Parcheesi* board.

"Waitresses don't get snow days." When had I sailed from salutatorian to waitress?

"Just a few more months," she says, echoing the words I keep telling myself.

"I don't want you driving those roads!" my aunt—probably attached to her curling iron—yells from the bathroom. "Why don't you call in and tell 'em you can't make it?"

I perk up at the pity, but my uncle says, "She can handle herself."

Suddenly, I don't feel so bad about going in to work. I tell Mindy to get dressed again because I know she won't want to stay alone on the farm. "You can help me wrap silverware in napkins."

Uncle Jarl started my truck and scraped its windows, so by the time Mindy and I step into the cold, the cab is warm. The drive to town is only fifteen miles. Up the dirt road onto the Hi-Line, which runs parallel to the tracks, which runs parallel to the Canadian border. The sky is white, the highway is white. The snowplow passed by earlier this morning, but the wind has already whipped the snow off the skinny shoulders and flung it back on the road. On days like this, the road feels narrower than ever, an ice rink rather than an artery that leads to the heart of town. I crawl along at forty, grateful my uncle has weighed me down with feedbags that stop the Ford from fishtailing.

We walk through the door of the Town Dump just as KSEN announces that the highway patrol decided to close the highway, 120 miles of whiteout. My first thought is, why couldn't they have decided before Mindy and I got in the truck? My second thought, as I pass behind the counter and hang up my coat, is that if the snow keeps up all day, we might be stuck in town and have to spend the night at Flo's. My third thought almost makes me drop the carafe as I pour myself a coffee. Among us is the killer. He can't get far and neither can we.

At the counter, Mindy swivels on the stool. The daily ballet begins. Though the wind revs up to forty miles an hour, locals aren't afraid to drive short distances. It feels like most everybody passes through for a cup of coffee or Flo's hot chocolate, to marvel out the window at the snow or to complain about winter before it even starts.

Rob comes in. "Hey, College Girl," he says, and I grin.

Flo notices us smiling at each other. "Maybe I should take the posse table for a while."

I shake my head, unwilling to give Rob up.

"Did you get that early admissions application in, College Girl? Did you . . ." Rob stops talking when John Junior sinks into the booth, still hungover. He should be just plain John—his dad's been dead for a decade—but we call him Junior because he's still the high school jock who copied Rob's homework.

"Pity he and Nancy never had children," Flo tells me. "Sometimes a man like that grows up at the same time as the kids."

Ever the real estate agent, Brad Halsted goes around to each table and hands out flyers with photos of the house his agency is selling, like we all haven't been inside the Thornton place a thousand times. He nods politely at Flo before sitting with Rob and John Junior.

We all watch the sheriff hold the door open for Deputy Dina. The holster at her waist accentuates the sway of her hips. Both of them look tired. The sheriff listens as she speaks. She's much younger than him. If he desires her, he hides it well. When I finish taking their order, Dina tells me the night before was spent trolling the highway and pulling out-of-staters from ditches. They are always looking out for us. If we go down the wrong road, they will bring us back. I feel safe when they are here.

The farmers come in next. My uncle pulls off his old work gloves. His callused hands cup the beige mug. County trucks sidle up to the café and work crews bring in gusts of cold with them.

"Close the damn door!" Meg Walker yells from a booth close to the entrance.

One of them is the fiancé who jilted her at the altar twenty years ago, so no one takes offense. Another flirts with me. I don't flirt back. He dated my best friend—she's at Carroll College now—and I know what's hidden behind those smiles.

"Leave her alone," Jim Ballestreri warns him.

"No way," Meg Walker tells her daughter as I set the bill between them on the table. "You're not quitting, I worked too hard to get you on the squad!"

Meg comes up to the register to pay. She digs around in her Dooney & Bourke, and I wonder if she really has a revolver in there. Finally, she finds her checkbook and writes out the exact amount, $8.53. Anyone else would have made it for ten. She has the money to buy a $150 purse but can never seem to find a few quarters for a tip. I imagine her riding in the car with the stranger, things not going her way. I wonder if they were lovers. When she leaves, I tell Flo, "It's easy to believe a bad tipper might be a murderer. No respect for rules or social contracts."

"Hon," Flo says, "it's more complicated than that."

But this is the lens through which I see people.

Snow is still falling, downy as dandelion fluff. It sticks to windshields, the parking lot, the wet sidewalk.

"Report came in yesterday," the deputy says, just loud enough for everyone to hear. An informal press conference. No one makes a sound. "The Smith & Wesson .357 revolver on the seat of the car wasn't the murder weapon."

"It was a Colt .45 automatic," the sheriff adds. He looks over at the posse. "A few folks around here have one." He ambles over to the men.

"I thought it was suicide," John Junior says.

"Oh, you thought," the sheriff scoffs. "We almost missed finding the .45's ejected shell casing way back under the front seat. The killing bullet blasted out the roof to who knows where, but the state crime lab in Helena says they can match the casing to the gun that shot it."

"We'll need to see your gun," the deputy tells John Junior.

"That's going a little far. You reading his rights?" Brad Halsted says. I'm surprised it is the real estate agent who speaks up for his friend, not the lawyer. My eyes skitter to Flo's, and it dawns on us that Rob knows something about the murder.

"You want to get involved in this?" the deputy asks Brad Halsted.

The sheriff has more cards than anyone in town and he knows how to stack the deck. Brad's son got a DUI his junior year of high school, and we're all pretty sure he forgot to mention it on his college applications. He has two more years to go at Cornell. One phone call might change that. Shaking his head, Brad folds.

So does John Junior. "Spent half an hour looking for that casing," he tells the sheriff. "It's always some little thing."

They escort him into the blizzard and the backseat of the squad car.

Someone exhales. I move to Mindy, still on the stool. She hugs me tight and I can feel her tremble. No one moves. No one speaks. For the first time, my uncle is silent. He sits in the booth, handkerchief in both hands, eggs over easy half-eaten on his plate.

There is no satisfaction. It's not like TV with a standoff between the criminal and the law. It's not an Agatha Christie novel with a soliloquy explaining why. Without a motive, it feels like a random game of *Clue*: the banker did it, in the field, with the automatic.

Over the next few days, facts flurry together. John Junior thought his wife was having an affair. He followed Nancy around town and saw her talking to Sullivan in his car, heads tilted together, behind the bowling alley. He didn't know that she'd been gathering information about the Bar None feedlot, where she'd snuck in and taken photos of forty dead horses rotting in pens filled with soggy manure. We learn that it was Rob who picked up John Junior from Sig's farm after the murder and drove him back to town. Not an accessory, but an accomplice nonetheless.

He still comes in early—*Hey, College Girl, have you signed up for your classes yet?*—trying to be friendly like before. We don't talk to him. Flo pours his coffee now.

We're glad Mindy's back to tending her steer. Good thing

too. It's almost fair time. Theodore's up to 1,200 pounds. She spends more time blow-drying his hair than I do mine. We still don't understand how the killer could be someone we know, someone who contributed to my college fund every morning. "I smiled at a murderer while serving him breakfast," Flo murmurs to herself. It's the first time we've ever seen her fazed. After the trial, John Junior ends up in the state pen. We feel sorry for his mother. Folks shake their heads and say this never would have happened if John Senior were still alive.

You can see the wind today. It whips car antennas in the parking lot, it turns the pasture across the highway into an ocean of light-green waves. Tumbleweeds blow by the gas pumps, through town, on their way to the rest of the world. Won't be long and I'll follow.

DARK MONUMENT
BY SIDNER LARSON
Havre

Back when I was alive, we knew better than to chase yes-terday, but here you are, blood of mine, a full-grown man with no more sense than those wandering orphan ponies we called catch colts.

I flew into Denver and then changed planes for Helena. It would take a couple more hours to get to Havre from Helena than from Great Falls, but I didn't mind because it would allow me to drive through the healing space of Wolf Creek Canyon and give me time to think. I upgraded to the biggest rental car available in case I needed to sleep in it, tossed my duffel bag in the backseat, and hit the road around six p.m.

Havre, Montana. Shit. After nearly thirty years gone and now sixty-some years old, I was on my way back to Havre. Havre of the underground tunnels where hookers and Chinese railroad workers once roamed. Havre where the Indians were treated so badly in the old days that the Catholic Church had to send Black Robes to intervene with the other whites. Havre where my great-grandfather was the government scout and packer who found Chief Joseph and the Nez Perce for General Miles at the time of their desperate flight to Canada.

Didn't like the son-of-a-bitch Miles, but I took a job, so I did it. Indians like me keep their word, Colt.

It was about ten when I arrived. I drove slowly through town toward the Montana Bar, shocked to see the entire block was now a parking lot. Back when, there'd been three bars and a hotel, with the Montana on the east end. Wiped from the face of the earth, I thought. Biblical. Or at least corporate, which does not reward family, community, or "cities" in the middle of nowhere with no industries or oil or glitter and populations the size of Havre's not-quite ten thousand souls.

I drove the rest of the way through town with the hair on the back of my neck standing up. It was like driving through a fog bank full of ghosts. I gripped the steering wheel, put my foot back on the accelerator, and emerged on the other side of town, headed for Chinook. The Bear Paw Battlefield was fifteen miles farther south, and I yearned to get out there to listen for the spirits on the morning breeze. I shit you not, when things are right you can hear voices along the creek below the monument.

I picked up my phone as the Plainsman Bar outside of Chinook came into view, eerie in the darkness and looking like it had been closed for quite a while. Elizabeth answered on the second ring and I said, "I just passed the Plainsman."

"Okay," she replied, "I'll meet you at the Chief Joseph Motel."

Motel? Man leads his tribe damn near a thousand miles, beating the hell out of the US Cavalry most of the way until I come along, then takes a stand and surrenders so his women and kids won't get killed, and what—they name a seedy motel after him? And you stay there?

It took me awhile to roust the motel clerk, a disheveled older woman who grumpily shoved the registration card my way, then went to the front window to see if I had a "floozy" in the car. Not that the clerk cared, as long as I paid.

The room smelled of dust that had probably been there since the eighties when Elizabeth and I first used these highway "cabins" as our rendezvous, our safe place. Tan bedspread, a couple of saggy pillows, a chair, a table, a TV on a chest of drawers (one wouldn't close), a bathroom with a shower that dripped. I tried not to pace a hole in the thin carpet as I left the room open to the night.

Elizabeth filled the doorway twenty-three minutes after I got there. Her hair was longer and darker, lined with silver, but she'd kept her elongated beauty. She still had full breasts and good legs.

We stood staring at each other like a couple of teenagers.

"Thanks for coming," she said. "And meeting me here."

"Why not in Havre?"

"I don't know, it's not like before, I guess."

Fine woman, bad liar, and you know it, but as usual you are letting her lead you on, Colt.

"Not like before," I said.

"When we were married to other people."

"We buried all of that. And both of them. It's too bad, but . . ."

"Yeah," she said. "But letting some secrets out on Main Street won't do anybody any good now."

You got no idea what she means, do you?

She sat on the chair. I sat on the bed.

"Besides, if you really can help, I don't want Bill to know you're going to *until.*"

"He has always considered himself bigger and better than anybody else *until,*" I said. "Especially when the *anybody else* is somebody like me."

I grew up part Gros Ventre Indian, on the Fort Belknap reservation in Montana, smack in the middle of the Grovons' ongoing battle with the modern world. All these hundreds of years since we were "discovered," many of us came from the mingling of blood, both a devastating and strengthening thing.

Least you got that right.

"Wild Bill" Wendland was a rich white kid from up on the Hi-Line—the stripes of highway and railroad that run across the top of Montana and smack through Havre. Bill had gone to law school someplace back east, then come home to claim his due. He'd been a customer when I ran a tavern, liked to hang out because Elizabeth and her husband drank there, even though there were classier joints in Havre. Elizabeth's husband never figured out why she preferred it, but Bill's eyes figured us out even as he brazenly put the moves on her in front of her husband. The husband was a "lots of potential" man who'd peaked in college. As Elizabeth worked her way up the academic ladder of success, eventually becoming a dean, she'd been unable to make him strong or successful, though part of his problem might have been the cancer slowly eating him. We didn't know about that until years later.

Wild Bill had been a bad customer in every sense of the word, even before his lecherous behavior toward the marriage-trapped woman I loved in secret until my own wife saved herself, dumped me, and I wandered away from Havre. I realized how deep Bill's badness ran in those confusing times one hot summer night in the parking lot outside my bar. I'd carried a bucket of beer bottles out to the trash and turned around to see Bill had left the jukebox country-and-western songs and followed, probably to mock or challenge me in that rich, small town–jerk way of his. But headlights caught us standing there before either of us could say a word.

The car rattled to a stop and out of the driver's side came JoeBoy Eagleman. There were a few Indians, like JoeBoy and me, who had been around both the white towns and the reservations since we were kids. He was a friend, about six feet tall and slender. He had a wooden crutch under his left arm, and his left leg was crooked below the knee, marking him as one of polio's last easy victims in America. He stood on the parking lot gravel in the headlights of his car and said in a singsong Indian brogue, "Hey, I'm lookin' for you, Bill, *ennit?*"

Bill, a good three inches taller and probably thirty pounds heavier, sneered at the Indian with the crutch. "Whyn't you come over here then?"

"I can't walk too good, *ennit!*" JoeBoy replied, limping ahead a couple steps.

"That's too bad, *ain't it?*" Bill said, mocking the all-purpose Indian phrase.

"Hey, I come to tell you to quit those lawsuit things you doin' on my brother Tennyson."

"The law's the law. Even for your kind." Bill grinned. "Maybe especially for your kind."

"What you doin', finding that shit to take him to court, bust him flat paying for lawyers so he's got to sell the land to you? That's what you're doin', *ennit?*"

Bill growled: "Fuck you, smoked meat."

"Hey, fuck you too, then."

Bill walked toward JoeBoy. "You better get outta here before I kick your Indian ass!"

"Come over here and make me then, *ennit?*"

JoeBoy moved back a step, tossing his crutch to the side. Then he crouched, putting weight on his good right leg while raising his fists. Bill punched with his right hand. JoeBoy deflected the swing with his left and hit him so hard on the chin that Bill dropped to the ground like a sack of potatoes.

JoeBoy nodded to me and picked up his crutch.

Splayed on the ground, Bill fumbled around under his

hips, reaching for his back pocket, where he could have—

JoeBoy swung the tip of his crutch through Bill's legs and slammed him hard in his crotch. Whatever Bill was reaching for got forgotten as the hotshot lawyer doubled up and grabbed his throbbing groin with both hands.

JoeBoy climbed in his car and drove off.

Bill slowly raised himself to his hands and knees. From where it had fallen on the gravel, he scooped up a short-barreled revolver like the cops carried on TV when we were kids. "You saw! That was assault and battery! Call the cops."

"*You* call the cops," I said. "I'll tell them and everybody else what I saw. You threatened him, he defended himself, and then you got your ass kicked by an Indian with a crutch and a bum leg." I laughed, even as the notion nudged my wandering *what if*'s: what could the law do?

Bill pushed himself to his feet. "You fucking . . . Indian!"

"Don't worry about your tab tonight. On the house."

The house of my bar and marriage lasted only another two years, but that was longer than JoeBoy's brother, who Bill hit with every possible lawsuit he and his money could conjure up out of life in Montana. But while the Eagleman family lost their ranch, they always told the part of the story where Joe-Boy kicked that lawyer's ass and I was the witness.

And that story is what sent JoeBoy's auntie to see me as I was packing up the last of my stuff in the bar to wander in a new direction. I was leaving Elizabeth, my ex-wife, and my tavern behind to become one of the oldest law students in University of Minnesota history, in an attempt to reinvent my life away from Havre.

Don't you know we never get to leave who we are, just like we never get to go back and be someone else? You think I didn't have regrets about Looking Glass?

A few weeks before I thought I was leaving Havre for good, Wild Bill was acquitted of raping an Indian girl from the Rocky Boy reservation.

JoeBoy Eagleman's aunt walked in through the front door I'd kept unlocked so I could carry boxes out to the U-Haul.

"Here," she said. "I want you to make that Wasichu suffer."

She handed me one of the Montana Bar jackets I'd bought for the softball team I sponsored over the years. Bill'd played on the team just long enough to get a jacket and piss off everyone in the league.

"This was in the backseat of the car the night Bill Wendland raped my niece. After he did it, she got away and ran off carrying it. She threw it away but I went back and found it."

"You should give this to the police," I told her.

"Hah, them were barely believing my girl, and she didn't think to tell me 'bout it until after that judge let him off." She shook her head. "You was witness once to him. That damn jacket's got the name of your place on it, so now your place is stuck bein' witness with it, too."

She walked out before I could figure out what to say.

I kept the jacket and held my tongue. I wanted to help but didn't know how, figured after I became a lawyer I'd find a way to right the old wrong. But that would have meant coming back to Havre. I never forgot about the girl but I never did a damn thing, either. I sure as hell never made Wild Bill suffer for what he'd done.

And now, thirty years later, Elizabeth and I sat in a cheap and musty motel out of sight of Havre's eyes as she told me what he'd been up to lately.

"All the time since you left, all the time even before my husband died, it didn't matter if one of his wives was around or not. Bill's . . . I don't think he even really wants me. He just wants me to suffer because I wouldn't say yes to him but I said yes to you." She shrugged. "I need a lawyer, one he doesn't own."

"You need a friend too, not just a lawyer. How bad is it?"

"Relentless. And invisible. Forget about whatever happens in the streets or grocery store. He's a big donor to the college, serves on all sorts of boards, they even give him an office, and yeah, maybe there's some way that's also spinning bucks for him, but mostly he does it because he loves the clout, the power. He's been pushing the college to 'modernize' by dumping my humanities programs to replace them with computer classes and how-to-be-a-cog business classes. He doesn't give a shit, but he lets me know that if I want to stop the squeeze and save the department so I'll still be a dean, what I have to do is . . ."

"You said stuff happens in the streets?"

"The usual harassment most women get, but a couple times . . . I've seen his car drive through the alley behind my house. Or parked just up the block with him sitting in it. I called the cops once and he told them he was pulled over to take a call, just like the law says."

He was stalking her at night. I couldn't say what I was thinking. Fearing. All I could say was: "I'll talk to him."

She laughed. "Like that'll do any good."

"Some words weigh more than others."

"But—"

"No. No more tonight. You called me to come help. I will."

Outside, the high prairie wind blew from the west, over the motel, toward Havre.

"It's late," I said. "Why don't you stay?"

"Aren't we kind of old for this?"

"Yes."

She looked at me a long moment, then took her purse into the bathroom.

I turned off the rest of the lights and sat on the bed, watching as she took off her clothes. I pulled back the covers and lay down. A few minutes later, she stretched out beside me.

We were still for a while and then I traced the contours of her face and breasts with my fingers. She was wet when I touched between her legs and I rose and settled on her like a dark bird seeking her white flesh. I entered her quickly, opening my senses at the same time, and knew that although time and distance had intervened, our old connection was still alive and well.

Afterward, we didn't talk about what was going on. I couldn't stop myself from telling her about my great-grandfather, Louis Shambo, and the Battle of the Bear Paw where he shot Looking Glass, war chief of the Nez Perce, as they tried to escape from Idaho to Canada.

When I was kid, my friends and I used to ride up to the battlefield to look for shell casings and smoke cigarettes in the willows along the creek below the monument at the top of the hill. People still leave offerings inside the wrought-iron fence that encloses the spot where my great-grandfather shot Looking Glass as he raised his head to look out of the rifle pit he had dug.

The next morning, Elizabeth and I bought coffee at a gas station near Havre after we left the motel. We filled our cups and sat, listening to news of the latest mass shooting on the radio.

"Jesus," I said, "what's the world coming to?"

"What do you think I should do?" she asked.

"Give me a chance *to* do," I told her.

"After all these years, now it's my turn?" she said.

"It was always your turn. Just never my time."

She shook her head but her face wouldn't tell me what she was really thinking.

Too late for that, Colt. Too late! So now be a warrior.

I sipped my coffee. "I'm going to look up Bill Wendland. You said his office is in Morrill Hall?"

"Yes," she said, her eyes wide. "What are you going to do when you see him?"

"I'm going to be who I am."

She didn't ask any more questions.

I followed her the rest of the way back to Havre and watched her make the turn toward her place. That could be a place to live. A place I could finally let go and settle down.

I kept driving, past the former site of the Montana Bar, then turned left toward the college that overlooks the town from the south.

I knew Central Montana had become mostly a vocational college, but back in the day there was a strong liberal arts focus to go along with the diesel mechanic school. The majority of the students were from Montana, white and Indian, now with a growing number of Latinos, all of whom needed the leg up in life—or at least the certification of success—that a diploma can provide. All of them needed someone with the good heart of Elizabeth to watch over them, teach them about life beyond dollar signs, and shelter them from academic wars and the power of nasty guys like Bill Wendland.

Morrill Hall was the centerpiece of the campus, an impressive Ivy League–looking structure with a big bell tower reaching for the sky. It was on top of a steep rise, with a large pond and fountain toward the bottom of the slope. I drove up the hill, around to the parking lot in back, and climbed the stone steps to the rear entrance. Another staircase with marble steps curved up and to the left, and as I made my way to the third-floor administrative offices, I could feel my adrenaline surge.

I walked down the hall past big oak doors with gilt lettering on them until I spotted the one with his name, just his name, on it. I opened the door and stepped inside, where I could see a receptionist's desk with a hallway beyond. I stood there, and after a couple of minutes a middle-aged woman emerged from the hall. She looked like a drill sergeant.

"Can I help you?" she asked.

"Yes, I'm here to see Bill," I replied.

"Your name, please?"

"Mr. Smith."

"Do you have an appointment?"

"Yes, I think we were set for ten," I lied.

"I don't see anything on his calendar. May I ask what this is about?"

"I'm from the Edsel Foundation, here about matching your donor contributions with our dollars."

That got her attention. "Let me go tell Mr. Wendland you're here."

She came back shortly. "His office is at the end."

I walked down the hall and into Bill's wood-paneled office. His back was to me as he rearranged twentieth-century file folders in a large cabinet. He heard me enter and turned.

"I'll be damned," he said, taking care to keep the desk between us.

I looked him straight in the eyes. "Long time no see."

He gave me the grin of a hungry spider. "Have a seat." He pointed to a leather chair.

I just stood there.

"I don't figure there's any foundation that sent the likes of you here, or anywhere, so what's up?" He smiled broadly, as if I was a long-lost friend or his next meal.

"Elizabeth."

"What about her?"

"Stop. Stop now and you still have a chance to keep all this glory and power. Stop messing with her, with her job and deanship. Stop hunting her in alleys and out of sight. Let her go, stay away, and keep her safe."

"Her safety has nothing to do with me." He sat in the leather-chair throne behind his big desk and grinned again. "I've done nothing wrong."

"Right or wrong, I've got something of yours."

His eyes narrowed. "What?"

"Meet me out at the Bear Paw Battlefield tonight."

"The Bear Paw Battlefield? What the hell's this all about?"

"If I was you, I'd be there, Bill," I said, turning around and walking out. "Before sunset so we can see what we've got to see."

I drove south from Chinook and turned off the highway toward the tourist facility on the edge of the battlefield. Across a coulee to the east, the monument sat on the highest point of ground. Farther to the east was a bare cutbank where I had buried the Montana Bar jacket in multiple plastic bags. My own private memorial on that sacred ground. My own feeble attempt to be a good witness and honor a victim.

Too many of what Bill called my "kind" had already been dishonored in history. I wanted him to represent his "kind" and answer for all that has happened to Indian people, to trapped women, to anyone his kind had abused. Even if I never got to crack his skull with the collapsible steel baton shoved in the back of my waistband.

Damn right, Colt, you take a job, you go in prepared and do it right.

I stood there waiting in the fading light. Thinking about Elizabeth. Me. Us.

With about a half hour of daylight left, I spotted the vehicle—a big black Suburban like the security guys in movies drive—heading south on the old highway coming from Chinook. It was going like a bat out of hell and careened off the blacktop onto the gravel road leading to where I was. When it straightened out again it raised a big plume of dust as it bore down on the tourist lookout point and skidded to a stop in the parking area.

Bill was out and on the ground before the car was fully settled to a stop, his red face nearly matching the tie loosely knotted around his beefy neck. He wore his hotshot lawyer suit, and I wondered if he still carried killer steel in his back pocket. He was breathing hard and didn't look happy as he stomped up the footpath to the lookout.

"I don't know what the fuck you're doing back here, or what you're up to, but I'm here to find out," he said, putting his hands on his hips as he stopped about ten yards from me.

"Leave her alone."

"Like you did. Like she is. Like she will be after you're gone again. All alone."

"You stop it all right now. No more going after her in any way, shape, or form. Or we'll see you in court. Win, lose, or draw there, your rep will be ruined, your clout will evaporate, and all your money will make you a big target that's been made weaker for every other person you've fucked with or fucked over all these years. They'll come out of the woodwork to go after you."

"What, you think you're a goddamn attorney or something now too?"

"Yup. University of Minnesota Law, class of '85."

"They gave you a law degree because you're a blanket-ass Indian son of a bitch?"

"Talk about blankets, Bill, I've followed your rape charge for a long time."

He looked at me incredulously. "So what," he finally said. "That's over and done with."

I reached into my shirt pocket, took out a folded piece of paper with three pictures printed on it, and handed it to him. The top picture was of the back of a satin warm-up jacket with *Montana Bar* silk-screened on it. The middle picture was of the front of the jacket, with *Bill Wendland* embroidered over the left breast. The bottom picture was of a dried stain below the name and above the left front pocket.

"You were a pretty good stick on that softball team, remember?" I said, as he looked at the pictures. "Those were nice jackets. Too bad yours has that stain on it. Like a stain on a blanket. What do think that is, DNA evidence maybe?"

"Statute of limitations," he shot back. "And even if that wasn't already up, I was found not guilty, and they can't try me twice for the same offense. The law's the law."

"True. But I bet I can get some DNA match from you somewhere—off a cup you drink coffee from, at your barber. You'll have to spend the rest of your life watching out for that."

You need more to nail him! You need—

"And even if I don't get the criminal science, the girl is a woman now and has heirs. Some of them live around here. I'll file a dozen civil lawsuits, spill out every accusation in subpoenas for evidence, and make it huge so it'll get in the papers. Sure, you might get every one of those lawsuits thrown out, but the evidence I'll introduce will create evidence others can use to, say, show a legally established pattern of propensity for . . . for whatever someone else accuses you of. With me as a witness to put it all in context, because the law is the law, *ennit?*"

"You come after me—"

"I come after you only if you keep after Elizabeth. If she so much as gets bit by a mosquito, I'm going to file some of the most beautiful briefs you've ever seen. And out of where I and my friends know it's hidden—"

"Shit, I know more than you know 'bout bluffing!"

"—I'll display that jacket at every press conference. Makes a great photo. Or hell, I'll post one online. New century, new ways, same old shit."

He made a move toward me.

The baton filled my hand and flicked out like a black stick to count coup. "Not quite a crutch, but it'll do," I said.

Whether or not he had iron in his back pocket, seeing the baton made him weigh his chances. "You keep all that yesterday shit to yourself," he said, "and she gets a clear road." Then he sneered the truth: "But the two of you, *never!* I won't let you win that much. You come around here, you take up with her, I'll spend every dime I've got making your lives miserable. Whatever smears you hit me with, I'll wipe twice as worse over the two of you. I'm a lawyer who's rich enough to afford my own cavalry of lawyers."

He stormed to his vehicle, got in, and tore off back toward the highway, throwing gravel as he went. I went back over to the lookout bench, sat down.

Guess this isn't win-win for you after all, Colt. You can't come back here, stop your wandering. You're like . . . You're my blood.

The lights of Havre were just over the hill from where I

sat. And now I was never going to grow old in their glow.

Or see again who I'd seen after I'd ambushed Bill in his office.

After that visit, I'd driven to Elizabeth's house, I don't know why—to warn her or to reassure or to just see her blue eyes again before I went off to battle. Maybe to find a reason to stop my wandering, even though I'd already figured Bill would do everything in his power to derail any plans I might have.

Then, as I turned the corner onto Elizabeth's block, I saw *him* coming out of her front door.

He was the same age as the years I'd been gone, a full-grown man with his mind and heart made up about who he was, and after I saw him wave goodbye to her without either of them seeing me, Havre's public library helped me track him down through Facebook and high school yearbooks. He'd grown up thinking that cancer had killed his biological father a long time ago. If I suddenly came into his life, he might hate his mother for lying and punish her in ways she didn't deserve. He'd take one look at me and wonder, but if he saw any paintings or pictures of my—our—famous great-grandfather, he'd know. And he didn't deserve to have the ground he called home pulled out from under him by that truth. That had already happened to enough of our blood.

As I sat there in the night, looking around the brown hills and at the two monuments, one of them visible only to my eyes, I thought about how remembrance is a piss-poor substitute for justice. I had lived into my own history, coming full circle, and now I was headed for the highway, driving away from another hand I couldn't beat. I felt the spirit of my never-met, long-dead great-grandfather, who for all he'd done right and wrong ended up wandering too. He would always be with me. The ghosts of who we come from are witness as we play the cards we're dealt and make monuments to what we did.

ALL THE DAMN STARS IN THE SKY

BY YVONNE SENG

Glasgow

Nora Jones began each morning much the same way since arriving on Montana's abandoned Glasgow Air Force Base, a rifle shot from the Canadian border. Stepping into her running shoes, she pulled a fleece over the sweats she slept in. Sipped cold coffee in the dark. Worked a wet washcloth across her face and shaved head, polishing the scar that still itched, avoiding the mirror, not turning on the light. Put on her watch cap, headlamp, gloves.

She shoved a log into the wood stove, stoked it against the spring chill that seeped through the thin walls. She paused outside her aunt's bedroom, drawing the door closed across the worn linoleum, smiling at the smell of senior sex and alcohol that wafted from the lumped-up quilt. Aunt Rosa and her boyfriend Phil. Phil—no illusions, just stubborn old love. Rosa—the reason Nora was there.

Stasi, Nora's doberman, sat erect by the front door, ears forward, waiting for the command. The dog was ready. A familiar spirit, silent, sleek, troubled.

In Vegas after the accident, Stasi had sat by Nora's bed for weeks, retrieving the phone when she dropped it, dragging up the covers and books that fell to the floor. The hospital wouldn't let the dog in, so Nora had gone home to a shitty apartment in the desert with an empty pool and Leonard Cohen's voice on repeat in the apartment upstairs. Stasi took up guard, kept visitors away, killed cockroaches. When restless, she'd leap through a neighbor's open window, bringing back a magazine for Nora, a packet of Cheetos for herself. Nora didn't ask questions.

Nora had liked it that way, just her and her silent guardian. Especially when her partner came to apologize. Nick, her aerial partner from Cirque du Somethin'. Nick who, stoked on early-morning coke, had forgotten to secure their practice cables and sent both the grapnel and Nora flying into the void. Scalped by the hooks, she broke bones, broke her heart. Something else too. At thirty-six, damaged, she was too old to fight the young wolves snapping at her heels. It was the end of Nick and Nora. The end of flying high.

The dog waited, silent, its eyes piercing the front door.

Nora whistled low and soft.

Stasi stood on hind legs and slid back the bolt with her teeth.

Nora had inherited Stasi from a friend doing time for burglary. Stasi, his assistant, had gone scot-free. Everyone in Vegas had a game. Stasi's was thieving. Which added a spark to their road trip back to Montana.

Outside, in the predawn dark, a billion cold stars pressed down, squeezing Nora's heart with their soft hum. As a child, she had wanted to fly among them, circling the earth, peering down on adoring faces looking up. Now she closed her eyes against the stars and concentrated on stretching out her hamstrings, checking the pins that held her body together.

Goddamn that endless Montana sky. Goddamn those stars. She had split because of those stars. A teenage runaway, fleeing into their embrace. She'd joined the circus. Not even original.

Now here she was, back again. Back to Aunt Rosa, her mother's sister, who'd taken her in after her folks died and left her alone to grow like a weed. Aunt Rosa, for whom neglect meant love.

Who'd said on the phone: "Get your sorry ass out here, girl. We're buildin' a dream and I need you."

Nora blew on her hands and started slow, Stasi tracking her left.

They ran the barbed-wire perimeter of the old air force base. Up here it was so flat you could see the curve of the earth. Bitter cold and clear skies. Decades ago, proud Cold Warriors floated three at a time on the sky's gentle arc, their planes idling among the stars, ready to speed across the Arctic and bomb the hell out of Russia at a moment's notice. Missile silos hid in wheat fields. Underground airmen, their fingers on the red launch button, stood ready to back up their airborne heroes, to bomb the shit out of a pigeon if they got the chance. The third-largest nuclear power in the fuckin' world, bragged the locals. With concrete sixteen feet deep, the jets' runway was long and strong enough for the thump of a landing space shuttle if needed.

Her cousin Frank, Rosa's son, had worked on that runway, shoveling cement the last summer of high school before he escaped to college, so she knew all about it. Only eight, she had a hard crush on Frank.

"Got a thing for your cousin, pet?" Rosa's only try at parenting.

Nora had blushed.

"First cousins," Rosa said. "Off limits. Taboo. Got it?"

Nora only glared. Unreachable, just like her mother.

"Can't say I didn't try," Rosa added with a shrug before walking away.

Nora rode Frank's lunch over every day, knobby knees bumping the handlebars of her outgrown bike. After work, he'd shower, back his pink-and-gold 1952 Dodge convertible out of the driveway, and she'd leap in. Pink tutu. Bare feet. Up the pin-straight highway, ripping past wheat fields, burning up the road to the Canadian border. He sweated out his anger while she swallowed her scream as they hit a bump in the road and went airborne, bending into the curve around a silo town. She soaked up Frank's approval: "Good girl, never show your fear."

"Hey, pipsqueak," he'd say as they approached the border roundabout, a casual thumbtack on the map before the world went crazy. "Ready?"

"Do it slow, Frank," she'd reply, cool as an Arctic breeze, lips pursed like she'd seen in the movies.

While he slowed the car to a crawl, she would stand in her seat, stepping over the windshield onto the hood, unfolding herself into a handstand. Spider legs in the air. Toes caressing the endless sky. Pink tutu fluttering like a spring blossom. They would slowly circle the border roundabout, past the cheering, dark-blue guards. An eight-year-old girl, hood ornament on a pink-and-gold convertible. Behind the wheel, a teenage boy in a checkered cowboy shirt, counting the hours to freedom.

On the road back, they'd give one final roaring yell before reaching the turnoff to the base. Slowing down, they'd salute the billboard that proclaimed: *This Is the Future.*

Proud days those had been for the residents of the base, who went to bed in their idyllic tract houses dreaming of that future. More than seven thousand brave souls, flyboys and their families, up there at the stark edge of the earth, beautiful except for the six months of winter, three months of mosquitoes, and the month of mud in between. Fewer than two hundred fools now slept in their abandoned beds.

Nora ran past the fenced-off runway and airfield. The Multinational Aerospace Corporation—MAC, Inc.—the world's second-largest aerospace empire, was using the airfield to test its latest technology up here in the cold, secret silence. Shiny new high-tech warehouses gleamed amidst the decay. Area Fifty-One-and-a-Half, the locals called it. Imaginations ran wild: UFOs, black ops, the Illuminati. Every few months, MAC, Inc. brought in a planeload of Germans or Japanese to check out the secret projects. A hundred of them at a time, the locals claimed, stayed a month in a nearby town, eating fat steaks and looking for cowgirls. Last week Nora had seen a convoy of rented cars with bewildered Asian faces behind tinted glass. Maybe they'd survive the month, but she doubted it. They'd die of boredom first.

Nora continued on through the fog that rose from the overgrown playing fields and headed back toward home. Night ghosts hissed at her. She couldn't begrudge their anger. She was alive. They were long gone but restless, their lives cut short by pink slips after the Cold War was forgotten. Most families had packed up their houses and transferred their dreams to warmer places. Some left their silverware in the sink as a gift to scavengers.

Except Aunt Rosa. Aunt Rosa would never have left her forks and furniture to be picked over, Nora mused as she cleared a rotted pole fence. Aunt Rosa had stayed put. Deciding not to go south with her flyboy husband, she got herself a county contract dismantling the commissary where she had once worked. She found a new boyfriend, then another one. And then Phil came along with his big dream.

Phil's dream wasn't even original. It was a hand-me-down from an old pal, a retired pilot who, thirty years ago, bought up the deserted houses, rechristened the base town St. Marie, and tried to build a refuge for right-living military retirees who wanted to hit golf balls over the horizon in peace and quiet. But the county raised the property taxes sky high. Bankruptcies, lawsuits, and liens followed. A luckless whore, St. Marie was once again abandoned. A few retirees hung on and Phil had seen opportunity in the isolation.

Phil's idea was short of work. He'd read a few business books on job retraining after the paper mill shut down and had a five-step plan. One: buy up the liens. Two: rebrand. Forget the golf course, build a shooting range to attract bird hunters. Three: horizontal expansion. Hunters need bullets. Maybe the government too, with all the wars it was getting itself into. He'd open a little manufactory in the empty commissary. Bring in some illegals, bunk 'em in the back, set 'em to work. Cartridges, casings, and slugs, all nice and quiet, off the map. Money from the cartridges would buy back the liens. Four: rename. No more St. Marie. Philson, Montana. He liked the sound of it. Five: he always forgot the fifth but loved the sight of his open hand.

"You're outta your mind," Nora had replied to her aunt's call to come home.

"You speak Mexican, doncha? We need you to handle the Mexicans."

"Salvadoran, Rosa, you said they're Salvadorans."

"Well, you speak Illegal, and that's good enough for me."

Shit, Nora thought as she replayed their conversation. Now here she was, up to her tits. Phil scouring the back road junkyards for brass and lead. Aunt Rosa handling the business end, Nora using her service-worker Spanish to oversee the men who poured the casings and the women who packed the cartons.

Phil wasn't the only one with a scheme. A couple years back, out-of-town suits arrived, bought back some houses from Jenkins at the bank, and moved motel furniture in. Shiny vans arrived in the middle of the night—dark glass, no number plates—to drop off passengers and suitcases. The next morning the town awoke to new residents. Sometimes it took a week for the new arrivals to come out into the sunlight, blinking at the endless horizon, the wheat-field ghost town with tumbleweeds whipping across the airfield.

For the most part, they kept to themselves. Always tetchy, always looking over their shoulders. Witness protection, the locals assumed, thereafter referring to them as the Witnesses.

Nora smiled to herself. What bright light in the feds had decided to dump a load of Witnesses on an abandoned air base in Montana? It was like some twisted, cosmic joke. Hiding in the wide open, spooked by the emptiness, afraid to leave. The Witnesses had bartered their lives for a death sentence in nowhere.

In the predawn, Nora and Stasi had the town to themselves. Lights flickered from a few scattered buildings as insomniacs twitched the curtains. Every seventh house or so was occupied. Early spring weeds poked through cracked roads. Some houses were immaculate, painted and polished. Others were lopsided, water stained, peeling.

The security light tripped on at Witness Mike Smith's small house and Nora caught the glint of his binoculars through the upstairs window. Always ready. An arsenal of guns in his garage. Late fall, Stasi had nicked a steak waiting by Mike's grill and the jerk had sworn he'd shoot the dog if she came in sight of his place again.

Winded, Nora slowed her pace on the edge of town. The

burned-out shell of the bachelors' quarters always spooked her, its jagged edges cutting the horizon.

Stasi sensed the presence before Nora. Ears back, her body a sleek arrow, she pointed movement at the corner of the carbonized building.

Nora narrowed her eyes, stopped in Stasi's frozen shadow. Smelled a whiff of cigarette smoke. Saw the red light of a draw.

High schoolers sometimes roared the twenty miles from Glasgow, up Zombie Road, they called it. They held all-night keggers in abandoned houses, had sex among the near-dead, and then torched the houses. Some tweakers had tried to move in and cook meth for the workers in the Bakken oil fields but blew themselves up. Now Philson had itself a repurposed fire truck, compliments of MAC, Inc., and a volunteer fire department, compliments of themselves.

Nora crouch-ran toward the safety of a dead cottonwood for a closer look. Her knee cracked and she cursed silently.

Among the ruins, hulking shapes from childhood memory. A tank. Convoy trucks. Vintage, as if from a black-and-white movie. She flashed on the air base doing military maneuvers: crisp uniforms, adrenaline smell, the thrum of convoy trucks. Her mental newsreel turned in the projector, motes of dust dancing in the light, as her young self sat squished between Rosa and Frank in the safe, warm dark.

But that was then. Like the billboard said, this was the future.

Beside the outdated convoys, a circle of new, mud-spattered pickup trucks. A glammed-up Humvee nearby. Not bird hunters—hunters of another kind.

She steadied her breath and lowered her temperature, an amphibian on a wire. Edging a few steps closer, she squatted down. Stasi quivered with readiness.

Nora clicked her tongue and released the dog like a silent missile. "Good girl. Bring me something."

Dawn leaked into day, pouring itself across the bleak ground. She picked out a couple of sleeping bags humped with blankets. Folding chairs blown on their sides. A head slumped against a truck window.

The breeze kicked up and chilled her sweat. Flapped the Confederate flag on the back of a pickup.

A truck door creaked open. Nora dropped low. Saw the leg—army boot, camouflage pants—coming down. Heard the hock of boozy phlegm followed by the sound of urine marking territory. Stasi hopped into the cab of the now-empty truck. Nora held her breath until she saw the canine shadow leap out.

Circling back to her, Stasi dropped the wad of paper on Nora's knee and waited for the handstroke on her forehead that said love.

Nora flattened out the paper and wiped away the dog saliva. She squinted at the blur of words.

WARNING! PRIVATE PROPERTY . . . You are hereby notified that the owner of this property requires all public officials, agents, or person(s) to abide by "THE SUPREME LAW OF THE LAND" . . . A person who knowingly enters unlawfully upon this property could place his/her LIFE AT RISK . . .

She stuffed the paper in her back pocket.

Militia. Nora had dated one once. A one-night stand, more like it, on the road home from Vegas. Too much booze, too many painkillers. She was lonely. He was in his midtwenties, on his way to Lincoln, Montana, to support some miners in an armed standoff against the Forest Service.

The militia were just regular guys, he'd told her: carpenters, drywallers, firefighters, EMTs. Even cops. Hard-working guys in a tough land. Vets from Iraq and Afghanistan. He'd done three tours. He was a concerned patriot who didn't like what our government was doing over there and liked what he saw at home even less.

I got no problem with Obama being black, he'd told her. *I fought next to his kind. But he's pushing un-Christian values.* Others in the militia thought Obama was the Antichrist. A front for the United Nations taking over the world or the Chinese buying America.

Someone's gonna get hurt, her new friend had said. She'd since met others like him. Locals who filled their freezers with deer and elk in the fall to feed the wife and kids. Stacked supplies in their sheds in case the feds took away their constitutional right to bear arms. They'd change a tire for you on a dark road, call you *ma'am,* and shoot you if you trespassed on their land.

Nora ran back through town to the house.

Aunt Rosa and Phil took up half the kitchen, two old crash cars in a fading carnival ride, brewing coffee, burning toast. Rosa, in the middle of pulling her long silver hair up in a ponytail, let it fall loose when she saw Nora in the doorway. Instead she pulled the threadbare kimono around her slight body and raised her coffee mug in the air, offering. At seventy, Rosa was flirting with twenty.

Nora nodded yes to the coffee and pulled off her watch cap. Stasi lapped water before bringing in her food bowl and dropping it at Nora's feet. Phil muted the local Fox News. A Botoxed face yapped in silence. Montana's congressman and an Asian trade delegation appeared on the screen.

"Look who's back," Phil said. "Fuckin' Yul Brynner."

Nora dried her bald scalp with Stasi's mud towel.

"Put some clothes on, fuckface," she replied. "Animal act is over."

Phil looked down at his ragged T-shirt, his paunch, his birdy legs that barely held his weight. He ran his hand through his thinning hair and tugged his stringy 'Nam ponytail.

"Girl, I love ya," he said, putting her in a headlock.

Stasi growled. Nora raised two fingers to signal she was fine and the dog sat.

"Cut it out, you two," Rosa intervened, her voice burred with sleep. "We've got work ahead."

Phil rubbed his face with his T-shirt, turned to Rosa who was scraping toast. "Got a spliff?"

"Not today, hon. Today's the big day. We're buying off the old man's liens. Tell her, Phil."

Nora pulled a parcel of chopped elk from the freezer to thaw for Stasi's dinner.

"Whoa, back up, girl," Phil said to Rosa. "Gonna be next week. Jenkins says more paperwork and then down to Great Falls for the big OK."

Aunt Rosa frowned. "Well, we're signing the bill of intent today, though. I hate all this waiting."

"Just one more week, love," Phil said. "Then Mailer and his militia can go eat shit. We beat them fair and square. This'll be ours, for our business, and no damn Constitutionalist militia is comin' in here and buildin' a compound."

Nora reached into her pocket for the piece of paper and handed it to him. "Too late," she said. "They're here."

Phil fumbled for his glasses. While he read, everything on him sagged: his jaw, his shoulders, the hula-girl tattoo on his arm.

Nora unscrewed a bottle of cheap bourbon, tipped coffee out of her mug, and added a generous shot. She broke a pain-killer in quarters, popped one, and washed it down.

"No way!" Phil shouted. "Not today! It's not happenin'!" He crumpled the paper into a ball and threw it at the unmarked cartons sitting near the door. "You know that bird-hunting group? The Duck Fuckers? They rented the range for today. Raffling off new guns for their fundraiser. Today! Money in the bank." Phil lurched toward the cartons and started pulling them apart. "Look! Springfield Stainless model 1911 .45 ACP!" He put it down, pulled a twelve-gauge shotgun from another carton. "Beretta A400 Xplor! Even has its own ducker serial number!"

Rosa balanced against the sink, her eyes as big as poached eggs. "Today was supposed to be our day, Nor. That money from the duckers puts us over the top."

"Browning bolt-action 7mm!" Phil ranted, spit flying.

"The duckers brought them here last night, so's we'd be all good and ready this morning." Rosa cocked her head toward the building where the illegals slept. "And the girls in the back are doing the food. Mexican. Real nice."

Nora heard sounds outside. A staple gun punching wood. Measured voices. Idling trucks. She held up her hand for quiet. "Shh."

"Shit, shit, shit." Phil paced. "And Bert's eightieth. The party."

"We hired those exotic dancers," Aunt Rosa explained. "From that white van. They're giving Bert a breakfast surprise."

Nora broke the bourbon bottle on the corner of the counter, loud as a hammer, shards and whiskey flying. "Shut. The. Fuck. Up."

"Don't talk to your uncle—"

"Mailer's militia. They know about the ammunition?" Nora asked. "The business? The illegals?"

Phil shrugged. "Fuck if I know."

"They want the UFOs," put in Rosa.

"The what?"

"The UFOs," repeated Phil, nodding at Rosa. "At MAC, Inc., Mailer's got this thing about the feds saying there's no UFOs when we all know they're everywhere. Says it's a secret base for a secret war and the Asians and the Germans are in on it too. They've got UFOs over there. Aliens too. And we're not talking fuckin' illegals."

"So Mailer doesn't want the town, he wants the UFOs?" said Nora.

"Take over the world, is what he wants," Phil replied. "He says if he don't fight back, the feds are gonna enslave the common man. The United Nations . . . the Chinese . . ."

Nora put her elbows on the kitchen counter, hid her head in her hands, her shoulders quaking. Tears of frustration and silent laughter sluiced down her face.

Schemers. Every goddamn one of them had a goddamn scheme. She had left Vegas to get away from the circus and here she was, back in the center ring.

"Now what, Phil?" demanded Rosa.

"Don't know, woman. You tell me."

Nora raised her head and wiped away the tears. She stood and kissed her aunt's forehead. "Call everyone and tell them to keep calm. We're having an emergency meeting."

"Even the Witnesses?"

"Yes, even the Witnesses. They may want to . . . duck." God help her. The absurdity of it all. "But first, get the sheriff out here."

"You really want that?" Rosa asked. "Him coming out here?"

Nora nodded. "No other choice. He's the sheriff."

"You know he's not a real sheriff, Nor. He's a doctor now. Real proud of him, we are. Just deputized a few weeks while Bert's off fishing."

"I said call him." She turned to Phil. "The banker lied to you. Ask the piece of shit how Mailer got there first."

"This is war!" shouted Phil.

"No, Phil. This is a problem," Nora countered. "The circus lion's loose, that's all." She clicked Stasi to follow, then stepped over shards of glass in a puddle of booze. Grabbing her daypack, she checked for her phone, fingered two keys on the chain around her neck, and made for the door.

"Take a wig," Rosa insisted. "Can't go out there lookin' like that."

Nora snatched the long blond one from the stands by the door—seven wigs, blond on Friday—and headed out. Stuffing the wig in her pack, she pulled on the watch cap.

"Think I'll call Fox News," Phil muttered.

Nora followed the thrum of idling vehicles, the *thwack* of notices being stapled to abandoned houses. A score of militiamen in army-surplus camo, semiautomatics slung across their shoulders, huddled outside the MAC, Inc. gate amid plumes of vehicle exhaust. In their center, Beau Mailer stood ramrod straight and flapped a large sheet of paper. He jabbed a finger toward three long buildings behind MAC, Inc.'s chain-link fence. He shook the paper at the barred gate. "Those buildings over there are ours. Part of the old man's lien. MAC, Inc. is on our land, men, and we have the right to occupy it."

One of Mailer's militia rattled the gate. "We're comin' in, fuckers!" he shouted up at the security cameras, then, grinning at the camera, he took aim and shot the invisible face watching through its lens. Everyone laughed. His eyes roved over Nora without seeing her.

She pressed herself into the rotting walls of the building. *Never show your fear, pipsqueak.*

Inside the fenced area, air force sirens wailed. A warehouse door rolled up. Two jeeps filled with athletic clones in black body armor drove across the tarmac, stopped a hundred feet from the security gate, and halted while the drivers waited for orders from their earphones.

Outside the gate, the pavement shuddered beneath Nora's feet. Expecting a lumbering circus elephant, she saw instead the militia's refurbished tank clanking toward them. The tank rammed the main gate and broke the guard bar. After two more runs, the machine ground to a halt, its elephantine trunk jammed into the chain-link fence.

"I think something's broke, boss!" the tank driver yelled over the MAC, Inc. sirens.

A voice behind Nora startled her: "What're you up to, ma'am?" He was young, feigning tough. Acne fighting through his downy whiskers. A pile of leaflets in one hand, a power staple gun in the other.

"Walking my dog."

He eyed the doberman. "You local?"

She nodded.

"Then where's this commissary place? Shit all looks alike 'round here." He showed her one of the leaflets. "Gotta post these warnings on the commissary."

The sirens were getting louder. Nora covered one ear and tried to think. The illegals were inside the commissary and God knew what Mailer's militia would do to them. And it was only a matter of time before they found Phil's munitions factory.

She pointed toward the decaying elementary school that had failed to contain her. "Down there," she said.

A cloud of dust rose from the state highway turnoff. A large black van was headed for the MAC, Inc. compound. Morning sun ricocheted off its tinted windows as it juddered over a pothole and flew toward the main gate, toward the stalled tank, toward the men in camouflage and their assault rifles.

The van pulled to a stop. Windows rolled down. Montana's smiling congressman rode up front. Dazed Asians sat in back. Hungover. Saki time in cowgirl land. Little sleep and no context.

"Fuckin' chinks!" one of the militia shouted at the Japanese delegation. He raised his rifle.

Nora took out her phone and dialed Rosa. *Pick up, Rosa. Pick up the goddamn phone.*

"Listen up," Nora told her. "Don't argue. Just do it. Now, goddammit!"

Another dust spiral from the highway turnoff. A blue light revolving on a beat-up pickup, its siren whining in the wind. Fifteen minutes since Rosa had called the new volunteer sheriff, and he'd beat the record from town.

Three brown high-powered SUVs slipstreamed the sheriff: duckers ready to test their new toys on the firing range they'd rented for the day from Phil.

Right behind them was a white van with four women hanging out the windows, shrieking up a party. Old Bert's birthday girls.

The sun topped the water tower.

"Fuckin' chinks!" the pin-eyed militiaman yelled again. He fired into the air, just missing the blades of the Fox News helicopter that chopped the sky.

How the hell did that get here? Nora wondered as the MAC,

Inc. sirens drowned out the world. She set Stasi loose. Smaller mass. Smaller target.

A pickup honked behind Nora, forcing her into a ditch. Mike Smith was at the wheel and the extended cab was packed with fellow Witnesses, armed for gang warfare. Gravel sprayed like buckshot as he shimmied to a stop in front of the militia's tank. The local volunteer fire engine rumbled behind, Phil riding shotgun, armed with the duckers' arsenal.

Phil was out before the engine stopped, his posse close behind. Jabbing Mailer's rooster chest with his fat ring finger. All set to press the red button on the console. *Ready! Launch! War!* Mailer stepped back slightly, then stepped forward and threw out his chest, smacking Phil in the nose. Mailer's militia pressed forward, weapons ready. Phil's posse raised theirs.

Nora stopped, closed her eyes, and waited for the violence. Instead of apocalypse, she heard a voice. *His* voice.

"Gentlemen."

Nora heard Leonard Cohen in her head. *Give me back the Berlin Wall*. Maybe it was the painkillers.

"Gentlemen," the voice said, gravelly, familiar, like the road home. "Let's be reasonable."

She opened her eyes to see the volunteer sheriff standing easily between two men ready to battle for their empires. His careworn face broke into rivulets of smile lines.

"Shall we try taking one step back in time?"

Phil and Mailer moved sideways, their heads high, their eyes small and threatening. Phil's posse and Mailer's militia lowered their weapons.

"Now, let's talk."

Nora stood mesmerized. Inside her head, she heard the hum of stars. Down by the commissary she saw Rosa's van, the Salvadoran families piling into the back, their arms loaded with children and bundles. She watched Rosa steer down the dirt road toward the state highway. Rosa would do them right.

Nora caught the shadow from the corner of her eye. Saw Stasi leap into the cab of one of Mailer's pickups, grab the Ray-Bans from the windshield ledge. Saw Stasi push off toward the ground.

Saw Stasi shudder in midair before she heard the shot.

"Fuckin' thievin' dog! Told you I'd kill her one day!" Mike Smith roared.

Mailer's militia took cover behind their tank. Phil's posse got behind the fire engine. When all the world's a target, there's no time to ask who fired the first shot. The duck hunters were on the radio for support. The Japanese were taking phone photos, sending them to the world. Oblivious, the congressman stepped out of the van, smiling for posterity. The Fox News helicopter hovered overhead, sending live video back to the station: *Congressman taken hostage by Montana militia.*

Radio static. Backup on the way. Federal. State. Extraterrestrial.

Behind the barbed-wire fence, MAC, Inc.'s warehouse doors rolled open, releasing strange aircraft like dandelions on the wind. Outside, the paid-for party girls stopped dancing and started screaming for real.

Armageddon in a blink.

Nora ran.

She followed the trail of Stasi's blood over a rise to the old barn she rented from a wheat farmer. The blood trail went through a broken board in the wall she'd meant to fix. Nora reached for the two keys on the chain around her neck. The first was for the padlock on the door. The second one she hadn't touched in years.

Inside, she threw on the lights even though she knew every inch of the barn with her eyes closed. Her high-wire rig was in place above a safety net and a sawdust floor.

She called Stasi. No reply. She followed the blood to the drop-cloth mound in the center of the room and raised the shroud.

Stasi lay against the car door.

A pink-and-gold 1952 Dodge convertible. An eight-year-old girl in a pink tutu doing handstands on the hood, her toes caressing the stars. A teenage boy racing time, racing to freedom.

Nora sat in the sawdust on the barn floor with Stasi's head on her knee. She pulled gauze from her backpack and swabbed the dog's wound. She didn't hear the approaching pickup or the footsteps.

"Hey, pipsqueak," said the voice.

She stroked Stasi's head. Took her time looking up. "'Bout time, Frank," she replied to the volunteer sheriff.

"You kept the car." He ran a finger along the side, slowly, as if he felt vibrations in the metal.

"You're a doctor now?"

He nodded.

"Then give me a hand."

Frank retrieved his emergency pack from his pickup. He wrapped Stasi's wound and gave the dog a shot.

"Your mother saved your car. She kept everything after you left." Nora bent her head and nuzzled Stasi.

Frank's eyes focused on Nora's skull, the raw cap of scar where her flesh had been pulled from her and she'd been turned inside out. He reached his fingers toward it. Touched her.

Nora felt the stars race through. "Six months, Frank. I've been back six months."

He traced a tear down to her lips. "Couldn't do it, Nora. Couldn't come close."

"Your mom got away."

"I saw her in the van with the illegals."

"You knew."

"I knew."

The sounds of Armageddon filtered into the barn. Jets. Helicopters. Gunshots. Screams.

Nora pushed herself to her feet, Stasi cradled against her chest. Frank held the car door while she laid the dog on the cream-leather seats.

"Feel like a ride?" said Nora. She opened the driver's side, taking the second key from the chain around her neck. It slid in smoothly and the engine turned. It purred. "Get in, Frank. I'm driving."

He leaned over and kissed the salt from her mouth. "I've seen the future," he whispered.

"It's murder."

"We're cousins," he said simply.

The words had sat between them for years, had driven her away, had kept him from her. Their own no-fly zone.

Nora touched the badge on his shirt, traced that star. "It's the law."

"Law goes where you take it."

Stasi stretched out on the backseat, enjoying the drugs.

Nora took a moment to pull on her blond wig and paint her lips pink in the rearview mirror. Satisfied, she put the car in reverse and backed it out the barn door.

The gunfire song of Armageddon played all around them and across the curve of the earth.

"Canada?" Nora asked. "Zombie Road?"

"Montana's a big state." He looked at her hands on his steering wheel.

"Don't worry, Frank," Nora said, lips pursed, cool as an Arctic breeze. "I'll do it slow. Real slow."

THE ROAD YOU TAKE

BY JAMES GRADY

Shelby

A big blue sky arced over that prairie highway driven by a lone white minivan.

Roxy rode behind DezAray who'd called shotgun when they left last night's motel in a pine-trees-and-good-money town across the mountains. Shotgun meant riding next to Bear, three hundred–plus pounds of *watch out* crammed behind the steering wheel. He stank of weed he wouldn't share, cigarettes, and whiskey, plus you might catch a paw if he thought you sassed or he simply got the itch to pop somebody, but DezAray packed sixty extra pounds of flesh on her five-eight-in-stiletto-heels frame and the big girl knew how to take a hit.

Cherry rode on Roxy's left, past the cooler, behind Bear. Her golden-blond dye job had more class than DezAray's motel-sink peroxide. Cherry craned to see where they were going as if there were some destination besides the next gig. She was a few high-school years ahead of Roxy, who wondered if somewhere under heaven there was a letter or e-mail inviting her real name to her class's ten-year reunion. That notion made Roxy sort of laugh as the white van rumbled her life away.

"What's so fucking funny?" mumbled Star from the way back, where she rode slumped amidst suitcases, sound system speakers, cables, minispots, makeup and costume bags, telescoping dancing poles, and the deflated ring for oiled-up bikini-wrestling gigs.

"What isn't." Cherry arched her back to stretch. Potholes on this two-lane highway across the top of the state rattled the minivan, but Roxy saw no tremble in the breasts some surgeon built beneath Cherry's red sweater.

Wonder if Cherry paid back the loan plus vig Luke fronted her for that work. Wonder how much longer I can keep him from "helping" me go under some knife.

Star said: "'Nothing funny 'bout one of you skimming my stash."

"Not me!" said DezAray. "And no way it's Bear: crystal'd make his heart fart!"

Whoosh came Bear's backhand toward DezAray—missed because a gopher ran across the road, made him swerve the minivan, and messed up his aim.

"Almost," said Cherry of the attempted varmint murder. "Star, Luke's rules say no rips, no hold-backs, so there's no thieves in this ride."

Bear growled: "Don't talk 'bout Luke. I'm road boss. And no more you askin' to drive or some *What the fuck you want?* and cozyin' up to the man."

"I'm just trying to stick to my place," said Cherry.

Roxy said: "Nobody's skimming you, Star. You could tell."

Tweakers know tweakers.

So far, Star'd steered clear of the needle and the pipe, only sniffing. She'd kept her high cheekbones, tawny-haired, stop-traffic beauty, her teeth, and her tight T&A, no tremor in her pony legs when she stripped. But her eyes were always black holes.

"Catch some sleep," Roxy told the beauty in the way back.

"Sleep is when they get you," said Star.

"You can really get got when you're tweaked," said DezAray. "Don't care then."

DezAray stared out the windshield: "There's a whole lot of *out there* out there."

The western third of the state was the Rocky Mountains marching down from Canada, pine tree crags soaring more than a mile above sea level. East of the mountains meant scrub-grass prairies and chessboard-brown-and-gold fields of rotated crops, which if you weren't born there looked like one terrifying, big empty.

In the two weeks Roxy'd gone to community college in Miles City, some 413 crow-fly miles from where the white van now rumbled, a teacher had said Montana held seven regions, each bigger than many other states. Where she was now was the Hi-Line, named for the railroad built after the Civil War by a tycoon who got free land along his tracks from the federal government, got the feds to create cargo and passengers for his trains with public-land giveaways to homesteaders who didn't understand it rained next to never out there. Before Roxy's lifetime when the glaciers melted, forty-below-zero blizzards roared over the prairies a few times a year. Most homesteaders fled, died, or went crazy. The ones who stayed leathered up tough.

Like me. Roxy's eyes found the van's mirror. What the locals saw when she stripped was some lanky bitch with chopped hair the color of dirt, nothing special behind, and up front too small for more than five-dollar tips. Ice eyes. And no matter the hoots, hollers, and creep games, nobody ever saw more than what she was tough enough to sell.

Except Paul.

Dead rabbit on the road.

Bear swerved to run over it. His mirrors showed mountains shrinking forty miles behind them. They'd rolled east out to the prairies, blew through Browning on the Blackfeet reservation, barreled through Cut Bank like that town wasn't there.

Coming up on the left horizon, Roxy saw three blue humps, the Sweetgrass Hills, mini-mountains left over from dinosaur days. Her heart punched her ribs. *Keep it together.* She stared out the windshield. "Here come the space aliens."

Like an army of giants ten stories tall, a hundred windmills with spinning white blades rose from the prairie, big-money invaders that—in harmony with Montana's history—were built elsewhere and sent electricity spun from the local wind out of state.

A dozen miles beyond the army of windmills waited Shelby. And Paul.

"Yay, I got cell service! Okay," DezAray said, waving her cell phone registered by Luke through some *gonna bust it* account, "promise I'll work my geeks, but first I need me some Candy Crush."

Every circuit girl had a website for credit-card chats and "private" downloads with viruses run by some hacker in Russia. Once Luke's crew had gotten all they were gonna get from a cyber-sex troll, that citizen might find his credit crashed and bank tapped, a touch of that coming back to Luke to be washed in his Payday Dollars Now yellow shack on Bozeman's strip of warehouses, seedy motels, and bars. Luke kicked a slice of the hacks' score to the women he put online, minus any vig they owed him.

Then there's the cash from dates.

Roxy didn't do that.

"Yet," Cherry had whispered to her a week before in Lincoln, the truckers' and Unabomber town in the mountains halfway—eighty-three miles—between Missoula and Great Falls, the city a hundred miles southeast of where Roxy rode in a white minivan. In Lincoln, Roxy'd caught Cherry sneaking back into the diner from the highway patrol cruiser parked out back, from the badge who had a kink Cherry parlayed into lawman tips that got her nods from Luke. But that badge wasn't clocked to meet up with Cherry on this circuit.

Cherry saw herself caught in Roxy's eyes, put her finger to her smeared ruby lips: "We all got secrets." Roxy ratted Cherry out to nobody. That night Cherry gave Roxy a nod, told her how life wasn't *yet*.

Now on that April morning, the white van rushed past the wind-farm army of towers. Shadows from the spinning blades slashed Roxy.

Cherry told the driver: "Your belt's packing the take just fine."

"Shut up 'bout my belt or you'll get it," growled Bear.

Cherry ignored him. Gave Roxy a look about . . . about the take?

There's *the take* and there's *the books*.

The books are the circuit's fee plus a cut of the door at bars, bachelor blowouts, or frat-house gigs, negotiated taxes on beers and booze, payouts for gas and motel rooms, and "independent contractor" fees to the stable. The books are for the law.

The take is everything else. A cut of all the presidents tucked into G-strings or tossed on a beer-stained floor. Half the dollars from dates cleared by the road boss that Roxy still said no to. DezAray said yes to such *gotta pay* dates from the kind of guys who mocked *fatty* back in high school, so who's laughing now, huh? "Cherry-picked," they all joked, referring to the big shots who were reeled in by the blonde with big breasts and big ideas. Star let any guy with the right cash hang her up in whatever night he wanted. But the major dollars in the take came from the envelopes that nameless mooks brought to Bear as they traveled the road, cash laundered into the books as gross income.

The books and *the take*—what they say you do and what you really get.

White letters on a green road sign: *Shelby, 7 Miles.*

Bear's eyes goaded Roxy from the rearview mirror: "Maybe I'll stop."

Shelby'd been a gig on the circuit last month.

A mesa rim flowed off to Roxy's left. Up on the right, she saw the truck-sized flapping American flag near the highway crossroads, one road through town, the other to Canada or toward Great Falls past the electrified chain-link fence of a private prison.

The books claimed they'd done great the first night of their double-header gig in Shelby at Jammers, a former trackside slaughterhouse renovated to a bar with a liquor license acquired from a gone-broke tavern in pollution-poisoned Libby, 246 miles away in the pine-forests-and-mountains northwestern corner of the state. Jammers' owner clung to Shelby's dreams that wind-farm workers and prison guards *someday* were gonna drop enough dollars in town to banish the whitewashed windows from Main Street.

Roxy woke up in a motel, Cherry asleep in the next bed, the others zonked in their rooms. The night before, opening night in Shelby, Roxy'd scanned a mere handful of faces nursing beers as Bear emceed "our Big Sky's best exotic dancers." They worked the poles, two shows, couldn't have pulled in enough legitimate dollars to pay for their motel rooms, but it wasn't worry about dollars that woke Roxy early, it was the wind.

"Fucking never stops blowing here," Bear'd grumbled.

The wind felt crisp and fresh, felt good, felt free on Roxy's face.

She did what you never do in a small Montana town: walked.

Near ten a.m. on a spring Tuesday, strolling the highway to where it curved into Main Street. Houses with peeling paint. Vacant lots. A church. A quarter-mile of flat-faced stores, a bank, empty curbs for parked cars. She thought about taking the bridge over the train tracks where a freight whistled through 'bout every other breath, but stayed on the main drag where teenagers cruised loops in quests they couldn't name. This town nestled in a rolling prairie valley supposedly housed three thousand–plus souls, felt shrunken from its *used to be*. As two white-haired ladies shuffled into the lone café, Roxy saw—

Her jaw dropped, gasps trembled her as she stared across Main Street to the brick building with a two-story tower, glass doors, and a yellow marquee.

A man's voice: "Are you okay?"

"That's me," she whispered. "The movie theater."

"You mean the Roxy? Been there since before we were born."

"I'm where people go to watch the movies in their heads."

"You're your own movie," said the man, maybe thirty, clean and lean, quiet looking, with a smile and eyes that seemed wide open.

She wanted to hit him. "You don't know who I am."

"I'm Paul."

"Good for you."

"Well, I should do better."

"Everybody should. Get over yourself."

"That's the whole point, right? Over yourself and with somebody."

"Look, cowboy," she said, and a smile twitched his lips, "I'm not in your movie."

"So where are you?"

"Walking. And I'm not gonna do whatever you wanna."

"I *wanna* walk with you, see my hometown through your eyes. 'Course, if you want coffee, we could pop into the Tap Room." His nod flicked her eyes to a bar beside them with its door open to the morning. "Just dropped off breakfast for Gary to get into Denny. Gary's the bartender, makes sure Denny eats, won't let him sit 'less he does. Or we could go 'cross the street to the café. You saw Teresa and Bev walk in for their every-morning go-to-coffee, they'd like meeting a new face that could be a granddaughter since all theirs aren't around."

"Doubt they'd like to have coffee with a stripper."

"Then we'll get another table."

Roxy blinked. She turned the way she'd been drifting. He fell in step beside her.

"What's with you and the theater?" he said as that building slid past on their left.

She kept her eyes on the road out of town to Jammers' slaughterhouse, heard the truth sneak out of her: "Roxy's not my real name."

"I've always been Paul. We keep going this way, you'll see the post office where I work."

"You're the mailman?"

"And here I am out for a walk. What was I thinking?"

Stop smiling at him. Ice eyes.

"Mostly I staff the counter or the sorting room. You like your job?"

"Are you crazy?"

"I'm here," he said. "Born and raised. Tried college, didn't feel right. I wasn't at home in other people's big ideas. Worked, saved up, drove around the country."

"What did you see?"

"That everyplace was someplace, even the road." He shrugged. "I took a chance. Came back here where 'least I am who I am."

They turned off the main drag. He pointed out this, told her about that, about the library where he'd get books—*only fictions, got enough facts just waking up*. That tan house was where Linda used to live, heartbreaker but worth it, moved three hundred miles away to Billings, married, kids. The Curtis boy came out of that peeling white paint place, marine, didn't make it back from Iraq. Paul's great-aunt used to live down that street, not far from the Methodist church that never was for him.

"What would your aunt say if she knew you were with me?"

"We can ask her, she's back that way in the Heritage, assisted living."

"Better spare her heart."

"Hell, the eyes in this place—by now, half the town knows we're out walking."

"Why are you doing this?"

"Because *there you were* in my *here I am*. Because you see more than just a theater. Because there's something about you that's nobody else's movie."

"No! I'm no rescue-me girl. I needed money, and *work one party* led to *work another*, then you're on the circuit, so what, I'm not poking a fast-food cash register, not some forget-it face behind a counter like they said I'd be, I'm . . . I'm . . ."

"Roxy," he said.

Their footsteps crunched gravel. Lilacs scented the wind. They'd die.

"I got nothing for you," she told him.

"I get to walk with you. Hear you. See you."

"You wanna see me, it's all out there for a five-dollar cover at Jammers, but tonight's the last night."

"I want to see *you*, not *it*."

Her bones cracked. *"Why?"*

"Might take forty, fifty years for me to answer that."

The wind blew dust into her eyes. She whispered: "Don't come tonight."

"Don't leave tomorrow."

Roxy said: "I don't believe in this kind of shit."

"How's the shit you believe in working out for you?"

She watched him scan his windswept town.

Then he walked backward facing her like some goofy teenager: "I don't know why you hit me like you do, but if the hit is all I get, 'least my hurt is earned and true." He swung around to walk beside her again.

Can't look at him, can't breathe, can't—

"You know what I want to do now?"

YES, I KNEW IT, HERE IT COMES, ALL HE EVER WANTED TO DO WAS—

"Listen," he said.

And he did. About her mother. That shit in high school. How her dad never backed down and seldom got it right, left her his IOUs. How she wouldn't walk away from what was owed to creepy Luke because that's not right or who she was, but the harder she worked to pay it off, the more she was who she wasn't. How she was tough.

"I believe you," he said.

Shelby was a small town. They didn't walk up Knob Hill or cross the tracks to the pink high school three times the size today's student population needed. They circled back to the west side of town and were crossing a truck stop's parking lot when the white minivan roared off the street, crunched gravel in front them, and slammed to a stop.

"Leave!" Roxy told Paul as Bear squeezed out of the van where Cherry rode shotgun. "I got nothing for you! I'm bad trouble!"

Paul stood beside Roxy. "And I'm right here."

Bear stomped closer: "DezAray's doing a date like she should, Star's got the shakes in the motel shower, Cherry and me figure to grab some breakfast, end up finding your ass out here with some dude ain't been road-boss cleared."

Roxy tried to stop Bear. "We're just walking!"

His paw spun her toward the van—she plopped on her bottom.

"No!" yelled Paul.

Under the law, he attacked Bear first when he grabbed him.

Whump! Bear's fist slammed into the mailman's guts, lifted him off the gravel.

Bear caught him on the way down, yelled, "Stop!" for witnesses to hear, tossed the gasping local guy smack into the closed sliding side door of the minivan—dented its white metal. Paul bounced off and fell to the ground. Bear gave him the boot.

On her ass in the gravel, Roxy heard a new voice yell: "Done!"

A brown-skinned man in blue jeans and a snap-button shirt loomed in front of Bear. "I seen Paul make his move, that's on him and between you two, but it's done."

"Says who?" growled Bear.

"Us," said another man's voice from the truck-stop café's stoop. A silver-haired guy in a windbreaker, his hands open and flat along his sides.

"Bet you got iron, maybe rigged in your van for easy grab. Go for it. Float with the others, the Mekong or the Marias," the silvertip said of the river running through trees seven miles south of town. "It's all the same to me."

Cowboy Shirt Guy said: "Time for you to be gone."

Roxy scrambled toward where Paul lay crumpled in gravel, but Bear pulled her up, shoved her toward the van and Cherry's waiting arms as he growled to the locals: "Fuck your nowhere town."

Cherry pulled Roxy into the van, whispered: "You got no win, not here, not now."

Roxy heard the van door slide shut on everything but where she was.

Jammers' owner didn't bitch when they pulled out an hour later and a gig early. Luke added that "projected lost revenue" and the repair of the white van's sliding door to Roxy's tab, though when they rolled out on the next circuit, the dent was still there.

On the circuit. A loop through the whole state, twenty-seven days of driving, one or two shows a stop, on the road like the sweep of a second hand around a clock, up the spine of the Rocky Mountains to where they were the night before, now headed east across the Hi-Line to go beyond Havre, into the bleak northeast corner, drop down to Glendive and Billings, then the long run west, maybe to state capital Helena with its cathedral and bureaucrats, its new wine bars and old money, of course over to haunted Butte and then back home to Bozeman, to the Payday Dollars Now yellow shack, to the trailer she shared with DezAray, to the tab Luke said he'd figure some way to let her work off.

Now here they were, back in Shelby.

Cruising past that truck-stop parking lot, a few parked cars, a pickup, nobody in sight. The road curved them onto Main Street. Bear made their machine crawl through the heart of the town to draw out Roxy's pain. She looked across the cooler, past Cherry, saw the reflection of the white van passing across the wall of windows of the lone café, wondered if Teresa or Bev would look up from their coffee to see her glide by.

Cherry said: "You're doing it smart, Bear. Don't even stop to take a piss."

Bear snapped his attention away from the old movie theater. "Hell, Roxy, now I know why you like this dump: they named that place after you!"

DezAray chirped: "Oh wow! How cool, Roxy!"

Someone whispered: "Leave it be."

The bleached-blond big girl blinked. "What'd I say?"

From the way back came Star's whisper: "I don't want nothing named after me."

Bear laughed: "No worries." He glared at Roxy: "Your worry is to ride the circuit right."

"Ignore them, Bear," said Cherry. "You're driving good for being shaky tired."

He frowned at her in the rearview mirror.

The white van cruised past the squat green visitors' center. Past the turn for the post office. Over a spur of railroad tracks as the highway followed the main track line and rolled the minivan toward the edge of town and the slaughterhouse turned into a bar called Jammers.

"Some gigs are worth losing," said Cherry. "Sometimes you gotta get up and go. Speaking of go—Bear, you gonna two-hour us all the way to Havre? I could give you a break, let you pee, drive, let you—"

Bear pushed the pedal to surge past the gray skyscraper-huge grain elevator before the turnoff to the county fairgrounds. "You aren't the one who *lets*."

"I know who I am," replied Cherry as the van rumbled up the east wall of the prairie valley. She smiled at Roxy: "You played that cool and smart."

Roxy mumbled: "I just sat there."

The van topped out of the valley, sun glistening off the train tracks to their left, the vast prairie rolling out before them like a golden sea to the long-gone horizon.

"Wow," said DezAray. "Imagine getting stuck out here? Hello, Mr. Serial Killer."

"You know what I bet?" said Cherry. "I bet the take in Bear's belt'd probably be enough to cover Roxy's line."

What?

Cherry shrugged for everyone to see. "Just saying, she threw in a big chunk."

Twenty-one bucks from last night's stripping tips is a big chunk?

Bear flicked his eyes to the mirror to—

"Cop!"

The police cruiser pulled around the white minivan, whooshed past, and sped away until it was a black dot vanishing on the long gray highway.

"Where'd he come from?" mumbled Star.

"You're in the way back!" said Bear. "You're supposed to be the lookout!"

"You got mirrors." Star stared at the ceiling of the van.

"Was that your trooper, Cherry?" asked DezAray.

"No," she replied. "He's got Wolf Creek Canyon patrol this month, remember?"

"I barely remember where we're going now!" DezAray giggled.

"Don't ever remember," said Star.

"I'm glad I remembered to pee." Cherry looked at Roxy: "You okay, girl?"

Like suddenly you care?

"Gotta do what we gotta do." Cherry smiled, her lips the color of her name.

DezAray, who kept looking for the TV cameras she *like totally* deserved, burst into the song that Luke wouldn't let her use in her routine, even though she did the swirl in high heels pretty good for a bleached-blond big girl and could whip off the sequined bikini top with flair as she belted out: "*I GOTTA BE ME!*"

"You strip so guys think they are who they wanna be," Luke had told her. "So no *gotta* for you."

But for that moment, that one April morning moment in a white van speeding east on a gray-snake, two-lane highway, DezAray *was*.

Blue sky arced above them.

Nothing to see out the windshield except the horizon rushing toward that glass.

Bear flipped up the turn signal. "Damn it!" His eyes glared at Cherry from the rearview mirror. "Barely a couple miles out of that shit-for-a-town and look what all your pee talk's making me do."

The white van glided off the highway to a graveled roadside historic attraction, a wooden sign burned black with letters about the Baker Massacre south of there at the Marias River where in 1870 the US Cavalry slaughtered 173 Blackfeet men, women, and children who were all innocent of killing one white man, the official motive for the military action. Bear stopped the van, turned off the engine.

"I gotta take a piss," he told the four women in the van. "You know the drill." He pushed his way out from behind the steering wheel.

Cherry watched Bear stomp around to the front of the van, said: "Pass me a Coke, would you please, Roxy?"

"*Please*," came Star's soft voice from the way back where her mind wasn't.

Roxy felt herself open the cooler, stick her hand into its motel ice, bottles of beer and soda and energy drinks that Bear always bought before hitting the road, lift out a Coke, and hold it across the backseat toward Cherry.

Cherry said: "Perfect of you to set it up for me, Roxy—isn't it, everybody?"

"Whatever," said DezAray as her thumbs and eyes played Candy Crush.

From the way back came the whisper: "Everything's so fucking perfect."

"You know the way it always works," said the golden-blond woman with red lips, steel eyes, and breasts she'd chosen herself. She took the bottle from Roxy, growled an imitation of their road boss: "*You drain the lizard, you gotta give him a drink.*" Cherry's eyes flicked between the windshield's view of a hulk with his back to the van and what she was doing that Roxy couldn't see. "You know, Roxy," she said loudly, stepping into a conversation they'd never had, "you might be right, could be lots of opportunities coming up in the company."

What? Roxy heard a soft pop.

Beyond the windshield, Bear's shoulders shook as he fumbled in front of himself.

"He likes to piss on things," said Cherry as that mass of flesh and fury turned to storm back to his command chair. "Here."

Roxy reached to take what Cherry's closed fist passed her.

An unlabeled pill bottle filled Roxy's hand. An empty pill bottle she'd just smeared with her DNA and fingerprints.

Cherry locked eyes with her, held the twist-cap Coke bottle out between them, shook it like a rattlesnake.

Bear jerked open the driver's door, glared at the women, stuck out his paw.

"Don't look at me," DezAray told him.

"You bitches all work for me," he snapped.

"Well, for Luke," said Cherry as she let Bear and everyone watch her open the Coke bottle.

"Life's a ladder, bitch." Bear grabbed the bottle. "And you ain't ever gonna climb above me."

Cherry said: "Don't stress. You're way too stressed, isn't he, everybody?"

"I'll show you stress." The open bottle of dark liquid trembled in Bear's paw as his eyes lashed Roxy. "And tonight I'm gonna show you what's what."

Cherry said: "A girl's gotta do what a girl's gotta do."

"You got it." Bear raised the bottle.

Roxy pictured that brown liquid glistening with skimmed and dissolved meth crystals, a hyperdrive solution destined for the hulk who smoked too much, an easy heart-attack verdict for whatever small-town law got the 911 about trouble on the road, highway patrol right there when the call came, nobody to tell the tale except women in the white van whose fingerprints and stories . . . She pictured herself knocking the bottle from Bear's hand. Him believing Cherry's lies and what truth DezAray and Star could tell, his temper exploding, his fists.

His promised *tonight*. She saw herself telling some cop that she'd been hands-on part of Bear's fate, but *I didn't do it, wasn't me after the money or because of . . . whatever.*

"Sometimes," Cherry said straight into the dawning light on Roxy's face, "you give somebody a chance."

"What chance've I got?" whispered Star.

Roxy imagined stories Cherry'd tell creepy Luke, the chance he had coming, the chances a situation named Roxy would have cupped in Cherry's red smile.

We all gotta do.

She said nothing as Bear tilted the bottle and glugged down what it held. He burped, wedged himself behind the steering wheel.

Whir went the dented side door of the white van Roxy threw open. She knew the only thing she could count on being there for her was the big sky. She stepped out under its blue forever anyway.

"What the hell!" yelled Bear. "Get your ass back in here!"

"Roxy!" cried DezAray as the escaping woman slid the van door shut. "Nobody will see you out here!"

"Nobody," sighed Star in the way back. "Cool."

"Bear!" yelled Cherry. "Drive off, leave her ass! Hell, you've already got her stash in the take, covers her tab, nothing to lose but her trouble!"

Roxy stalked to the other side of the highway.

Cherry's shouts boomed from the van: "Show the bitch who leaves who. Get down the road, make one of us take the wheel while you call Luke, then—"

"Shut up!" yelled Bear.

Cherry yelled louder than she needed to: "You got it!"

I got it, thought the woman standing on the side of the road.

The van spun gravel as it sped back onto the road, a white blur on the gray-snake highway, shrinking, going, gone.

The woman stood watching with only the clothes she wore and the secrets she bore, alone on the side of a two-lane state highway that scarred the golden prairie beneath that massive blue sky. She heard a meadowlark whistle. Smelled the earth, the oil of the blacktop road, knew where she was, the direction of a face and a town where people lived.

She shouted her true name to the wind.

Started walking.

PART III

CUSTER COUNTRY

THE DIVE
BY JAMIE FORD
Glendive

3 Wins, 1 Loss

Carla "Train Wreck" Lewis bought her whiskey at ten a.m., right when the state liquor store opened for business. Not because she was eager for a breakfast of barleycorn mash, but because she didn't like to show her face in Glendive anymore, especially since she'd had her nose broken in her last fight. Getting KO'd in an unsanctioned MMA tournament held in the parking lot of some Chickasaw casino had altered her brooding good looks as well as the trajectory of her fledgling career—if you could call getting shinned in the head a vocation.

The Liquor Store Lady raised a concerned eyebrow. "I don't mind taking your money, honey, but if you keep coming in here every day for a bottle, it's gonna become a habit."

The silver-haired woman behind the counter had a good Christian name and probably an interesting life to go along with it, but everyone Carla knew back in high school just called her the Liquor Store Lady.

"And what kind of habit would that be?" Carla asked, an unlit cigarette dangling from the corner of her mouth.

"The kind your mother wouldn't approve of."

Carla removed her sunglasses to reveal two black eyes— the unwanted offspring of a nose that now pointed ten degrees to the left, the result of fighting a southpaw for the first time.

Carla gained new respect for the Liquor Store Lady when the woman didn't even blink at the temporary ruin of her face.

"My mother doesn't tend to approve of anything I do," Carla said with a shrug. "Never has. Lucky for me, the feeling's mutual."

The Liquor Store Lady bagged the bottle of Roughstock. "Yet here you are, back in town. When I heard you won a couple of them crazy fights, I figured you'd left Dawson County for good this time. I didn't think you'd let a beating in the ring send you running back home." The woman cocked her head and raised a concerned eyebrow. "Or did some boyfriend lay hands on you?"

"I don't have a boyfriend." The words hurt more than the pain in Carla's blocked sinuses. Especially since her ex-boyfriend, Sturgill Runyon, had also been her trainer and manager. The moment her perfect 3–0 record took a hit, he'd dropped her off at the nearest hospital before skipping town with her show money and the redheaded lefty who'd spilled Carla's blood all over the canvas. Carla didn't bother finishing Sturgill's *we can still be friends* texted apology. Instead, she deleted all his messages and blocked him on her phone. A final lesson in self-defense.

The irony was that Sturgill said they'd been offered five grand for a worked fight and begged Carla to take a dive. She refused and took a beating anyway.

"And I'm guessing you know why I'm back in town," Carla said as she grabbed the bottle by the neck. "There aren't many secrets around here."

"Oh, you'd be surprised," the Liquor Store Lady chuckled. "That being stated, I am very sorry about your mother's present situation."

Carla nodded her gratitude. "Been a long time coming.

But she's got a few more days left in her—weeks maybe. I swear she's just holding on to make sure the *Ranger-Review* gets her obituary right. Even on her deathbed—"

"No, dear," the Liquor Store Lady interrupted. "I'm sorry she's still married to your stepfather. Word is, that bastard from North Dakota got your mom to change her will and now she's leaving everything to him: your family's ranch, the oil rights, the Lewis Mansion, everything—lock, stock, and barrel. That's what I hear, anyway."

Carla bit down on her cigarette, tasted the bitter tobacco. The Liquor Store Lady sighed. "This bottle's on me."

3 Wins, 2 Losses

The afternoon sky was beginning to purple as Carla left the unopened bottle in the passenger seat, stepped out of her truck, and stood in front of the three-story building that had been built by her great-grandfather and namesake, Charles Lewis, a train conductor turned sheep baron. The old brick manse was nothing like the sprawling estates back east, the kind she'd seen in magazines. In fact, the building might pass for a guesthouse in the Hamptons. But in Glendive, Montana, the place stood out like the Hope Diamond in a dusty coal bin, and had just as many stories told about it. Some were apocryphal, others merely the cud chewed by local gossips, but as Carla spotted a kettle of turkey vultures circling a nearby field, she knew that just as many were true.

Even though Carla had grown up here, she still called the place by its formal name. Especially after her father committed suicide years ago and her mother married their attorney from Watford City, a business partner who called himself Arnold H. Chivers, *Esquire*. Since then the Lewis Mansion had felt even less like a real home.

"About time you showed up," her stepfather snapped as he opened the front door and met Carla on the porch, which was littered with cigar butts. He tried not to grimace when he saw her broken nose and bruised cheekbones but failed miserably. If masking emotions had been an Olympic event, Arnold Chivers would have scored a 3 out of 10, with perhaps a generous 4.5 from the Irish judge.

He shook his head and glanced at the time on his cell phone. "I don't even want to know. Your mother's been asking for you nonstop, so get in there and be the prodigal daughter you always thought you were. I'm heading to my office to get some papers notarized. I'll be back in a little bit. I expect she's—"

"She's in there dying," Carla said flatly. "And you're screwing her one last time, with your fountain pen. This building and every acre is part of *us*, built by and for my family." Carla felt herself rising on the tide of emotion left over from losing her last fight. She used that anger as a cudgel, digging her forefinger into her stepfather's chest. "I'll see this place burned to the ground before it belongs to you."

This was the longest conversation she'd had with her stepfather since she was twelve, when she came back early from Lincoln Elementary, heard strange noises, and walked in on her stepfather having sex with their young German housekeeper. He'd sent Carla to the family cabin on the Yellowstone River. When she returned three days later, the housekeeper had been fired and given a one-way ticket on a Greyhound bus. Carla's mother had been a riot of drunken apologies but refused to leave the man or kick him out. Since then, the house had felt like a mausoleum, smelled like dust instead of wood soap, mold and mildew instead of scented candles.

As Arnold collected himself, Carla remembered how he

was the first person she'd ever hit. It was an awkward, ugly, overhand right, straight to his neck-beard, when she was sixteen and he was . . . where he wasn't supposed to be.

She never talked about that night to anyone, just quit FFA and took up wrestling. Then boxing. Then left town after graduation, never to return.

Until now.

"Look," Arnold said, "I know you don't think highly of me."

"I don't think of you at all."

There was a crack of gunfire and they both glanced at the field. Two boys were shooting gophers, sighting their rifles for Glendive's annual coyote hunt.

"This situation with your family's estate isn't my doing," said Arnold. "Believe it or not, your mother had her will changed of her own volition and without my knowledge. I just found out yesterday. I didn't expect it, I didn't ask for anything beyond my stake in the business, but I'll gladly take everything—if that's your mom's dying wish." He shoved his way past Carla. "And good luck trying to stop me."

3 Wins, 3 Losses

Alyce Lewis had withdrawn from the world from time to time even before she got sick. Carla suspected it was because her mother enjoyed the drama her absences created. There were small-town rumors: Alyce had gone to New York City, worked in off-Broadway musicals under a stage name, and flamed out before coming home to Glendive in shame. She'd suffered a bad bout of plastic surgery in Mexico and now went to bed wearing her makeup. She'd had an affair, which was why her husband blew his brains out during harvest. As Carla walked into the parlor, she smelled dead flowers in vases filled with fetid water. She saw the spent oxygen bottles and listened for the grandfather clock, which had stopped working. She was reminded that nothing is as simple as gossip.

The truth was that Carla's father had killed himself after learning the pipeline he'd built on their land had leaked benzene into the groundwater. Nearby homes and ranches were contaminated. Three newborn babies died. Arnold settled with the families, buying their silence. But when Alyce got sick, her heartbroken father took matters into his own hands. Arnold cleaned up the mess, literally and figuratively.

The affairs came later. Many of them.

"Hello, dear," her mother rasped, staring out the front window into the dark clouds that had put out the sun. "People kept calling all week, telling me you were back in town. If I had known dying would have brought you home so quickly, I would have got on with this business years ago."

Carla thought her mother looked like an aging movie star in repose. She was wearing silk slippers and a long ivory negligee whose plunging back showed her jutting shoulder blades, revealing how much weight she'd lost during her eight-year battle with leukemia. Alyce took a long drag on her cigarette, heedless of the wheeled oxygen tank at her side. The hose curled up beneath the nape of her neck, disappeared into the long blond tresses of her wig, and then reappeared just below her nose. Curlicues of smoke drifted up and caressed a ceiling the color of coffee-stained teeth.

"I think you died when you married Arnold," Carla said. "I'm looking at a ghost who's made some very bad financial decisions."

"So you've heard." Her mother fought a cough, then smiled through cracked lips. "Yes, everything that rightfully belongs to you, my dear. Everything your grandparents fought for during the Dirty Thirties when the weaker fled, everything your father endured those long winters for, so he could make this place what it is—I'm leaving it all to your stepfather."

"If you're doing this to hurt me—"

"I'm doing this to save you. Oh, I knew what he did to you, darling." She paused to let that sink in, flicking her cigarette into a cracked ashtray. "And I know how that must make you feel. But if I'd left him, if we divorced, he would have ended up with half of everything and I just couldn't allow that. So I waited and put it all in his name. People will think he forced me to change my will—they already do. Then when he returns, everyone in town will say that's why I did this."

Alyce opened a drawer. Inside was an old Colt .32 with black tape on the handle. Carla knew the gun—it was her father's.

"I'm just a sick woman who is sick of dying," her mother continued. "And sick people do terrible things when they're not in their right minds, like protecting what is theirs." She coughed until her eyes watered; it was the closest she ever got to crying. "And paying people to lose fights. So they'll come home where they belong. I never thought you'd turn the money down and take a beating. Just look at you."

Carla stared at her as thunder rattled the windowpanes and the electricity flickered. The Lewis Mansion creaked and groaned as wooden joists settled like the timbers of an old sailing ship heaving in the wind.

Alyce wiped her eyes without a hint of apology. "I'm dying but I'm not above trying to make amends. And I couldn't wait any longer. I'm too old for the Make-A-Wish Foundation, and even if I wasn't, I doubt they'd fulfill my desire to put an end to your philandering stepfather. With Arnold gone, when I'm laid to rest, everything will be yours. And you can fix that broken nose."

She stubbed out her cigarette and lit another, coughing as she puffed away.

Carla went to close the drawer. Hesitated. She picked up the revolver and felt its weight. It didn't seem real until she opened the cylinder and saw the gun was loaded. She trailed her fingers along the oiled barrel while her mother kept talking, wheezing, lecturing, until her voice became the sound of a drunken fight crowd throwing plastic cups of beer, screaming for Carla to step forward, to press on, to walk through the punishment. She heard Sturgill shouting from outside the ring, urging her to circle to her left, away from the gloved fist that kept coming out of nowhere. Carla closed her eyes and smelled her stepfather's aftershave amid the smelling salts. When she opened them she saw a trail of dust out the window as Arnold turned down the lane toward the house. Her knuckles were white, laced around the grip. Her finger was on the trigger.

Her mother was smiling.

The room fell silent except for the soft hiss of the oxygen tank.

Carla sighed and her shoulders sagged. "That was a very nice speech, Mother. I bet you practiced it for days. But you should have just come out and asked. Instead of pretending you were going to do something noble for a change."

Carla's mother tried to look insulted. But she never had been an actress.

"I almost believed you," Carla said. "Almost."

She put on her sunglasses, popped her neck, and walked outside, gun in hand, as a stray dog barked in the distance.

3 Wins, 3 Losses, 1 Draw

Carla walked into the stubble field where her father had taken his own life. Where his body had been found at sunset, arms and legs akimbo.

She heard gravel spray as Arnold pulled up in his Cadillac.

She heard the car door slam as he began shouting for her to come inside, telling her that her mother needed her and it would soon be raining, hailing, or worse. She kept walking as lightning flashed on the horizon. She stared ahead at the furrowed ground, remembering how she used to wander these fields in the spring as a little girl, spending long afternoons looking for dinosaur bones and meteorites. But all she ever found were gophers and jackrabbits, tumbleweeds and the occasional rattlesnake.

Carla heard her stepfather stumbling behind her, babbling threats about legal precedents and powers of attorney. Reminding her that she'd run away and telling her she'd never wanted any of this to begin with. He finally stopped talking when Carla turned around and he saw the gun tucked into her waistband. Where his hands had once been.

Carla enjoyed the long moment of silence. She needed a moment to clear her head. To feel this place again.

She licked her lips and drew the pistol. She stepped forward and touched the barrel to the bridge of her stepfather's nose. She closed one eye and cocked the hammer with a satisfying click, like the sound of an ambulance door closing, the latch of a coffin lid, or an expensive fountain pen snapping in two, splattering red ink all over the page.

Arnold froze. He sucked air past clenched teeth. He swallowed and his Adam's apple rose and fell. "Look," he whispered, "we can make a deal. I'll give you anything you want. You don't have to do this."

"I don't have to do anything anymore," Carla said as she slowly lowered the gun. "And you have nothing to give." She looked over her stepfather's shoulder, toward the house. Her feeble mother was on the porch, mouthing the words, *Do it.*

She offered the gun to Arnold. "My mother wants you dead."

Her stepfather hesitated, not trusting her. She lifted the Colt slightly. *Take it.*

"But I'm not my mother."

He took the revolver in his trembling hands, quickly pointing the business end at her as his face showed fear, confusion, and relief. He chewed his lip while dust from the field settled into the beads of sweat on his forehead.

"You won't get off that easy." Carla reached out, placed her hand over Arnold's, and squeezed his trigger finger.

Carla didn't hear the gun go off. But she heard the ringing in her ears, her mother's shouting. She thought she saw her stepfather smiling as her body bent in half and she tumbled to the ground. She closed her eyes and waited for the bell.

1 Win, 0 Losses

Two months later Carla limped back into the state liquor store.

The Liquor Store Lady was reading the morning paper and Carla couldn't help but smile when she saw her stepfather's face on the front page. The headline read: ATTORNEY GETS 15 YEARS IN DEER LODGE FOR ATTEMPTED MURDER. FRAUD TRIAL PENDING.

Carla owed the boys in the field for stopping the bleeding and saving her life. Especially for testifying that they'd heard a single shot that stormy afternoon and seen Arnold Chivers, Esquire, standing over Carla's body with gun in hand.

Her stepfather swore that he'd been set up, of course. But the dying testimony of Alyce Lewis, a heartbroken woman so in love with the man she'd put her entire estate in his name, removed all doubt from the jurors' minds.

"Nice to see you walking around under your own power," the Liquor Store Lady said. "I'm sorry you couldn't be there for your mother's funeral."

Carla shrugged. She felt the loss. But she had a bottle of Percocet to dull the pain from two surgeries and her memories of this town that she loved and hated. A place where you could buy shotgun shells along with chewing gum at the local diner. Where second-graders visited a museum featuring dinosaurs and Noah's Ark side by side. Where poaching applied to mule deer, elk, and the occasional person.

Her family's estate was in turmoil, and probably would be for years, but Carla didn't care. She had better things to do.

"Back to the old standby?" the Liquor Store Lady asked.

Carla shook her head and placed an unopened bottle of Roughstock on the counter. "I don't need it anymore. Figured I'd just return it to the source."

The Liquor Store Lady nodded her head. "Given up drinking, have you?"

"I've given up losing," Carla said as she left.

Driving east, she thought about the redheaded lefty who was out there somewhere. Along with the ex-manager who owed her.

And Carla "Gut Shot" Lewis was looking for a rematch.

BAD BLOOD

BY CARRIE LA SEUR

Downtown Billings

The elders lined up in ergonomic conference-room chairs, birds on a wire, careful not to touch the sleek ash table that made Jimmy Beck so proud. Elbow to canvas elbow, braids down their backs like a fringe on the row, they watched the court reporter set up her machine and did not look at Vera. She was free to study their faces, which were the color of ripe acorns, and the river drainages mapped across their cheeks.

She had dressed down to the extent tolerated at Bennett & Haversham, LLP—a silk blouse and black trousers, expensive but not eye-catching. The satellite offices monitored appearances even more closely than the LA headquarters, to avoid the PR office's microscopic attention.

Yet this was Billings, her hometown. LA had no context for the people in front of Vera today. If they were preparing for trial, Rita from Santa Monica with the improbable eyelashes would dress up these reluctant witnesses. She'd Hollywood-ize them with beads and make them speak in parables. It would be unbearable, alien. Still, Vera checked her cuffs and smoothed her gold collar necklace. Beyond the plate glass nine stories up, postcard views extended from sandstone cliffs to the north and southeast down to the swift Yellowstone fringed by refineries. *This town,* she thought. Country clubs and nickel casinos, half the folks trying to be something fancier than they were and the other half just trying to get by. PR would never understand that they'd have more credibility here in boots and jeans than suits.

At a nod from the court reporter, Vera stepped up to the table. "Thank you for coming. We've all spoken by phone, so you know what to expect today. I'm Vera Ingalls, the lawyer who called. I've reviewed all the documents forwarded to me and there's no record of any applications for homestead patents by your ancestors, but we have good evidence that they did homestead in the area you've identified. The army has records of the promises made to honor homestead rights, and there's the Indian Homestead Act itself. We'll start with that and take your oral testimony. This is Kristie, who'll be taking down everything you tell her. She has instructions about what we need. I'll be just down the hall in my office if any questions come up. Is there anything you want to ask before we start?"

Shifting and sidelong glances moved up and down the row. Finally, a heavy man in a denim work shirt and a white cowboy hat leaned on his forearms. "We want copies of the testimony," he said. "For each of us and for the tribal college. For the history department."

"Certainly." Vera ran an expectant look along the row of faces. They raised and lowered their eyes, but no one spoke. "Okay then. My assistant will be in around eleven thirty to take lunch orders if you're still going."

Beck was coming up the hall as she emerged from the conference room.

"This that pro bono project?" He slowed, but Vera still had to quicken her pace to join his efficient progress toward the restroom in order to have a conversation with him.

"They're recording oral history today. What they told me by phone backs up the archived documents, so I'm getting it down."

"Good stuff. LA wants this in the news as soon as you can get the complaint filed. We're getting hammered—all the media wants to cover is those damn Navajo protestors. We need the redirect." Beck halted at the restroom and put his hand on the doorknob to let her know the consultation was over.

"I'm on it, but we don't have any record of homestead applications. That's the real problem. Army generals making empty promises to Indians isn't exactly a federal case."

"I get it. But we need a win here. Your partnership review is coming up and LA is big on team players. Knock it out of the park for us, kid." He raised a fist to her shoulder but didn't punch it like he used to. A big sexual-harassment payout against one of the Denver partners had recently created a new, and welcome, force field around the associates. Beck disappeared into the restroom and Vera unconsciously rubbed her shoulder.

If the elders had been paying clients, she would have stayed to hold their hands and rack up billable hours, but they'd be fine. Vera had heard too much on the phone to hanker for the live performance.

"My ancestors traveled to Fort Keogh to meet with General Miles, before the reservation time. They promised peace and he promised land . . ."

"The soldiers gave no warning. They came with horses and wagons and told all the families east of the river they had to move to the new reservation west of the river . . ."

"The babies were buried down there, near the river. We had to leave them. We still go, for ceremonies. It is a sacred place . . ."

Anybody who grew up around here was raised on the litany of white savagery against the local tribes—what more was there to say, Vera asked herself, but mea culpa, mea maxima culpa? It was a bloodstain better assigned to the past. No present guilt could change it. Knowing the outcome, the century of community her ancestors and their neighbors had built, she wasn't sure that changing it would be for the best anyway. Jimmy Beck and the management were so smug, so sure that they knew better than the locals how things should play.

"You don't own me," she whispered to the innocuous Western landscape art.

Her office had a glass door and wall onto the corridor. Nothing hidden. The managing committee frowned on the use of the blinds by associates. *We thrive as a partnership in an atmosphere of maximum transparency*, the employee handbook read, when what it really meant, Vera had discovered by observation, was maximum transparency for associates while the equity partners operated from the security of an absolute black box.

She glanced up and down the empty corridor, stepped into her office, and snapped the blinds shut. She had only just opened the complaint document when knuckles rapped the glass, a knock she recognized. Vera held a hand to her forehead, coughed, and said, "Come in."

Peter was in business casual for the flight.

"Hi." He greeted her in that tentative voice he used around women. It used to fool her, but since she'd met him she'd come to understand that the unassuming manner was a deliberately disarming front for Peter's litigating MO, which was to reach down his opponent's throat and rip his beating heart from his body.

"Moving up to the big leagues," she said. He checked the time on his smartphone.

"Flight's at eleven. Just turned in my keys." He advanced to stand before her desk as if inviting some gesture from her, but she stayed seated, half turned toward her monitor.

"Good luck."

He sighed. "Vera, can't we put things behind us and be friends? I don't want to leave bad blood between us."

But he hadn't seen the blood, had he? He wasn't there when the toilet filled with blood like some cheap effect in a horror movie. He couldn't spare the time to hold her hand as the gyno completed nature's messy work, because it had all been her mistake. He'd made that clear.

"There is no us, Peter. Go to LA. Have a nice life." She indicated the door with head and eyebrows.

Another sigh, this one more aggressive. "Fine. Just remember, you're the one who wanted to leave it like this."

She held her peace as Peter stalked out and enjoyed the little victory of the door whispering shut on its strong hinge in spite of his best attempt to slam it. The complaint sat before her, uninspiring, for the next half hour or so, until finally she went to check on progress in the conference room.

She was back at her desk, boxed salad open in front of her, when the phone rang. Muriel had instructions to take messages today while Vera drafted the complaint, but calls from her great-uncle Marshall were different. He was as likely as not calling from the hospital, after he or another aging relative wound up in care. Since her parents migrated to Scottsdale a few years earlier, Vera batted cleanup at home in Montana.

"Everything okay, Marshall?"

"Oh, just fine. How about yourself?"

She turned to her salad. "I'm fine. On a deadline, as usual."

"I know how busy you are, but I got to thinking after we talked last weekend about that Indian case. Maybe I have something that could help."

"Oh? What's that?" Vera took a big bite and clicked *Pause*

on her timekeeping software. Might as well eat while Marshall rambled.

"Grandad kept all his records for the old place in that sea trunk I've got in the basement. Down there I don't know how long, but it'd all be from that area you're talking about, along the Tongue River. That's right where they homesteaded. Anything happened out there back around the turn of the century, he'd have something on it. Old man was a real pack rat. Guess I got that from him. Can't stand to get rid of any of this stash I've got. Maybe you could help out and go through it to see if there's anything worth keeping. I'd kind of like to use that trunk. I've got a bunch of LPs—"

"Yes, that sounds interesting," Vera broke in. "What if I stopped by tonight after work?"

"Oh!" Marshall's voice pitched up with excitement. "Oh, I'd like that. Maybe you can stay and watch the game with me."

Vera wedged another bite of salad into her cheek. "Let me see how things go this afternoon. There's something I have to finish before I can relax. But there could be something in the trunk. Maybe he traded with the families or something. It could help prove where they were living."

This could be the break she needed, Vera thought, as she gently excused herself and clicked the line shut. New evidence from her own family archive had *partnership* written all over it.

When Kristie poked her head in to say that the elders' testimony was complete, Vera went to thank them for their efforts and accept the cool press of their hands, not quite handshakes. From the window she watched them file down the street toward the Lucky Quarters just out of sight, where Vera knew the marquee advertised a five-dollar senior meatloaf special and SLOTS! THAT! PAY!

She had walked to work from the bungalow she rented just west of the business district. The early autumn was trying out a new crispness in the evenings. Vera left her office sweater on under her jacket and pulled on running shoes from the selection under her desk for the longer walk to Marshall's on the near south side. She'd have to pass the rescue mission, but there was nothing dangerous about the route, just a depressing tour of blocks beyond the tracks that resisted gentrification. Her colleagues all lived in thousands of square feet in the western suburbs with garages full of toys and lawns that someone else tended. They drove full-size pickups to work and kept vacation homes in the mountains. Vera could have afforded some version of all that by now but she preferred the feeling of lightness in knowing that she could box up her few possessions, turn in her keys, and walk away. It was worth it to listen to Jimmy Beck give orders like she was a creature he'd personally shaped from clay and think, *Maybe I will, and then again, maybe I won't.*

The streets of Billings drew her in as they always had. They were homey small-town streets, even with the population topping a hundred thousand these days, full of people who smiled and said hello even to strangers. Vera had seen cruelty and prejudice here, but surely that was mostly behind them as a city. There had been so much progress since the days when her grandparents, raised on ranches east and south of town, told her mother they'd disown her if she married a black man or a Catholic. When a chronically homeless man died here, a crowd of downtown workers who had been his friends came forward to testify to the value of his life. When a beloved independent bookstore closed, its bereft customers formed a cooperative to open a new one. Artists created their own open studio space. Churches transitioned struggling families from shelters into their own homes. Small businesses were passed down from generation to generation. It was not a town of big money, just small efforts day after day, by people who would never see their names recorded, until it all compounded into a sense of powerful resilience.

Marshall was in a plastic lawn chair on the front steps in his shirtsleeves when she arrived with her briefcase and a canvas bag from the food co-op.

"What are you doing? Aren't you freezing?" Vera had her hands in her pockets and her collar turned up as the quick fall of night sucked more heat from the air by the minute.

"I was over at the senior center and when I got home it was colder than a witch's tit inside," he said as she nudged him to the door. "I went down and lit the furnace and came back out to catch the last of the sun."

"You've got to do something about that furnace. You need one that comes on automatically, and one day the city's going to crack down on you for burning coal." Vera followed him in, where the air was indeed no warmer than outside.

"I'll take care of that out of my trust fund," Marshall said as he shut the door. "Lucky for me, hay's doing well this year and I've still got a few acres out at the old place. Otherwise it'd be magical fruit out of a can three times a day for me."

Vera rolled her eyes at Marshall's habitual exaggeration of his poverty. He wasn't willing to spend what money he had. Any more would only pad his mattress. She headed for the kitchen.

"I brought groceries."

"Twinkies?"

"Salad. And ground beef." She had a frying pan on the stove already for the one meal Marshall would reliably eat: instant mashed potatoes, a hamburger, and a small salad drenched in ranch. She cooked on autopilot while he talked about the Packers, then fed him, like she did several times a week.

"Best meal in town," Marshall said as he wiped his mouth on a paper towel he'd carefully torn in half to make it go further. Vera smiled. For reasons she couldn't have articulated, watching the old man eat a good meal satisfied her in a way her crisply written complaint did not.

"Now," she said while Marshall topped up their Folgers, "show me that trunk. I have to get back to the office tonight."

"I dragged it out from under the steps and put it under the light." In the tiny kitchen, Marshall only had to stand up and turn around to hold open the basement door. His silhouette hung in the doorway as Vera descended toward the single bare bulb in the middle of the hand-dug cellar not six feet deep, steps protesting as she went. The furnace was an apparition from her childhood nightmares, exactly as she remembered. Its whooshing, clanking, leering presence could draw her in and consume her whole, like a crematorium, she had always felt sure. It was the fire that burned clean, that consumed all it touched. Nothing it swallowed could survive.

Vera turned her back on the conflagration visible through the isinglass window and kneeled in the dirt. The trunk lid rose with a banging of buckles at her push. Marshall had spoken the truth. From well to arched vault, yellowed papers crammed every available inch. There was no visible mold—not in this climate—but a smell of age emerged, acids breaking down organic compounds. Vera reached for a stack of seed receipts.

The fire was warm at her back and the dirt almost forgiving after she padded it with her sweater and jacket. She grew comfortable as she bent and lifted and read and sorted. There was a whole world here, every little transaction that had made up her ancestors' days. She felt quite transported by the time she reached the bottom and found a leather binder in among some land documents, deeds for small parcels that had long since passed out of the family's hands. The binder was so close to disintegration that it looked at least as old as the trunk itself, like it might contain the original owner's manual: *Load up all your belongings. Leave your homeland. Never look back.* How had they done it?

The binder sloughed off dry leather particles when Vera drew it from the trunk.

"My my," she said. "What could you be?"

A rawhide thong secured the flaps but tore in two at Vera's first tug. She set aside the coverings and blinked at the first page. It was—it couldn't be, but it was—an application for a homestead patent along the Tongue River by someone named Little Trees. And then one of her recent phone calls came back to her with a woman's voice saying, *My name is Camille Little Trees, the great-granddaughter of the first Little Trees, who homesteaded at the mouth of Hanging Woman Creek.*

Here it was, the evidence, not of trading but of the land patent applications themselves, completed but never sent to Washington. Here was the evidence of a crime committed against the tribe over a century ago. The documents bore the seal of the Fort Keogh land patent office. The government had received and acknowledged them, then somehow the papers had found their way to the bottom of a white homesteader's sea trunk in a dark basement and stayed there as whole lifetimes passed above ground.

Vera sat back and knocked her funny bone hard against the steel handle of the furnace. She turned her head to peer fully into the flames for the first time. She had been avoiding them out of her silly childhood phobia. Now she looked for real. The coals were red hot and the fire flickered blue and white at its heart. She felt its ferocious appetite.

From the tall stack of receipts for equipment long since abandoned, seed long since sowed, Vera took a thick wad. She pulled open the furnace and tossed in the papers. They made a satisfying little whistle as the fire rendered them white ash in an instant. She took up more of the pile—advertisements for implements, Norwegian-language newspapers already falling into unintelligible shreds—and threw them in as well, more and more, until her own breath seemed in rhythm with the fire's, in and out, inhaling everything, exhaling only heat.

At last, her hand fell to the binder. It was light, as if it held nothing at all, but Vera of all people understood the significance of the land descriptions it contained. They were all the neighbors' riverfront ranches, the oldest and best water rights, flood-irrigated, her family's old place that cousins still worked, the best land in the valley—even those hay fields Marshall relied on. They had worked that land for generations, learned its sacred secrets, drained their sweat and blood to keep it. No piece of paper could make it any less theirs.

Vera thought of the land, its prairie-dog towns, unmarked burial sites, and crenellated buttes, and of the elders lined up at her conference table that very day. She thought of Jimmy Beck in the hallway, always pushing, so sure of her craven loyalty to the firm, and his implied threat about her partnership review. She thought of the lost baby and Peter's plane touching down at LAX that night. She thought of boxing up the rest of what she had found and leaving it for another generation to puzzle over. Upstairs, Marshall shouted something at the TV. Soon he would notice her long absence and shuffle to the top of the stairs. Now was the time for decision.

Her hand moving almost on its own, she opened the furnace. The documents she'd fed it had already disappeared like so much steam. There was nothing at the center of the fire but pure heat, pure hunger, avarice itself, like the flame of history that burned everyone, sooner or later. Down deep where she had protected her soul from all the coups counted against it, a few things sheltered. The family. The land. There was no law, no rule, and no duty beyond that, only the primal ruthlessness that won the West. *Mine*, she breathed.

In one determined movement Vera took the whole stack, leather binder and all, and flung it at the hottest place where the fire swallowed once, just as she swallowed hard while watching, and left nothing behind.

She pushed to her feet and gathered the small stack of papers put aside for saving, including the old deeds from the very bottom of the trunk. She set the lid to without a noise, picked up her sweater and jacket, and carried everything up to the kitchen table.

"Find anything good?" Marshall asked from his recliner. He took his eyes from the game and followed her progress from door to table to sofa.

"Nothing special. I cleaned it out for you." Vera kicked off her shoes, sat on the far end of the sofa, and curled against the arm. The Packers' offensive line filled the screen as something unreadable passed across Marshall's face, another hidden thought in a lifetime of hiding thoughts, nothing he would ever allow her to extract.

"Atta girl," he said, and turned the volume higher.

OASIS

BY WALTER KIRN

Billings Heights

O asis Pizza never closed. It was open all night and it delivered anywhere. That was its edge, the way it stayed in business. Unlike the shops that belonged to national chains, it served the grimmest parts of Billings, from meth-lab motels to pit-bull trailer courts to dirt-floor shanties by the river. The pizza itself was overpriced and awful. The crust was soft and starchy and the red sauce was a smear of tasteless paint. Worst of all, the pizzas had little cheese. Ray Rogers, the owner, who'd bought the place at thirty with money from a personal-injury lawsuit involving a runaway Polaris snowmobile, was too consumed by his video keno habit to buy mozzarella in sufficient quantities. Some nights the shop ran out of cheese entirely, forcing us, the drivers, to buy our own cheese and sprinkle it on en route. People won't tip for a pizza without cheese, and our tips were all we had. Our wage was six dollars an hour, pitiful, and sometimes—as often as he could away with it—Ray paid us nothing. He gave us pills instead. Adderall. Dexedrine. Soma. Percocet. We took them too, especially the night crew. At four in the morning, lost on a dark street in a car that reeks of grease and garlic, a guy will do anything for a burst of energy, or even for just a new, distracting thought. That was the danger driving for Oasis: You ran out of thoughts. You forgot you had a mind. Except when it ached, which was almost all the time, you forgot you had a head.

In the nine months I worked there, which sounds like a short time to people who've never worked jobs that start at midnight and end when the rest of the world is waking up, I only made one friend. His name was Crush. I assume he named himself. I've always been drawn to people of that type, the ones who start life as Dale or John or Brad but reach a mysterious crisis point that leads them to retake control of how they're viewed. But what did *Crush* mean? He never told me. Was it intended to emphasize his strength? He was certainly broad in the shoulders and chest, and yes, it stuck with you when he shook your hand or clapped you thunderously on the back, but to me his most striking quality was his enormous capacity for pity. He felt sorry for people other folks detested, including Ray Rogers, who treated us like slaves and stole from the world with his cheese-free, doughy pizzas. "I love Ray," Crush told me once. "I love his cruelty. So afraid he'll be hurt if he doesn't hurt you first."

Crush was a tip monster. He knew all the tricks. He taught them to me during my first two weeks, when he persuaded Ray to let me ride with him rather than learn the business on my own. His best trick was flapping open the pizza box when a customer met him at the door, supposedly to make sure the order was right but actually to stun the person's nostrils with a warm Italian herbal cloud. Another trick was to show up out of breath, as though he'd sprinted from the car. If it was cold out, he wore a heavy coat buttoned right up to his chin, dramatically shivering as he made change. Quite often, his customers let him keep it. Sometimes his tips were as much as the whole bill, and sometimes they were more. His most generous customers were drunks and stoners, who he learned to identify by the toppings they ordered, which tended to be complex and over-rich. Pineapple chunks and jalapeños, say, or barbecue chicken with Canadian bacon. He scrapped with the other drivers to make these runs, and so did I, once I learned what they were worth. To hungry druggies at their euphoric peaks, a twenty is just a pretty piece of paper. If they pay you in coins, even better. They'll hand you jars full. And one pound of quarters is a lot of cash.

Though sometimes they robbed you. Not often, but now and then. "Cooperate," Crush said, concluding my week of training over a cup of black coffee in the shop. "Hand it all over and never call the cops."

I asked him why.

"In my experience, the same ones who rob you, you often meet again, and when you do, you find out it wasn't personal. They needed something and had no way to get it. Tires for their car, child support. Who cares? Is money your god?"

"Not exactly. Maybe sometimes."

"Not mine," said Crush. "My god is love."

Was Crush a Christian? I braced for a full sermon. They spring them on you, I'd discovered over the years, usually just when you think you're safe with them. I was only nineteen, but I'd done a lot of living, some of it on a juvenile work farm, thanks to a shoplifting ring I got drawn into during my sophomore year of high school. The work farm was full of religion. I'd learned to fear it.

"Do you have a lady?" Crush asked me. "A lady beautiful?"

"Not right now," I said.

"Well, I do. You'll meet her sometime. She lights my way. She's the reason I work here, to give her what she needs. I very much hope that you find one of your own. I'm saving to pay off her Jeep Grand Cherokee."

"That's a lot of deliveries. A lot of tips."

"Fortunately, I'm highly disciplined."

"What's her name?" I asked.

"Beth. Beth Louise. But she dances under Cassandra."

A stripper. Poor Crush. I found it hard to look at him. It would have been better if he were born-again.

"I love it at night," he said, gazing out the window, which was fogged from his coffee breath, and dusty too. The stacks of the refinery flared red and orange. "Or maybe it's that I hate the sun."

"How come?"

He shrugged his big shoulders inside his army jacket. It smelled of oregano and it fit him wrong, suggesting that another, smaller man had earned its profusion of stripes and patches. "Because I'm a true romantic, I suppose. Sunlight diminishes people. It steals their dreams."

Ray Rogers liked to raid the till to gamble. The Magic Diamond Casino—half gas station that sold sundries, half liquor store—stood kitty-corner across the street from us, allowing him to pop over at any time—he just locked the front door for ten minutes and disappeared. That's why the empty cash drawer didn't faze me. Our pizzas had been cheese-free for a month, indicating that Ray was on a spree. With video keno, the way Montana laws worked, you couldn't bet more than eight quarters at a time, but as my great-uncle, a bank manager, once told me, it's slippage that bankrupts people, not huge mistakes.

I was making good coin, having mastered Crush's system. One night I earned 180 bucks. Some delinquents were throwing a party in a parked bus. It took me a solid hour to find the thing because, of course, I had no address, just a treasure-map set of directions based on landmarks: a billboard for a dentist, a row of garbage cans, a tree with a plastic bag stuck in its branches. The pizzas were cold and hard when I arrived but mounded with cheese from the two-pound bag I carried. The kids were impressed. They were snorting ketamine. They passed a hat around to pay the check and collected three times what they owed. I'd learned to count money with a glance by then. I refunded them fifteen dollars to seem honest and pocketed the extra sixty-two.

I boasted to Crush when I got back to the shop, thinking he'd be proud of me. Instead he acted weird. "If you were a decent guy, with principles, you'd have given me half of that when you walked in here, without me even asking, as repayment. Was I not your mentor?" he asked me. "Yes, I was."

I peeled a twenty off my roll, not because I felt indebted to him but because of his wrinkled, disgusted look. It scared me. I wondered if he was getting sick. He'd lost weight in his face but bulked up around his hips. Plus, he was losing his eyebrows. They'd gone patchy.

"Thanks," he said, taking the money from my hand. I didn't expect it. I'd thought that he was bluffing. He brought out his own roll from his jacket, wrapped it in my ransom, and put it back, keeping his hand in his pocket afterward as if to go on fingering his loot.

Hoping to calm things, I asked, "How's Beth Louise? You two still going out?"

"Cassandra and I don't *go out*. We keep things private. She has to seem unattached, for business reasons."

I said I understood.

"She's a child," said Crush. "Incredibly naïve. We'd be married already if it were up to her."

"Really?"

"She's in her earning years. No reason to blow it. Our love will always be there."

Behind us, the phone started ringing, but with Ray at the Magic Diamond for a quick game, it was okay to lose the order. Our cook had just quit and neither Crush nor I liked the smell of garlic on our hands. The caller hung up but tried back a moment later, and this time, out of annoyance, I picked up.

"Is Crush there?" a young woman's voice asked. She sounded angry, like someone who'd been tricked and wanted vengeance. Her tone was the reason I didn't have a girlfriend and wasn't seeking one.

I covered the phone with my hand. "I think it's her."

"It can't be," he said. "She only calls my cell." He spoke in a whisper, as though he feared discovery. Was he ducking another girlfriend? A wife, perhaps? I realized I knew very little about my pal—I couldn't even guess his age. His smooth, undamaged skin made him look thirty, yet his air of prolonged rumination on major life themes seemed to fit a man in his midforties. But how could that be? He delivered pizzas. At nineteen, I was already plotting my next move: helicopter flight school. My dad used to fly one before a rocket got him when I was eight years old. His Marine Corps buddies sent me pictures.

"Who is this?" I said. "I'll pass along a message."

"Tell him it's me and his phone's dead and I'm done. Tell him he missed his last payment. They'll take the Jeep." The woman—Cassandra, obviously—hung up then. She hung up hard, in a way that hurt my ear.

Crush felt this somehow and slipped off to the bathroom. I didn't hear a flush, just running water, which was still going when Ray returned from keno. His eyes were twinkling, which meant he'd lost a pile.

It was two in the morning, when the bars clear out, and in

ten minutes, as happened every night, big orders from all over Billings would pour in. It would be my best night since I started, as I said, but not for Crush, who clocked out early, complaining of diarrhea and a stiff neck.

He didn't come in the next night either, a Saturday. This told me his lady troubles were truly grave. Saturdays at Oasis were cash bonanzas, so much so that Ray kept his gun on him while cooking instead of leaving it stashed beneath the counter. When Crush didn't show or answer when we called him, Ray fell quiet, a brooding, fretful silence that lasted until the calls stopped around dawn.

"I'll be honest," he said. "I thought he'd stick us up. He hasn't missed a Saturday in years. Plus, he's been pilfering lately. Something's wrong."

"He's dating a stripper. She's bleeding him."

"Crush is gay," Ray said. "I found his porn once. Country boys. Cowboys. He likes them blond and buff."

"Maybe he's branched out since then."

"That's rare, I've been told. Have you met this woman?"

"No. But I do know her name. And I think I've heard her voice."

"If she dances, it's either in Laurel or Lockwood. There are only two joints. Try and find her for me, would you? The man is deteriorating. We need facts."

"They'll card me. I'm underage. I won't get in."

"Bring some free pizzas over. Bribe the door guys. Say someone canceled an order and you have extras."

I said I'd try.

"Her name's not Lexus, is it? Like the car? Or Mango? Is it Mango? Like the fruit?"

"It's Cassandra, I think."

"She must be new in town. They float over from North

Dakota, from the oil patch. There's not much money there now, with crude so low."

"You're sure the porn was his?" I said. "Where did you find it?"

"In the men's room trash can."

"Then it could have been anyone's. A customer's."

"Except that I don't serve that type," said Ray.

I ignored this remark and headed home, back to my basement apartment in the Heights. Too many late nights, too much coffee, too many pills, and people start saying things just to wake their brains. Whatever you hear after five a.m., it's garbage, and whatever you say to others is garbage too. It's the same way with pizza, which isn't really food, just something to chew so you can feel your mouth move. Pizza is crap. A lot of things are crap. It's okay, though—it's fine. Crap won't kill you, so it's fine.

What will kill you are rockets fired from hidden positions in countries that your country is trying to save.

The first place was dead, with no one on the stage, just two girls at the bar with a trucker type between them dealing out fives and tens for their tequila shots and paying more attention to the TV—which was showing a ball game—than to their tits and babble. I ordered a beer and inquired after Cassandra, whom the bartender said had been fired over a year ago for biting the face of an off-duty state trooper who'd begged her to pee on him in a private room. I asked the bartender if he knew Crush and he said that he did but only by reputation, though what sort of reputation he didn't specify. When I brought out a twenty and pressed him for details, one of the girls leaned over, snatched the bill, and dragged me off to a booth in a dim corner, where she asked for another twenty to tell her tale. I could see by her unfocused eyes she didn't have a tale but was laboring to dream one up. In the meantime, she straddled my lap and went to work, grinding away with her coltish little ass and tickling my ears with precision bursts of breath that raised goose bumps on my neck and scalp. I liked her a lot. She had spirit. She had ideas. It made me feel less judgmental about Crush. I could see how the skilled devotions of such a girl—she reminded me of a nurse, this one, so dutiful and thorough—might rouse an impulse of selfless generosity.

During a pause to cool off, I mentioned Crush again, this time supplying a physical description.

"No eyebrows?" she said. "Or very little eyebrows? And stuck on Cassandra? And huge, with veiny hands?"

"Yes." She was simply repeating what I'd just told her.

"No. Never met him."

"But you know Cassandra?"

"I did. Before she hurt that guy and left."

"Does she still dance?"

"Not publicly. You have a phone?"

I nodded.

"There's no signal in this place. If you can wait five minutes, I'll grab my real clothes and we can do this from the truck stop. I'm finished tonight. I took a Molly, but it wore off. Now I want pancakes. Do you want pancakes? I do. A short stack of pancakes loaded with chocolate chips."

"Do *what* at the truck stop?" I asked her.

"Get online."

The girl, who went by Ultra, used my debit card to register with the website. Our booth faced a window that looked out on the interstate where three police cars with whirling colored lights were involved in some sort of major enforcement action against the obese male driver of a green hatchback. Once we entered the site, a grid of photos appeared that showed up poorly on my phone, whose screen was cracked and slightly wet inside. Ultra tapped on one of the pictures several times before the shaky image of a woman sitting cross-legged on a bed appeared. She was dressed in a red bra and panties and held a teddy bear whose head lolled sideways as if its neck was broken. She was pretty enough, with high, curved cheek-bones, but her hair was dyed blue and cut short, down to the roots, with lots of random tufts and fuzzy spots.

"Interact with her," Ultra said.

"You. I've never done this."

"She can't see you, don't worry."

"Where is she?"

"Interact!"

"Hi out there. What's your name?" Cassandra asked us. She stroked the dead bear and bit her lower lip. "Are we going to play tonight? I like to play."

"It's Ultra. From the Fox Hole," Ultra said.

"Ultra," Cassandra repeated. She looked confused. Behind her small bed was a poster of a boy band popular with seven-year-old girls.

"I'm here with a guy who says he wants to meet you—a guy from the club. He knows a friend of yours. I'm turning this over to him so I can eat."

Our waitress approached with a thermal coffee pitcher but took in enough with one glance to understand that earning her tip meant ignoring us tonight.

"Cassandra, my name is Brian Schick," I said. "I work at Oasis Pizza with your friend Crush. He didn't show up for work last night. We're worried."

Cassandra set the stuffed animal aside, rolled off her panties over her long legs, and intimately displayed herself. "You like it? It's yours if you want it. Check it out." She reminded me of a 4-H kid with a prize rabbit. There was genuine pride in her face, a kind of glow.

"I'm wondering if we could meet somewhere and talk. Like a restaurant," I said. "Tomorrow. Somewhere real."

"This is *my* real."

"I'm serious. I'll buy you lunch," I said.

"Impossible. I'm no longer based in Montana. I haven't been there for sixteen months. You're reaching me in a coastal Southern state famed for its theme parks and laid-back way of life."

"You're not in Billings?" I looked over at Ultra, who ignored me, cutting up her heap of sticky pancakes. These ladies stuck up for each other, which I admired.

"As for Crush," said Cassandra, "there's not much I can tell you. I really don't know him. We've never met in person. Only like this, like you and me right now. He says he used to watch me dance, but I don't remember. The lights were in my eyes."

"But he's paying for your Grand Cherokee," I said.

"He's been lagging on that, if you want to know the truth. I had to deactivate him."

"Deactivate?"

Cassandra reached over and retrieved the bear. She stood it between her legs to block my view and then held up one of its arms with her right hand and waved goodbye with it. "I'll catch you later, Brian. Have Ultra explain real life to you someday." She switched off her feed and my screen displayed the bill: $27.50.

Ultra said, "Check your statement for that card. Close the account if you start to see weird charges. That probably wasn't the most secure transaction."

"No, it didn't feel like it." I drank the rest of my coffee, which was cold. The creamer had formed a skin across the top that stuck to my lip in a wrinkled little sac that I picked off and set on a napkin. Horrible.

"Let's go to my place," said Ultra. "Let's keep this rolling. Drop some Molly. Drink a little wine."

"I'm broke," I said.

"This is friends. This isn't business. This is two adult individuals in Billings who don't keep normal hours or have relationships and may as well pass out together, not alone."

"Romantic," I said.

"I think it's romantic. I think it's about as romantic as it gets."

Years later, when I was living in Las Vegas flying Grand Canyon tours for a nice salary that could have supported a family if I'd had one, I thought back to that line and realized she was right.

When Crush reappeared a week later, a Friday night, his eyebrows were completely gone. He looked like a man who'd been sleeping in his clothes and eating out of a microwave, sporadically. His earlobes were badly sunburned, which seemed strange, since Billings had been cold and overcast, and his fingernails were different lengths, the ones on his right hand trimmed, the left ones long. I asked him where he'd been, what he'd been up to, but he busied himself with his orders and blew me off. Oasis was crazy that night, a pizza jam, as though there was no other source of food in Billings. Coming and going with our deliveries, we repeatedly missed each other in the shop, and not until five or so did business slow down enough for me to try to question him again.

This time he answered. "Tarpon Springs," he said. "A

Greek sponge-fishing village on the Gulf Coast. Except now there aren't many sponges left. Fished out."

"You went to Greece?"

"It's in Florida." He bit his left thumbnail down to match his right one as Ray ghosted by with his haul from the night's frenzy, headed for the Magic Diamond, jazzed. The machines had been good to him lately, but still no cheese. He'd learned to count on us to handle that part.

"Florida," I echoed once Ray was gone. I'd never visited and didn't plan to. My dad had lived there, near Pensacola. Florida is the state we stage our wars from. Florida and Texas. Consistent weather.

Crush brought out his phone, a new model, extra wide. He typed with his left hand, with his long nails. It made a bony clicking sound, so ghastly. I recognized the website when it popped up. First, there was a tiny pink heart, which beat, grew larger.

"You should see this," he said. "It's what happened to our love. It's what happens to love in general now."

"That's okay," I responded quickly, but Crush went on ahead. I'm sure that he'd heard me, but he was being hateful. And he knew it was late enough that I'd look at anything— the garbage hour, when your mind is empty and people like us hardly care what fills it up.

She wasn't okay. That was clear from the first frame. Was it live or a recording? Like I'd ask him. She lay facedown on the bed under the poster, her naked legs tight together, mermaid style. Her hair was Ronald McDonald red. A wig? I knew it wasn't a still shot because a meter was clicking away in the corner of the screen, racking up the charges for our visit. I waited for her to move. I got my hopes up. She didn't move. Her bear was at her side. It looked cuter than last time, fluffier, less crumpled. I concentrated on its little paws, or at least I tried to. It was late. The brain goes wherever it wants at that hour, seeking energy, seeking a target, seeking heat.

"I'm sorry I'm making you watch this," Crush said, sighing.

"It's okay," I replied.

And it was in a way, I've decided, since we weren't there.

MOTHERLODE

BY THOMAS MCGUANE

Jordan

Looking in the hotel mirror, David Jenkins adjusted the Stetson he disliked and pulled on a windbreaker with a cattle-vaccine logo. He worked for a syndicate of cattle geneticists in Oklahoma, though he'd never met his employers—he had earned his credentials through an online agricultural portal, much the way that people became ministers. He was still in his twenties, a very bright young man, but astonishingly uneducated in every other way. He had spent the night in Jordan at the Garfield Hotel, which was an ideal location for meeting his ranch clients in the area. He had woken early enough to be the first customer at the café. On the front step, an old dog slept with a canceled first-class stamp stuck to its butt. By the time David had ordered breakfast, older ranchers occupied several of the tables, waving to him familiarly. Then a man from Utah, whom he'd met at the hotel, appeared in the doorway and stopped, looking around the room. The man, who'd told David that he'd come to Jordan to watch the comets, was small and intense, middle-aged, wearing pants with an elastic waistband and flashy sneakers. Several of the ranchers were staring at him. David had asked the hotel desk clerk, an elderly man, about the comets. The clerk said, "I don't know what he's talking about and I've lived here all my life. He doesn't even have a car." David studied the menu to keep from being noticed, but it was too late. The man was at his table, laughing, his eyes shrinking to points and his gums showing. "Stop worrying! I'll get my own table," he said, drumming his fingers on the back of David's chair. David felt that in some odd way he was being assessed.

The door to the café, which had annoying bells on a string, kept clattering open and shut to admit a broad sample of the community. David enjoyed all the comradely greetings and gentle needling from the ranchers, and felt himself to be connected to the scene, if lightly. Only the fellow from Utah, sitting alone, seemed entirely apart. The cook pushed dish after dish across her tall counter while the waitress sped to keep up. She had a lot to do, but it lent her a star quality among the diners, who teased her with mock personal questions or air-pinched as her bottom went past.

David made notes about this and that on a pad he took from his shirt pocket, until the waitress, a yellow pencil stuck in her chignon, arrived with his bacon and eggs. He turned a welcoming smile to her, hoping that when he looked back the man would be gone, but he was still at his table, giving David an odd military salute and then holding his nose. David didn't understand these gestures and was disquieted by the implication that he knew the man. He ate quickly, then went to the counter to pay. The waitress came out of the kitchen, wiping her hands on a dishcloth, looked the cash register up and down, and said, "Everything okay, Dave?"

"Yes, very good, thanks."

"Put it away in an awful hurry. Out to Larsen's?"

"No, I was there yesterday. Bred heifers. They held everything back."

"They're big on next year. I wonder if it'll do them any good."

"They're still here, ain't they? I'm headed for Jorgensen's. Big day."

Two of the ranchers had finished eating and, Stetsons on the back of their heads, chairs tilted, they picked their teeth with the corners of their menus. As David put his wallet in his pocket and headed for the door, he realized he was being followed. He didn't turn until he was halfway across the parking lot. When he did, the gun was in his stomach and his new friend was smiling at him. "Name's Ray. Where's your outfit?"

Ray had a long, narrow face and tightly marcelled dirty-blond hair that fell low on his forehead.

"Are you robbing me?"

"I need a ride."

Ray got in the front seat of David's car, tucked the gun in his pants, and pulled his shirt over the top of it, a blue terry-cloth shirt with a large breast pocket that contained a pocket liner and a number of ballpoint pens. The flap of the pocket liner said, *Powell Savings, Modesto, CA.*

"Nice car. What're all the files in back for?"

"Breeding records—cattle-breeding records."

"Mind?" He picked up David's cell phone and, without waiting for an answer, tapped in a number. In a moment, his voice changed to an intimate murmur. "I'm there, or almost there—" Covering the mouthpiece, he pointed to the intersection. "Take that one right there." David turned east. "I got it wrote down someplace, East 200, North 13, but give it to me again, my angel. Or I can call you as we get closer. Okay, a friend's giving me a lift." He covered the mouthpiece. "Your name?"

"David."

"David from?"

"Reed Point."

"Yeah, great guy I knew back in Reed Place."

"Reed Point."

"I mean, Reed Point. Left the Beamer for an oil change, and Dave said he was headed this way. Wouldn't even let me split the gas. So, okay, just leaving Jordan. How much longer, Morsel? . . . Two hours! Are you fucking kidding? Okay, okay, two hours. I'm just anxious to see you, baby, not being short with you at all."

Lifting his eyes to the empty miles of sagebrush, Ray snapped the cell phone shut and said, sighing, "Two fucking hours." If it weren't for the gun in his pants, he could have been any other aging lovebird. He turned the radio on briefly. *Swap Shop* was on the air: *"Broken refrigerator suitable for a smoker."* Babies bawling in the background. He turned it off. David was trying to guess who Ray might really be—that is, if he was a fugitive from the law, someone he could bring to justice, in exchange for fame or some kind of reward, something good for business. He had tried everything he could to enhance his cattle-insemination business, even refrigerator magnets with his face on them that said, *Don't go bust shipping dries.*

He asked, "Ray, do you feel like telling me what this is all about?"

"Sure, Dave. It's all about you doing as you're told."

"I see. And I'm taking you somewhere, am I?"

"Uh-huh, and staying as needed. Jesus Christ, if this isn't the ugliest country I ever seen."

"How did you pick me?"

"I picked your car. You were a throw-in. I hadn't took you along, you'd've reported your car stolen. This way you still got it. It's a win-win. The lucky thing for you is you're my partner now. And you wanna pick up the tempo here? You're driving like my grandma."

"This isn't a great road. Deer jump out on it all the time.

My cousin had one come through the windshield on him."

"Fuckin' pin it or I'll drive it like I did steal it."

David sped up slightly. This seemed to placate Ray and he slumped against the window and stared at the landscape going by. They passed an old pickup truck, traveling in the opposite direction, a dead animal in the back with one upright leg trailing an American flag.

After they'd driven for nearly two hours, mostly in silence, a light tail-dragger aircraft with red-and-white-banded wings flew just overhead and landed on the road in front of them. The pilot climbed out and shuffled toward the car. David rolled down his window, and a lean, weathered face under a sweat-stained cowboy hat looked in. "You missed your turn," the man said. "Mile back, turn north on the two-track."

Ray seemed to be trying to send a greeting that showed all his teeth but he was ignored by the pilot. "Nice little Piper J-3 Cub," Ray said.

The pilot strode back to the plane, taxied down the road, got airborne, and banked sharply over a five-strand barbed wire, startling seven cows and their calves, which ran off into the sage, scattering meadowlarks and clouds of pollen. David turned the car around.

Ray said, "Old fellow back at the hotel said there's supposed to be dinosaurs around here." He gazed at the pale light of a gas well on a far ridge.

"That's what they say."

"What d'you suppose one of them is worth? Like a whole Tyrannosaurus rex?"

David just looked at Ray. Here was the turn, a two-track that was barely manageable in an ordinary sedan, and David couldn't imagine how it was negotiated in winter or spring, when the notorious local gumbo turned to mud. He'd delivered a Charolais bull near here one fall, and it was bad enough then. Plus, the bull had torn up his trailer and he'd lost money on the deal.

"So, Dave, we're about to arrive and I should tell you what the gun is for. I'm here to meet a girl, but I don't know how it's gonna turn out. I may need to bail and you're my lift. The story is, my car is in for repair. You stay until we see how this goes and carry me out of here, if necessary. My friend here says you're onboard."

"I guess I understand, but what does this all depend on?"

"It depends on whether I like the girl or not, whether we're compatible and want to start a family business. I have a lot I'd like to pass on to the next generation."

The next bend revealed the house, a two-story ranch building with little of its paint left. Ray gazed at the Piper Cub, which was now parked in a field by the house, and at the Montana state flag popping on the iron flagpole. "*Oro y plata*," he said, chuckling. "Perfect. Now, Davey, I need you to bone up on the situation here. This is the Weldon Case cattle ranch, and it runs from here right up to the Bakken oil field, forty miles away, which is where all the *oro y plata* is at the moment. I'm guessing that was Weldon in the airplane. I met Weldon's daughter, Morsel, through a dating service. Well, we haven't actually met in real time, but we're about to. Morsel thinks she loves me, and we're just gonna have to see about that. All you have to know is that Morsel thinks I'm an Audi dealer from Simi Valley, California. She's going on one photograph of me standing in front of an Audi flagship that did not belong to me. You decide you want to help, and you may see more walkin'-around money than you're used to. If you don't, well, you've seen how I put my wishes into effect." He patted the bulge under his shirt. "I just whistle a happy tune and start shooting."

David pulled up under the gaze of Weldon Case, who had emerged from the plane. When he rolled down the window to greet the old man again, Case just stared, then turned to call out to the house.

"It's the cowboy way," Ray muttered through an insincere smile. "Or else he's retarded. Dave, ask him if he remembers falling out of his high chair."

As they got out of the car, Morsel appeared on the front step and inquired, in a penetrating contralto, "Which one is it?" Ray raised his hands and tilted his head to one side, as though modestly questioning himself. David noted that the gun was inadequately concealed and turned quickly to shake Weldon Case's hand. It was like seizing a plank.

"You're looking at him," Ray called out to Morsel.

"Oh Christ!" she yelled. "Is this what I get?" It was hard to say whether this was a positive response or not. Morsel was a scale model of her father, wind-weathered and, if anything, less feminine. Her view of the situation was quickly clarified as she raced forward to embrace Ray, whose look of suave detachment was briefly interrupted by fear. A tooth was missing, as well as a small piece of her ear. "Oh, Ray!"

Weldon looked at David with a sour expression, then spoke, in a lusterless tone: "Morsel has made some peach cobbler. It was her ma's recipe. Her ma is dead."

Ray put on a ghastly look of sympathy, which seemed to fool Morsel, who squeezed his arm and said, "Started in her liver and just took off."

A small trash pile next to the porch featured a couple of played-out Odor-Eaters. David wondered where the walkin'-around money Ray had alluded to was supposed to come from.

"Place is kind of a mess," Morsel warned. "We don't collect but we never get rid of."

As they went into the house, Weldon asked David if he enjoyed shooting coyotes. He replied, "I just drive Ray around"—Ray turned to listen—"and whatever Ray wants I guess is what we do . . . whatever he's into." David kept to himself that he enjoyed popping coyotes out his car window with the .25-06 with a Redfield range-finder scope and a tripod that he'd gotten from Hill Country Customs. David lived with his mother and had a habit of telling her about the great shots he'd made—like the five hundred–yarder on Tin Can Hill with only the hood for a rest, no sandbags, no tripod. David's Uncle Maury had told him a long time ago, "It don't shoot flat, throw the fuckin' thing away."

David, who enjoyed brutally fattening food, thought Morsel was a good cook, but Ray ate only the salad, discreetly lifting each leaf until the dressing ran off. Weldon watched Ray and hardly said a word, as Morsel grew more manic, jiggling with laughter and enthusiasm at each lighthearted remark. In fact, it was necessary to lower the temperature of the subjects—to heart attacks, highway wrecks, cancer—in order to get her to stop guffawing. Weldon planted his hands flat on the table, rose partway, and announced that he'd use the tractor to pull the plane around back. David was preoccupied with the mountain of tuna casserole between him and the peach cobbler and hardly heard him. Ray, small and disoriented next to Morsel, shot his eyes around the table, looking for something he could eat.

"Daddy don't say much," Morsel said.

"*I* can't say much," Ray said, "with *him* here. Dave, could you cut us a little slack?"

"Sure, Ray, of course." David got up, still chewing.

"See you in the room," Ray said sharply, twisting his chin toward the door.

Weldon had shown them their room by walking past it and flicking the door open without a word. It contained two iron bedsteads and a dresser, atop which were David's and Ray's belongings, the latter's consisting of a JanSport backpack with the straps cut off. David was better organized, with an actual overnight bag and a Dopp kit. He had left the cattle receipts and breeding documents in the car. He flopped on the bed, hands behind his head, then got up abruptly and went to the door. He looked out and listened for a long moment, eased it closed, and shot to the dresser, where he began rooting through Ray's belongings: rolls of money in rubber bands, generic Viagra from India, California lottery tickets, a passport identifying Raymond Coelho, a woman's aqua-colored wallet with a debit card in the name of Eleanor Coelho from Food Processors Credit Union of Modesto, Turlock grocery receipts, a bag of trail mix, and the gun. David lifted the gun carefully with the tips of his fingers. He was startled by its lightness. Turning it over in his hand, he was compelled to acknowledge that there was no hole in the barrel. It was a toy. He returned it to the pack, fluffed the sides, and sped to his bed to begin feigning sleep.

It wasn't long before Ray came in, singing "Now Is the Hour" in a flat and aggressive tone that hardly suited the lyrics: "Sunset glow fades in the west, night o'er the valley is creeping! Birds cuddle down in their nest, soon all the world will be sleeping. But not you, Dave. You're awake, I can tell. I hope you enjoyed the song. It's Hugo Winterhalter. Morsel sang it to me. She's very nice, and she needs a man."

"Looks like you got the job."

"Doing what? Hey, here's what's going on with me: I'm starving."

"I'm sure you are, Ray. You ate like a bird."

"I had no choice. That kind of food gathers around the chambers of the heart like an octopus. But right behind the house they got a vegetable garden, and my plan for you is to slip out and bring me some vegetables. I've been told to stay out of the garden. Don't touch the tomatoes—they're not ripe."

"What else is there?"

"Greens and root vegetables."

"I'm not going out there."

"Oh yes you are."

"What makes you think so?"

Ray went to his pack and got out the gun. "This makes me think so. This will really stick to your ribs, get it?"

"I'm not picking vegetables for you, or, technically speaking, stealing them for you. Forget it."

"Wow. Is this a mood swing?"

"Call it what you want. Otherwise, it's shoot or shut up."

"Okay, but not for the reason you think. I prefer not to wake up the whole house."

"And the body'd be a problem for you, as a house guest and new fiancé."

"Very well, very well. This time." Ray put the gun back in his pack. "You don't know how close you came."

"Whatever."

David rolled over to sleep, but he couldn't stop his thoughts. He should have spent the day at Jorgensen's with his arm up a cow's ass. He had a living to make and if it hadn't been for his inappropriate curiosity about Ray and Morsel, he'd already be back in Jordan, looking to grab a room for the night. But the roll of money in Ray's pack and the hints of more to come had made him wonder how anxious he was to get back to work. There was opportunity in the air and he wanted to see how it would all play out.

"Ray, you awake?"

"I can be. What d'you want, asshole?"

"I just have something I want to get off my chest."

"Make it quick. I need my Zs."

"Sure, Ray, try this one on for size: the gun's a toy."

"The gun's a what?"

"A toy."

"You think a gun's a toy?"

"No, Ray, I think *your* gun's a toy. It's a fake. And looks like you are too."

"Where's the fuckin' light switch? I'm not taking this shit."

"Stub your toe jumping off the bed like that."

"Might be time to clip your wings, sonny."

"Ray, I'm here for you. Just take a moment to look at the barrel of your so-called gun, and then let's talk."

Ray found the lamp and paced the squeaking floorboards. "Taking a leak off the porch. Be right back," he said. Through the open bedroom door, David could see him silhouetted in the moonlight, a silver arc splashing onto the dirt, his head thrown back in what David took to be a plausible posture of despair.

By the time Ray walked back in he was already talking: "... an appraiser in Modesto, California, where I grew up. I did some community theater there, played Prince Oh So True in a children's production and thought I was going places, then *Twelve Angry Men*—I was one of them, which is where the pistol came from. I was the hangman in *Motherlode*. Got married, had a baby girl, lost my job, got another one, went to

Hawaii as a steward on a yacht belonging to a movie star who was working at a snow-cone stand a year before the yacht, the coke, the babes, and the wine. I had to sign a nondisclosure agreement, but then I got into a fight with the movie star and got kicked off the boat at Diamond Head. They just rowed me to shore in a dinghy and dumped me off. I hiked all the way to the crater and used the restroom to clean up, then took the tour bus into Honolulu. I tried to sell the celebrity drug-use story to a local paper, but it went nowhere because of the confidentiality agreement. Everything I *sign* costs me money. About this time, my wife's uncle's walnut farm was failing. He took a loan out on the real estate, and I sold my car, which was a mint, rust-free '78 Trans Am, handling package, W-72 performance motor, solar gold with a Martinique-blue interior. We bought a bunch of FEMA trailers from the Katrina deal and hauled them to California. We lost our asses. The uncle gasses himself in his garage, and my wife throws me out. I moved into a hotel for migrant workers, and started using the computers at the Stanislaus County Library and sleeping at the McHenry Mansion. One of the tour guides was someone I used to fuck in high school and she slipped me into one of the rooms for naps. I met Morsel online. I told her I was on hard times. She told me she was coining it, selling bootleg OxyContin in the Bakken oil field, but she was lonely. It was a long shot. Montana. Fresh start. New me. Bus to Billings and hit the road. I made it to Jordan, and I had nothing left. The clerk at that fleabag barely let me have a room. I told him I was there for the comets. I don't know where I come up with that. Breakfast at the café was my last dime and no tip. I had to make a move. So what happens now? You bust me with Morsel? You turn me in? Or you join us?"

"You pretty sure on the business end of this thing?" David asked, with a coldness that surprised him.

"A hundred percent, but Morsel's got issues with other folks already in it. There's some risk, but when isn't there, with stakes like this? Think about it, Dave. If you're at all interested in getting rich, you tell me."

Ray was soon snoring. David was intrigued that all these revelations failed to disturb his sleep. He himself was wide awake, brooding over how colorless his own life was in comparison to Ray's. Ray was a con man and a failure, but what had *he* ever done? Finish high school? High school had been anguish, persecution, and suffering, but even in that he was unexceptional. He'd never had sex with a mansion tour guide. He'd had sex with a fat girl he disliked. Then the National Guard. Fort Harrison in the winter. Cleaning billets. Inventorying ammunition. Unskilled maintenance on UH-60 Blackhawks. Praying for deployment against worldwide towel heads. A commanding officer who told the recruits that the president of the United States was a "pencil-wristed twat." Girlfriend fatter every time he went home. He still lived with his mother. Was still buying his dope from the same guy at the body shop he'd got it from in the eighth grade.

Perhaps it was surprising he'd come up with anything at all, but he had: Bovine Deluxe, LLC, a crash course in artificially inseminating cattle. David took to it like a duck to water: driving around the countryside detecting and synchronizing estrus, handling frozen semen, keeping breeding records—all easily learnable, but David brought art to it, and he had no idea where that art had come from. He was a genius preg-tester. Whether he was straight or stoned, his rate of accuracy, as proven in spring calves, was renowned. Actually, David *preferred* preg-testing stoned. Grass gave him a greater ability to visualize the progress of his arm up the cow's rectum. His excitement began as soon as he donned his coveralls, pulled on his glove, lubed it with OB goo, and stepped up to the cow stuck in the chute. Holding the tail high overhead with his left hand, he got his right hand all the way in, against the cow's attempt to expel it, shoveled out the manure to clear the way past the cervix, and finally, nearly up to his shoulder, grasped the uterus. David could nail a pregnancy at two months, when the calf was smaller than a mouse. He never missed, and no cow that should have been culled turned up without a calf in the spring. He could tell the rancher how far along the cow was by his informal gradations: mouse, rat, Chihuahua, cat, fat cat, raccoon, beagle. Go through the herd, or until his arm was exhausted. Throw the glove away, write up the invoice, strip the coveralls, look for food and a room.

Perfect. Except for the dough.

He'd once dreamed of owning jewels, especially rubies, and that dream was coming back. Maybe glue one on his forehead like a Hindu. It'd go over big on his ranch calls.

Morsel made breakfast for her father, David, and Ray—eggs, biscuits, and gravy. David was thinking about Ray's "last dime" back in Jordan versus the rolls of bills in his pack and watching Weldon watch Ray as breakfast was served. Morsel just leaned against the stove while the men ate. "Anyone want to go to Billings today to see the cage fights?" she asked. David looked up and smiled but no one answered her. Ray was probing around his food with his fork, pushing the gravy away from the biscuits, and Weldon was flinching. Weldon wore his black Stetson with the salt-encrusted sweat stain halfway up the crown. David thought it was downright unappetizing, not the sort of thing a customer for top-drawer bull semen would wear.

At last Weldon spoke at top volume, as though calling out to his livestock: "What'd you say your name was?"

"Ray."

"Well, Ray, why don't you stick that fork all the way in and eat like a man?"

"I'm doing my best, Mr. Case, but I will eat nothing with a central nervous system."

"Daddy, leave Ray alone. You'll have time to get to know each other and find out what Ray enjoys eating."

When Morsel brought Ray some canned pineapple slices, he looked up at her with what David took to be genuine affection.

She turned to David and said, "It's all you can eat around here," but the moment he stuck his fork back in his food she put a hand in his face and said, "That's all you can eat!" and laughed. David noticed her cold blue eyes and thought he was beginning to understand her.

To Weldon, she said, "Daddy, you feel like showing Ray 'n' 'em the trick?"

Weldon stopped his rhythmic lip pursing. "Oh, Morsel," he said coyly.

"C'mon, Daddy. Give you a dollar."

"Okay, Mor, put on the music," he said with a sigh of good-humored defeat. Morsel went over to a low cupboard and pulled out a small plastic record player and a 45, which proved to be a scratchy version of "Cool Water" by the Sons of the Pioneers. Weldon swayed to the mournful tune and then seemed to come to life as Morsel placed a peanut in front of him and the lyrics began: *Keep a-movin', Dan, / Don't you listen to him, Dan. / He's a devil not a man.* Weldon took off his hat and set it upside down beside him, revealing the thinnest comb-over across a snow-white pate. Then he picked up the peanut and, with sinuous movements, balanced it on his nose. It remained there until near the end of the record—*"Dan, can you see, / That big green tree, / Where the water's runnin' free"*— when the peanut fell to the table and Weldon's chin dropped to stare at it. When the record ended, he replaced his hat, stood without a word, and left the room. For a moment it was quiet, and then came the sound of Weldon's plane cranking up.

"Daddy's pretty hard on himself when he don't make it to the end of the record," Morsel said glumly, as she cleared the dishes. Heading for the living room, she added, "Me and Ray thought you ought to see what dementia looks like. It don't look good and it's expensive."

David had taken care to copy out the information from Ray's passport onto the back of a matchbook cover, which he tore off, rolled into a cylinder, and put inside a bottle of aspirin. And there it stayed until Ray and Morsel headed off to the cage fights. David used his cell phone and 411 Connect to call Ray's home in Modesto and chat with his wife or, as she claimed to be, his widow. It took two calls, a couple of hours apart. The first try, he got her answering machine: *You know the drill: leave it at the beep.* On the second try, he got Ray's wife. David identified himself as an account assistant with the Internal Revenue Service and Ray's wife listened only briefly before stating in a firm, clear, and seemingly ungrieving voice that Ray was dead: "That's what I told the last guy and that's what I'm telling you." She said that he had been embezzling from a credit union, left a suicide note, and disappeared.

"I'm doing home health care. Whatever he stole he kept. Killing himself was the one good idea he come up with in the last thirty years. At least it's kept the government from garnishing my wages, what little they are. I been through all this with the other guy that called, and we have to wait for his death to be confirmed before I get no benefits. If I know Ray, he's on the bottom of the Tuolumne River, just to fuck with my head. I wish I could have seen him one more time to tell him I gave his water skis and croquet set to Goodwill. If the bank hadn't taken back his airplane, I would have lost my house and been sleeping in my car. Too bad you didn't meet Ray. He was an A-to-Z crumb bum."

"I'm terribly sorry to hear about your husband," David said mechanically.

"I don't think the government is *terribly sorry* to hear about anything. You reading this off a card?"

"No, this is just a follow-up to make sure your file stays intact until you receive the benefits you're entitled to."

"I already have the big one: picturing Ray in hell with his ass *en fuego.*"

"Ah, you speak a bit of Spanish, Mrs. Coelho?"

"Everybody in Modesto *speaks a bit of Spanish.* Where you been all your life?"

"Washington, DC," David said indignantly.

"That explains it," Mrs. Coelho said, and hung up.

Of course he had no car when we met, David thought. No need to leave a paper trail by renting cars or buying tickets on airplanes. He'd got done all he needed to get done on the Modesto library computers, where he and Morsel, two crooks, had found each other and gone into business without ever laying eyes on each other.

Before heading to Billings, Morsel had told David how to get to the Indian smallpox burial ground to look for beads. Otherwise, there was nothing to do around here. He wasn't interested until he discovered the liquor cabinet and by then it was early evening. He found a bottle marked *Hoopoe Schnapps*, with a picture of a bird on its label, and gave it a try: "Bottoms up." It went straight to his head. After several swigs, he was unable to identify the bird but he was very happy. The label said that the drink contained *mirabelles*, and David thought, *Hey, I'm totally into mirabelles.*

As he headed for the burial ground, David was tottering a bit. Rounding the equipment shed, he nearly ran into Weldon Case, who walked by without speaking or apparently seeing him. Behind the ranch buildings, a cow trail led into the prairie, then wound toward a hillside spring that didn't quite reach the surface, visible only by the greenery above it. Just below that was the place that Morsel had told him about, pockmarked with anthills. The ants, Morsel claimed, carried the beads to the surface, but you had to hunt for them.

David sat down among the mounds and was soon bitten through his pants. He jumped to his feet and swept the ants away, then crouched, peering and picking at the anthills. His thighs soon ached from squatting, but then he found a speck of sky blue in the dirt, a bead. He clasped it tightly in one hand while stirring with the other and flicking away ants. He didn't think about the bodies in the ground beneath him. By the time it was too dark to see, his palm was filled with Indian beads and he felt elevated and still drunk.

As he passed the equipment shed, he made out first the silhouette of Weldon Case's Stetson and then, very close, the face of Weldon himself, who gazed at him before speaking in a low voice. "You been in the graves, ain't you?"

"Yes, to look for beads."

"You ought not to have done that, feller."

"Oh? But Morsel said—"

"Look up there at the stars."

"I don't understand."

Weldon reached high over his head. "That's the crow riding the water snake," he said, and turned back into the dark.

David was frightened. He went to the house and got into bed as quickly as he could, anxious for the alcohol to fade. He pulled the blanket up under his chin, despite the warmth of the night, and watched a moth batting against an image of the moon in the window. When he was nearly asleep, he saw Morsel's headlights wheel across the ceiling, then turn off. He listened for the car doors, but it was nearly ten minutes before they opened and closed. He rolled close to the wall and pretended to be asleep, while the front door opened quietly. Once the reverberation of the screen-door spring had died down, there was whispering that came into the bedroom. He felt a shadow cross his face as someone peered down at him. Soon the sound of muffled copulation filled the room, stopped for the time it took to raise a window, then resumed. David listened more and more intently, until Ray said, in a clear voice, "Dave, you want some of this?"

David stuck to his feigned sleep until Morsel laughed, got up, and walked out with her clothes under her arm. "Night, Ray. Sweet dreams."

The door shut and, after a moment, Ray spoke: "What could I do, Dave? She was after my weenie like a chicken after a june bug." Snorts, and, soon after, snoring.

Morsel stood in the doorway of the house, taking in the early sun and smoking a cigarette. She wore an old flannel shirt over what looked like a body stocking that revealed a lazily winking camel toe. Her eyes followed her father while he crossed the yard very slowly. "Look," she said, as David stepped up. "He's wetting his pants. When he ain't wetting his pants, he walks pretty fast. It's just something he enjoys."

Weldon came up and looked at David, trying to remember him. He said, "This ain't much of a place to live. My folks moved us out here. We had a nice little ranch at Coal Bank Landing, on the Missouri, but one day it fell in the river. Morsel, I'm uncomfortable."

"Go inside, Daddy. I'll get you a change of clothes."

Once the door had shut behind him, David said, "Why in the world do you let him fly that airplane?"

"It's all he knows. He flew in the war and dusted crops. He'll probably kill himself in the damn thing."

"What's he do up there?"

"Looks for his cows."

"I didn't know he had cows."

"He don't. They all got sold years ago. But he'll look for them long as he's got fuel."

Morsel turned back to David on her way inside. "I can't make heads or tails of your friend Ray," she said. "He was coming on to me the whole time at the cage fights, then he takes out a picture of his wife and tells me she's the greatest piece of ass he ever had."

"Huh. What'd you say to that?"

"I said, *Ray, she must've had a snappin' pussy because she's got a face that would stop a clock.* He didn't like that too much. So I punched him in the shoulder and told him he hadn't seen nothing yet. What'd you say your name was?"

"I'm David."

"Well, Dave, Ray says you mean to throw in with us. Is that a fact?"

"I'm sure giving it some thought."

David was being less than candid. He would have slipped

away the day before if he hadn't felt opportunity headed his way on silver wings.

"You look like a team player to me. I guess that bitch he's married to will help out on that end. Long as I never have to see her."

David had an unhappy conversation with his mother, but at least it was on the phone, so she couldn't throw stuff.

"The phone is ringing off the hook! Your ranchers are calling constantly, wanting to know when you'll get there."

"Ma, I know, but I got tied up. Tell them not to get their panties in a wad. I'll be there."

"David!" she screeched. "This is not an answering service!"

"Ma, listen to me. Ma, I got tied up. I'm sparing you the details but relax."

"How can I relax with the phone going off every ten seconds?"

"Ma, I'm under pressure. Pull the fucking thing out of the wall."

"Pressure? You've never been under pressure in your life!"

He hung up on her. He couldn't live with her anymore. She needed to take her pacemaker and get a room.

That week, Morsel was able to get a custodial order in Miles City, based on the danger to the community presented by Weldon and his airplane. Ray had so much trouble muscling Weldon into Morsel's sedan for the ride to assisted living that big strong David had to pitch in and help Ray tie him up. Weldon tossed off some frightful curses before collapsing in defeat and crying. But the god he called down on them didn't hold much water anymore, and they made short work of the old fellow.

* * *

At dinner that night, Morsel was a little blue. The trio's somewhat obscure toasts were to the future. David looked on with a smile; he felt happy and accepted and believed he was going somewhere. His inquiring looks were met by giddy winks from Morsel and Ray. They told him that he was now a "courier," and Ray unwound one of his bundles of cash. David was going to California.

"Drive the speed limit," Ray said. "I'm going to get to know the airplane. Take it down to the oil fields. It's important to know your customers."

"Do you know how to fly it?" This was an insincere question, since David had learned from the so-called widow about Ray's repossessed plane.

"How's thirteen thousand hours sound to you?"

"I'll keep the home fires burning," Morsel said, without taking the cigarette out of her mouth.

David had a perfectly good idea of what he was going to California for, but he didn't ask. He knew the value of preserving his ignorance. If he could keep his status as a simple courier, he was no guiltier than the United States Postal Service. "Your Honor, I had no idea what was in the trunk, and I am prepared to say that under oath or take a lie-detector test, at your discretion," he rehearsed.

He drove straight through, or nearly so. He stopped briefly in Idaho, Utah, and Nevada to walk among cows. His manner with cattle was so familiar that they didn't run from him but gathered around in benign expectation. David sighed and jumped back in the car. He declined to pursue this feeling of regret.

It was late when he got into Modesto, and he was tired. He checked into a Super 8 and woke up when the hot light of a California morning shone through the window onto his face. He ate in the lobby and checked out. The directions Ray had given him proved exact: within ten minutes, he was pulling around the house into the side drive and backing into the open garage.

A woman came out of the house in a bathrobe and walked past his window without a word. He popped the trunk and sat quietly as she loaded it, then closed it. She stopped at his window, pulling the bathrobe up close around her throat. She wasn't hard to look at, but David could see you wouldn't want to argue with her. "Tell Ray I said be careful. I've heard from two IRS guys already." David said nothing at all.

He was so cautious that the trip back took longer. He stayed overnight at the Garfield again, so as to arrive in daylight, and got up twice during the night to check on the car. In the morning, he skipped eating at the café for fear he might encounter some of his rancher clients. Plus, he knew that Morsel would take care of his empty stomach. He was so close now that he worried about everything, from misreading the gas gauge to flat tires. He even imagined the trunk flying open for no reason.

He had imagined a hearty greeting, an enthusiastic homecoming, but the place was silent. A hawk sat on the wire that ran from the house to the bunkhouse, as though it had the place to itself. It flew off reluctantly when David got out of the car. Inside, there were soiled plates on the dining room table. Light from the television flickered without sound from the living room. David walked in and saw the television first—it was on the Shopping Network, a closeup of a hand dangling a gold bracelet. Then he saw Morsel on the floor with the channel changer in her hand. She'd been shot.

David felt an icy calm. Ray must have done this. He checked the car keys in his pocket and walked out of the house, stopping on the porch to survey everything in front of him. Then he went around to the equipment shed. Where the airplane had been parked in its two shallow ruts lay Ray, also shot, a pool of blood extending from his mouth like a speech balloon without words. He'd lost a shoe. The plane was gone.

David felt as if he were trapped between the two bodies, with no safe way back to the car. When he got to it, a man was waiting for him. "I must have overslept. How long have you been here?" He was David's age, thin and precise in clean khakis and a Shale Services ball cap. He touched his teeth with his thumbnail as he spoke.

"Oh, just a few minutes."

"Keys."

"Yes, I have them here." David patted his pocket.

"Get the trunk for me, please." David tried to hand him the keys. "No, you."

"Not a problem." David bent to insert the key but his hand was shaking and at first he missed the slot. The lid rose to reveal the contents of the trunk. David didn't feel a thing.

PART IV

RIVERS RUN

TRAILER TRASH

BY GWEN FLORIO

Missoula

The graduate writing program at the University of Montana turned Benson down the same day it accepted his friend Gary.

"Me too," Benson lied into the phone when Gary called with the good news. Gary whooped. Benson held the phone away from his ear and imagined sticking Gary with something thin and sharp, an ice pick—no, too clichéd—or maybe a good fillet knife, freeing all that ego in a single, deflating *pffft*. "But I've decided I'm not going."

"Dude. The hell?"

"No money. Only way to go was if I got funding."

"Fuck that. You're coming with me. Worse comes to worst, you spend the first semester working and start a semester late. I'll share all my stuff with you, the assignments and everything, give you a leg up."

So Benson spent the last of his money on gas, horsed his embarrassing pinkish-purple 1998 Chevy Cavalier up and over Snoqualmie Pass, and gambled what was left of his luck on the switchbacks skirting Lookout, engine coughing and complaining, steering wheel juddering in his hand, coasting into Missoula on fumes and a busted transmission, only to find that Gary's offer to share did not include his digs.

"Dude." Gary stood barefoot on an unpainted porch dominated by a sprung sofa. Only the most determined rental agent's squint could have seen Gary's description—*a cool Craftsman, near the U*—in that cramped, sagging square. The bones of the same bungalow showed in the homes that flanked it, but those dwellings had been expanded up and out in a sort of Prairie-gone-vertical style, their smooth stuccoed walls crowding the limits of the landscaped lots.

"Lawyer." Gary jerked his thumb toward the house on the left. Then he pointed right. "Professor. I was lucky to get this place. Doubt it'll be here next year. Somebody will buy it for the lot, scrape this place and put up one of those. I'll be out on my ass, just like you."

Benson's laugh joined Gary's a beat late. The naked light-bulb above picked out the goose bumps on his arms, raised by a twilight chill that belied the mid-August date. Blades of wind skated off the bald hills that bordered the town, spearing street trash and depositing it around their feet. Gary kicked it away. "They call it the Hellgate wind. Named after the canyon."

He gestured to the cliffy walls of gabbro-striped quartzite just to the east. The river running through them widened and flattened once it escaped their grasp, flowing tame past the campus and through downtown, unabashedly picturesque, a chamber of commerce wet dream.

"It funnels the wind right into town. Freezes your ass off soon as it's dark. Winter should be a treat. Anyway, I got company, man." He held his hands before his chest, sketching breasts, then moved them down and out. Hips. "What happened to the Dainty Lady?"

The car—its unwelcome nickname bestowed by Gary back in Enumclaw—sat ticking in a miasma of exhaust and something more ominous. "It started making a noise just over the Idaho line. Some red lights came on. And I'm about out of gas. Just a couch, man. That's all I need."

"Say no more." Gary disappeared indoors. The home's scabby facade, so dispiriting as the car sputtered up to it, now beckoned with the promise of warmth and Benson-sized horizontal surfaces. Benson heard a girl's high, protesting voice and Gary's soothing tones. He turned sideways to the wind, his T-shirt and shorts an inadequate defense. Sweats lurked at the bottom of his duffel. He'd retrieve them once he got settled on Gary's sofa.

The door opened. Benson stepped toward it. Gary's outstretched hand, a twenty-dollar bill snapping in the wind, stopped him. "This should cover gas, couple of beers besides. This town is crazy friendly. Hit up anybody in a bar, you'll find that couch. That's how I got this place. Ask around about jobs, too. That's the quickest way to get one. Catch you in a few days. Oh, and hey—welcome to Missoula."

Benson's hands twitched. He imagined shredding Andrew Jackson's face, tossing the pieces at Gary like handfuls of dirt flung into an open grave. "Keep your fucking money." That's what he *should* have said.

He took the cash.

A shit job—lobbing rolled-up newspapers from the Dainty Lady onto the chemically treated lawns of the old folks who were the only ones subscribing to the *Missoulian* anymore—was easy to find. A shit place to live, not so much. Although the job eventually led to the place.

For the privilege of earning twenty cents an hour over minimum, forget about benefits, Benson rolled out of the backseat at three-dark-thirty. He coaxed the Dainty Lady, with the rebuilt transmission that had maxed out his only credit card, through fog-shrouded streets to the *Missoulian*'s loading dock, where stacks of newspapers awaited. There, Benson spent a couple of hours rolling and rubber-banding them, leaving his hands sore and swollen and slippery-gray with ink.

He'd have taken longer still but for Harlan, the guy assigned to train him. Papers flipped and spun in Harlan's hairy hands, rubber bands snapping like a teenager's gum. "Got to be quicker," Harlan said. "We ought to've hit the road by now."

The papers were supposed to be on doorsteps by six thirty, latest, but they didn't even head out until six. Harlan, knowing the route, held out his hand for Benson's keys. He pointed the Dainty Lady up a hill stair-stepped with asbestos-shingled split-levels showing their age, cars sardining their driveways, the street lined with overflow, as though every house had thrown a party at the same time.

"Students," Harlan said. "They pack them in there, charge them God knows what. You see all those cars in front of a place, keep driving. Not a one of them takes the paper."

"Then where are we going?"

"There." Atop the hill, a sign proclaimed, *Mansion Heights*.

Benson winced at the violation of *show, don't tell*. The homes, steroidal versions of the stuccoed boxes taking over Gary's neighborhood, told plenty. Wraparound decks that took advantage of the hilltop views nearly doubled the already excessive square footage. Naturally uninhabited at the early hour, the decks gave the appearance of permanent disuse, bereft of chaise longues or barbecue grills or other signs that anyone actually took his ease there. Benson tossed a half-dozen papers in front of three-car garages.

"Who lives here?"

"Nobody who wants to stay." Faded FOR SALE signs adorned several yards. Unsold lots, thick with weeds, abounded. "Recession hit before they finished this place. It's hardly worth the drive up here."

It was nearly eight by the time light spilled like skim milk over the summits, playing catch-up with the Dainty Lady as Benson and Harlan headed for the far side of town, trying to make up time, speeding past the acres of apartment complexes beyond the chain restaurants and big-box stores. A few subscribers lived out by the dump, in the fast-built and faster-falling-down developments that housed the families who'd never make it into the striving neighborhoods closer to the university.

Benson rubbed his pitching arm. He was supposed to work with Harlan for a week, but told him never mind after the guy broke into a rasping fit of giggles on their way back to the newspaper.

Benson thought Harlan was laughing at him because, even after two hours on the route, his papers sailed into aborvitae and petunias, even into the yards next door. But Harlan disabused him of that notion: "Let the biddies walk."

"Then what's so funny?"

"That right there." Harlan jerked his head toward an elementary school. In the playground, slides and swings awaited tiny bottoms. "I'm not supposed to be within a thousand feet of that place. And yet here I am. Bite this, judge!" He grabbed his crotch with both hands.

"Jesus Christ." Benson caught the wheel just in time to avoid sideswiping a parked car. The Dainty Lady had a wicked pull to the right. Benson knew only one reason a judge would order someone away from places with little kids.

"Heh-heh-heh." The seat shook with Harlan's laughter.

"I think I've got this down. You don't have to come with me tomorrow."

The silence went on and on, broken only by the *thwack* of a few final papers.

"Looky there. Over by those widowmakers." Harlan lifted a paw and pointed. A *FOR RENT* sign leaned against one of the towering cottonwoods that flanked the entrance to a trailer park. The trees, notorious for a shallow root system prone to giving way in storms, stretched outsized limbs capable of crushing the mismatched dwellings below.

The car rolled past. Nobody living in a trailer had money for the *Missoulian*.

"You said you were looking for a place to live? Might be that back there is your new home. Heh-heh-heh."

"Dude. It's not even ironic." Gary jammed his car key into the bottom of a can of Hamm's (which *was* ironic) and shotgunned it, his idea of a dramatic gesture to underscore his revulsion as he scanned the Mountain View Mobile Home Park.

Three doors down, a row of purple-headed irises bobbed beneath the ministrations of a woman with a watering can. Her short skirt crawled north of decent over meaty thighs as she bent to pluck a few weeds. "Check out the cougar. Talk about a walking STD."

The woman straightened. Shot them a look.

Benson waited for a smile, a shrug, maybe even a *Sorry*, from Gary. But he turned his attention back to the trailer, a camper, really. "Don't tell the group you live here."

The "group" being some of the others in Gary's classes. They convened at his apartment in the bungalow on Sunday nights to critique one another's stories before turning them in for the verdict of the whole class. Benson had learned his lesson that first night on Gary's porch. He didn't ask to be included; just showed up after Gary let slip about the gathering, then sat back while Gary stammered his way through the whole here's-my-friend-sitting-out-the-semester explanation. Benson even brought a submission, typed on a library computer and printed out for ten cents a page. Gary was old-school that way, wanting hard copies of everything. Easy for him. The money Benson spent copying a story for each of the eight people in the group would have funded a half-tank for the Dainty Lady. *Money wasted*, he thought after the first Sunday night.

"Your protagonist. What's his name again? Harold." Nathalie, pale of face and eye, twisted white-blond dreads around her finger. "He's a sex offender?" She gave the Medusa 'do a rest and pulled an apple from a bowl of fruit. Apparently Gary had taken one look around Missoula after his arrival and gone as crunchy-granola as the rest of his part of town. Everybody else—except Benson—had brought something to drink. Lots of microbrews, along with PBR and more Hamm's. Irony abounded.

"And all he does is drive around delivering newspapers?" *Crunch*. The waif's little white teeth opened a wound in the apple. "Why doesn't he try to molest the guy riding with him? I mean, if he's a sex offender, he's got to offend, right? That would ratchet up the tension."

"Because he didn't try anything." Benson grabbed at the air as though to recall the words. Too late.

"Underfictionalized!" the group chorused. Even though that was the most fictional part of his submission. Gary looked at him with eyes full of pity. Benson imagined putting a thumb to each of those eyes. Pressing hard.

Gary handed him the fruit bowl. "Grape?"

Benson's new neighbors would have cussed him twelve ways to Sunday if he'd shown up with a fruit bowl.

"Hey, boy, get on over here. You look like you need a beer, and we've got beer. And snacks." It was ten in the morning, but for Miss Mary, the yardarm constituted Mount Sentinel, the hill on the college side of town with its whitewashed concrete M—for the University of Montana—where the sun now sat comfortably ensconced.

Miss Mary lived in the trailer next door. Only a single-wide, but someone had affixed a porch, its boards gone so gray and warped that the woman spent most of her days sitting on the sturdy cinder-block steps. There she held court, sparkle-dusted pink Crocs on her feet, pink bandanna on her bald head, a cigarette in one hand, beer in the other. Given that she apparently spent most of her Social Security check on beer, Miss Mary frequently had company. Usually it was Velma, she of the cosseted irises, a divorcée in her forties whose life of child-rearing had left her ill-equipped to counter the husband who'd sprung for the sort of lawyer who guaranteed he kept the house. Even though Velma, with no job and none of the skills that commanded pay for a woman her age, had ended up in this shithole of a trailer park, she retained enough suburban sensibilities to know that when someone else supplied the beer, it was only right to offer up some eats. A green plastic bowl of sour-cream-and-onion-soup dip sat on the step between Velma and Miss Mary, along with a party-size bag of ruffled and ridgy Lay's, not the limp, inadequately salted supermarket variety that sometimes made an entire meal for Benson.

"Here." Miss Mary extended the smoke, its ends loosely twisted, with an illegal smile.

"Damn, girls." Benson sucked deep. Possibilities caromed around his brain. Fuck Harlan/Harold. Miss Mary and Velma— now *here* were some worthy protagonists.

"Hey. Hey." Velma snapped her fingers in front of her face. "Shit's good, but not that good. Where'd you go?" She liked the sound so much that she kept snapping, arching her back and swaying to the beat, so that Benson couldn't help but notice that Velma had herself a fine pair of titties. *Tick-tock*, he thought, before he wrenched his eyes away from the motion.

"Writing. I'm writing in my head."

Snap, snap. Both hands raised high. "Respect."

He could talk about his writing with the girls. Unlike the group that gathered at Gary's, they took it seriously. He passed the joint to Velma.

"How's the book coming? What's the latest?"

Early on he'd intimated that he was writing a book, a fabrication that required endless embroidery. "George is working Benjamin's last nerve."

Velma picked a fleck of bud from her tongue and flicked it away. Her lipstick was harlot scarlet, matching the polish on her fingernails and toes. He'd have to tone her down for his story, Benson thought.

"I hate that George. He's a privileged little shit and a bully. Reminds me of my ex. Is Benjamin gonna kill him?" She looked at her watch. Velma favored peasant blouses over short stretchy skirts with nary a hint of a panty line and, when sitting outdoors, religiously recrossed her thighs every ten minutes to keep her tan even, magnetizing Benson's gaze with each shift change. He took cloudy days as a personal affront.

A little broad in the beam, Velma, and nearly twice his age. Still, Benson couldn't deny he'd thought about it, in convoluted musings that involved those sun-coppered legs scissored around his skinny white frame, Nathalie's whispery drawl in his ear. He bit into a chip laden with dip and savored the smooth and salty crunch. Not like that weak-ass fruit bowl at Gary's, all waxed skin and no flavor.

"No," he said. "Killing him is too obvious."

* * *

"Ahhhbvious," Nathalie sighed her opinion of the revisions to Benson's sex-offender story, glancing at Gary for confirmation.

Benson had written a new section where the man's hand had clamped around his—his protagonist's—dick, fingers corpse-cold even through his jeans, freezing him into momentary immobility.

"I thought she'd like it," he told Gary later.

"Me too. Because if there's one thing that girl likes, it's dick." Gary made an O of his mouth. Pumped his fist in front of it. "Last week," he said, "after everybody else went home." Seeing the look on Benson's face, he added, "Sorry, man. I didn't know. Can't say I blame you. She's a few steps up from that trailer-trash hottie, am I right? Go for it."

"No way," said Benson. *Way*, he thought, and went home and wrote a new story for Nathalie. Which she dismembered the following Sunday with all the finesse of a child yanking the head off a Barbie doll.

"These women. You did everything but have them slinging hash in a diner. Aren't we over Raymond Carver yet?" She cast a sidelong glance toward Gary as she pulled apart paragraph after paragraph.

Benson imagined the doll's limbs flying: arms first, then legs, nothing left but a torso with Velma-worthy boobs and a sexless crotch.

"I know it's cliché"—*clichéd*, damnit, Benson thought—"but why don't you try writing what you know? Dig deep." Nathalie pounded at her skinny chest with her fragile white fist, stopping just short of actual contact. "Get past these caricatures and write something real. This verges on genre." At *genre*, a collective shudder ran through the room. "What's next—ending with, *In the distance, a dog barked?*"

"Nathalie's got a point." Gary, that fucking hypocrite. As

if he hadn't hightailed back to his side of town, irony foaming in his wake, after the *real* of Benson's trailer, of Velma. "You might want to think about taking a couple weeks off from the group, find your focus."

Nobody laughed until the door closed behind Benson. Maybe they'd forgotten about the open windows. Or maybe that was the point.

"Benjamin could shoot him."

Miss Mary cracked the beers even earlier than usual after Benson let drop he'd been informed that his services as a newspaper carrier were no longer needed.

"You don't mope around after getting shitcanned. You celebrate your freedom . . ." Her words trailed off into a cough so violent that the pink bandanna slid sideways on her shiny pate, giving her the look of a pirate accessorized by Mary Kay.

Velma hustled over with Cheez Whiz and Doritos and the optimism that had kept her married far too long to the asshole. "Now you'll have more time for your book. It's going to make you a millionaire. But only if Benjamin kills that jerk George. I'm with Miss Mary: shoot his ass."

Benson canted his head back, held the Cheez Whiz over his mouth, and jammed a finger against the spout. "Too messy." He spoke around the gooey blob. "Blood spatter. Same with stabbing. And anyway, George is his best friend. They're like brothers, always together. He'd be the first suspect. He'd never get away with it."

"Aw, honey. There's all kinds of ways to get away with murder."

Miss Mary made a gun of her hand and aimed it at Velma. "Then why didn't you murder the dickhead? You'd still have your house."

"I probably should have," Velma agreed.

"How?" Benson asked.

"How should I have murdered him?"

"How would you get away with it?"

"Whatever the cops ask you, just look them in the eye and tell the truth. Take your book. Say George is lying on the floor full of holes and Benjamin's standing over him, blood up to his ankles and a gun in his hand, and Mr. Cop asks, *Did you kill that man?* What's the only answer?"

"I don't know."

Miss Mary's fingertips, when she adjusted the bandanna, were blue but for the liverish circles of nicotine. "I'm guessing that's the wrong answer."

Velma looked at Benson. He shrugged.

"You say, *No sir, I did not kill that man.*"

"But he did kill him, right?"

Velma handed him another beer. "No, he did not. The gun killed him." She and Miss Mary traded fist bumps. "You just got to have the right moves." Velma's cheeks hollowed as she sucked Cheez Whiz from a crimson-tipped forefinger. She looked at her watch and executed a slow-motion leg cross. "Know what I mean?"

Benson was pretty sure he did.

Benson angled the Dainty Lady into a parallel-parking space in front of Gary's place. The Cavalier's purple ass stuck out about a foot into the street. He didn't care. Maybe somebody would hit it hard enough to total it. Insurance could pay for a new car. Except that he didn't have insurance. "Oops," he said aloud. He said it again when he tripped on the steps. Pages flew from his hand. The Hellgate wind snatched them and hurled them high. They drifted down onto the porch, the patches of grass, the bushes.

"What the hell?" Gary stood in the open doorway.

Benson started to laugh. He couldn't stop. "My story," he choked out. "For tonight."

Gary stalked past him, gathering pages. "There's no meeting tonight," he called from the yard. "We changed it. Jesus. How'd you get so plastered on that horse piss you drink?"

Benson stopped laughing. "Nobody told me."

Gary came back and stood at the bottom of the steps, the pages crumpled in his fist. "I talked to Jeanine last week."

"Who's Jeanine? Nathalie's replacement?"

"The administrator at the writing program. I was trying to do you a solid, find out if you'd gotten funding for next semester." The Hellgate wind took another try at the papers in Gary's hand. His fingers whitened around them. "She didn't know who you were. She had to look you up. She said you'd never gotten in at all." He thrust the pages toward Benson.

Benson hauled himself to his feet and ignored the unspoken invitation to leave. He walked toward the open door. "She in there?"

"Nathalie? No. Look, you can't leave your car like that." He was talking to Benson's back.

Inside, the fucking fruit bowl sat on the table. Benson selected an apple, turned, and drew his arm back. He was drunk, but not so drunk that he didn't nail Gary right in the middle of his fat mouth when Gary walked in behind him.

The Dainty Lady took the gravel road like a champ, even after it went to a two-track with autumn-brittle grasses making blackboard screeches along her rusted undercarriage.

The ruts ended atop a cutbank by the river. The water muttered and churned below, nothing like the lazy gleaming expanse that wound through town, its glittering surface festooned with neon-colored kayaks and paddleboards, along with the patched inner tubes from Benson's neighborhood.

"It's deep down there," Gary had said at the bluff weeks earlier. He'd taken Benson fly-fishing, back when he'd thought Benson was still salvageable. "Watch where you step. You end up in one of those holes and lose your balance, the current will take your carcass all the way to the Pacific."

There'd been no danger of Benson stepping in one of the holes that day. He didn't have a fly rod and, after an initial venture into the icy water, declined Gary's offer to share. He climbed back onto the bluff and watched Gary, mentally adding up the cost of his waders and special boots and vest and fly rod and license and even the flies themselves, and figured out that the fish they'd eat that night would be worth a few hundred bucks apiece. Except that they didn't even eat them. "Catch and release, dude," Gary had said, as a fish flashed jewel-like in his hand for the moment it took him to snap a photo.

"Catch and release," Benson said now. He hauled the tarp and its burden from the trunk. He'd considered a blanket before remembering how they were always talking about fibers on those police shows.

He unrolled the tarp. It had been a job wrestling Gary into the waders, the vest, the felt-soled boots. He grabbed him under the arms and dragged him to the lip of the cutbank. The hole below was especially deep. "Where the big ones hide," Gary had told him that day, although he'd been unable to entice any onto his fly.

"Here's a big one," Benson said, and heaved.

The fly rod went next. Benson watched as it caught the current and sailed out of sight. Gary rocked along behind it, bouncing in slow motion off the rocks, making his ungainly way toward the Pacific.

* * *

The tarp had required some back-and-forthing, first to the trailer to get it, then the return to Gary's house, cutting through downtown each way. The streets—lined with restored brick buildings that housed the brewpubs and distilleries where Benson couldn't afford to drink, the outdoor-gear stores where he couldn't afford to shop, and the cafés where he couldn't afford to eat—were deserted except for the bums sleeping it off in doorways, awaiting the return of not-Bensons who might toss a few spare bucks their way. The sky shaded gray as Benson left the river, reminding him of his paper-delivery days. By the time he got back to the Mountain View Mobile Home Park, the sun hung above Sentinel, the M gleaming its promise to the fortunate who lived at its feet. Benson cut the gas and popped the trunk.

"Need a hand?"

He hadn't heard Velma behind him until she was so close her breasts brushed his elbow when she leaned over to study the contents of the trunk.

"I'm just taking this tarp inside. I've got it."

But she'd already grasped two corners, backing up, motioning him to bring his own two corners in, pulling him toward her until the fold hid the still-damp blotch between them. Their hands touched, Velma so close he could smell the beer on her breath. He'd missed the morning session on Miss Mary's stoop.

"You got in late last night."

"More like this morning," Benson acknowledged.

"And went right out again. With something under your arm, all folded up. Just the way we're folding this." Her thighs pressed against his. He felt their heat even through the double thickness of the tarp.

She took it from him, making the last folds herself. "Maybe I'll just take this back to my place. I'm painting my kitchen. It'll come in handy." Her gaze lingered on the dark places on his shirt and pants. "I got a washer-dryer. I can take care of those. You don't want to leave them too long. Stain'll set. Come on."

He'd never been inside her trailer. She had a rare double-wide, carpeted, clean, smelling of air freshener.

"Well?" she said, and waited.

"What?"

"Can't wash your clothes if you're still in them. Here's how this goes. Let's see if you remember."

She stripped down first.

He concentrated on undoing the buttons of his shirt, grateful for the reason to look away.

Nathalie showed up a couple of days after Gary disappeared. She lifted a shredded Kleenex to her raw little nose as she choked out questions.

Behind him, Benson heard the metallic pop and hiss of opening cans. He didn't dare turn but knew Velma and Miss Mary were taking in the dreads snaking around Nathalie's bony shoulders, the loose halter dress, the skinny legs disappearing into the cowboy boots. When she bent to dig a fresh tissue from her purse, Benson could see down the front of the dress, nipples like cinnamon gumdrops on a flat, pale expanse.

"I've called and called and called. His roommates think he went fishing. All his gear is gone. But his car's still there."

"Maybe he hitchhiked. He's been known to do that."

"He has?"

No, he hadn't. But she didn't know that, and no one else did, either. None of these people knew Gary the way he did.

"Maybe he's just moved on to someone else. He's been known to do that too. Although, for the life of me, I can't imagine why." Benson put his fist to his mouth. Pumped. "You know?"

"You're horrible!" *Hahhhrible*.

Slow claps from Miss Mary and Velma as Nathalie boo-hooed her way to her car.

The knock Benson had been expecting came when he was at the camper's drop-down table, finally writing out in longhand the story he'd been spinning for Miss Mary and Velma. He closed his notebook.

"I'd rather talk outside," he told the cop. "I could use the fresh air."

The cop raised an eyebrow. "You been out yet today?"

The weather had changed overnight and the Hellgate wind blustered past, tearing leaves from the cottonwoods. They piled up against the trailers, a jackpot shower of gold. The Mountain View Mobile Home Park had never looked so good. But the sun was a tease, winking from a blue, blue sky, promising relief that never arrived. Down the row, Velma fussed over her dead irises. She wore a jacket that failed to cover her bare thighs, mottled with cellulite and cold. The officer stamped his feet and beat gloved hands together. Between questions, his gaze strayed to the fading bruise along Benson's cheekbone, his skinned knuckles.

Yes, Benson had seen Gary the night before he'd disappeared.

Yes, at Gary's place.

No, no one else had been around.

No, no idea where Gary was. Maybe he'd gone fishing? Nathalie had said his gear was gone. As to Gary's car sitting under its own blanket of leaves in front of the house: "He was always a big hitchhiker. Me? Hitchhike with him? Do I look like I can afford to fly-fish?"

"Officer?" Velma sashayed toward them, smiling, coat open. The cop looked, smiled back. "Anything I can help you with, officer?"

Plenty, according to his expression. "You know this guy?"

"Depends on what you mean by *know*." Velma cocked a hip.

Benson watched the cop trying to work it out, looking his way and rejecting the obvious implication. "You see any unusual activity over at his place a couple of days back?"

Benson had left Velma's while she slept, pulling his damp clothes from the dryer, hustling back down the row to his camper, thankful Miss Mary wasn't on her step. He hadn't gone out since. Sweat pricked his hairline.

"Anything unusual? I don't think so. Not that I remember." Benson breathed.

"But I might think of something later. You got a card?"

He did. The blouse beneath the parka was scooped low. The card disappeared into all that abundance. "See you later, hon," she said. Maybe to Benson. Or maybe the cop, who watched her ass all the way back into her trailer. *Tick-tock,* Benson thought. The woman had mastered the art of the sway.

The cop pulled a glove from one hand and wrote in a narrow notebook. "There was blood on the rug at your friend's place. We're going to test it. You up for a DNA sample?"

"Sure. But you don't need to take a sample. At least some of that blood is mine."

"Say what?"

"We had a fight." He held out his hand, scabbed knuckles up, pointed to his cheek, stopping himself just in time from adding a Nathalie-esque, *Ahhbviously.*

"What about?"

"Love." Because wasn't that what it was, the writing? The Unattainable One they chased, wooed, fought for and over? "Any idea where he is, officer?"

"None. I'll be honest: it doesn't look good. He hasn't showed up at any of his classes, and he'd never missed any until now. Nobody's used his credit cards or his phone. Nobody's heard from him. Those things usually add up to somebody being dead. Hard to know for sure, though, without a body." He slapped his notebook against his thigh. "So I'm just going to come right out and ask. Did you kill him?"

Benson locked eyes with the cop. He shook his head long and slow. "The last time I saw Gary, he was alive."

Benson had never thought much about the term *dead weight* until he'd wrestled Gary out of the car and toward the lip of the cutbank.

"How'd you get so heavy eating all that goddamn fruit?" he asked the back of Gary's lolling head. It would have been easier to drag him faceup but he couldn't stand the thought of Gary's dead eyes staring at him.

"Hunh?" Gary said.

Benson dropped him and jumped back, teetering on the edge of the bank. "Jesus Christ!"

When Benson was a boy, he'd gone duck hunting with his dad. Try as he might, he hadn't been able to get the hang of leading them as they coasted in toward the decoys. All his shots went wild. But his dad was a good shot, and as Benson had stuffed the mallards into a sack, their rich brown breast feathers still soft and warm, the blood on them only beginning to stiffen, he'd accidentally squeezed one. For years, his father retold the story of how Benson burst into tears when the dead duck emitted a final quack as the last of its breath was forced from its lungs.

Benson nudged Gary with his toe. Nothing. He nudged him harder, finally working up the nerve to turn him over. Gary's lips moved. "Dude. The fuck?" He stared up at Benson. His eyes widened as he went over the rim.

"That Benjamin. He's a better man than me," Miss Mary said.

Than I, Benson thought.

Miss Mary spoke from inside a pink parka that looked like it had swallowed her whole. Fuzzy pink socks warmed her feet inside their sparkly Crocs. Her skin seemed grayer than usual next to all that color. Velma had finally traded in her skirts for seam-stretched jeans. The cottonwoods, limbs creaking a warning, stood bare against a sky that spat snow.

"George was his best friend," Velma said. "Even if he was a shitheel, it makes sense that Benjamin was all broken up when George killed himself. Look at Benson here. He's still messed up over that college boy who . . . went missing. Aren't you?"

"Yeah. Well. It's hard, not knowing what happened."

Miss Mary's cackle competed with the rattle of dried leaves. "Nothing hard about not knowing. Look all around you. It's the easiest thing on earth." *Not dead yet*, she liked to say about herself. *Not by a long shot.*

"It's all about how things end." Velma leaned back and stretched her legs as though the sun still shone upon them. "Like the ending to your book. It got me." She took Benson's hand and laced her fingers through his, speaking the words like a vow. "*In the distance, a dog barked.*"

CUSTER'S LAST STAND

BY DEBRA MAGPIE EARLING

Polson

Nina Three Dresses worked at a fast-food stop called Custer's Last Stand at the edge of Polson, a mean little joint where the cars parked in a circle and blistered picnic tables sat squat beneath a stingy strip of shade. The road sign couldn't be missed: three white-bulb arrows falling in perpetual motion toward a round building made to look like a drum. They served up coffee drinks with lame names like SacaJoewea and Joeranimo, and cups of grainy soft ice cream with tomahawk sprinkles. Wednesdays it was "scalped" potatoes and red dogs. Oddly enough, it'd become an Indian hangout. I was drawn to the place by a sense of irony.

I'd had trouble I couldn't shake. Got myself arrested for walking out on a steak and a bottle of whiskey at the Depot Restaurant. Thrown in the hoosegow for a quick wink, then told to get out of town. No sentencing, no arraignment. Just a night of steel bars and Pine Sol dreams.

I didn't want to hang around Missoula anyway. I hated the hippies and the high-school university, the lazy-ass writers writing about lives they'd never led, the college kids with rich parents and low IQs, the shit-asses who hang out at breweries and call recreation a living. I hightailed it back to the Flathead to get a job and lay low.

It's the shitty little things that dog a person. Three years back, I was arrested in Butte for breaking a bottle on the sidewalk and not for the real crime I'd committed there. Hit-and-run. The guy's shoe landed topside up on my hood where I found it the next morning when I woke to a belch of bad memory, recollecting a sound like a pig squeal, the image of a man's crazy eyes as he looped in the air. I ditched my truck and headed farther west.

Custer's Last Stand was a new joint, a shitty idea dreamed up by a loser. When I first visited it, I made the dumb-ass comment to a big Indian behind the counter that the local Indians didn't even fight Custer, so why this stand here? It's way out of place, I told him. Rightfully belongs in Crow Country, I said. The big Indian in his Flathead Braves T-shirt stared at me from behind the counter, then placed a weak espresso in front of me with three packets of Coffee-Mate. "Yeah, well," he said, "just so you know, *you're* out of place." And he closed the serving window on me.

A few weeks later, Nina showed up and the little stand became my haven. She'd slide that serving window open and poke her head out, shield her eyes with her slim hands, and in a shivering half-whisper say, "Looks like it's going to be a scorcher." She'd wink at me and the world took on new meaning.

She's what drew me to Custer's, her calm demeanor. I felt right at home at those peeling picnic tables with a cup of steaming coffee, my morning paper, and a cigarette. I'd stop in once a week, sometimes twice, and for hours at a time if I was feeling lonesome.

The joint was run by a jaded cop who'd fled from Missouri to Montana all for the love of a Merle Haggard song. I'd been off the Flathead since I was a teenager but remembered there'd been others like him over the years. A woman who'd started a pancake house in a concrete teepee on the east shore of Flathead Lake. A couple who'd dyed their hair black, wore headbands with feathers, and had the balls to sell "Indian" beadwork they'd made themselves at the Crazy Daze festival in Ronan.

But Custer's Last Stand was another thing altogether—an anomaly three hundred miles out of place. Eavesdropping on the old Indians who slurped coffee, I heard about the history of the place and plenty more. Apparently, Officer Verlin Custer, the proprietor, was a character. A mean SOB who waved Indians through yield signs and then pulled them over for traffic violations. There was talk he had some deal going with the smoke shops, kickbacks from cigarettes sold for triple the price to lazy gamblers at the Wolf Den. Pissy penny-ante shit that would eventually turn to bad-ass shit. All his workers called him Squint—even in his presence—but he was too arrogant, too much of a prick, to appreciate their own stand against him.

Nina's "coworkers" were a joke: a big smiler named Toolbox, and a tattooed half-breed called Smug who had the longest cleavage I'd ever seen. Those knuckleheads would sit outside and smoke while Nina flipped burgers and cut fries.

Around eleven in the morning the gang would show up. Indian girls plinked away on cell phones, flirted with plump-ass boys, and picked flecks of eyeliner from the corners of their eyes. Surly girls who wore black hoodies, smirked instead of laughed, jiggled their keys like they were going somewhere but instead ordered yet another coffee with whipped cream and crushed-candy toppings.

Nina was immune to their jittery talk. She must have been twenty-five. She had a wicked scar that dented her left cheek, a dusting of freckles across her nose. Whenever work slammed the counter, Nina floated from task to task as if she had all the time in the world, and that grace made her seem far wiser than the others, especially when she served the boss.

She delivered every item to Squint with a cool countenance, and then double-flicked her wrists. It was a secret language he was too dumb to get. His coffee, flick flick, *nothing here;* his coffee straws, flick flick, *no more;* his steaming butterhorn, flick flick, *all gone.* Her nonchalance was natural, an easy read. *Nothing here for you, buster.*

He'd stop by every morning at nine a.m. to inspect the place, except for good days when he'd roar by the stand, his siren wailing: *MeMEmeeeeEEE.*

Squint didn't know enough about weights to exercise for health. He worked out to strut bulging thighs, lifted heavy to have arms that strained against his sleeves like tethered mutts. His neck bulged against his uniform collar as he leaned on the service counter to perform semi-push-ups.

"How's business?" he puffed. "Are you smiling for our customers?"

He wiggled a toothpick between his teeth and squinted at Smug's cleavage. He grabbed Nina's hands and traced his thumbnails along her palms to read her misfortune.

"One day a handsome man is going to snatch you up," he said. "And it may very well be me." Folks knew he was married to a battle-ax who made her profit off the sale of waterfront property that rightfully belonged to the Indians.

The old Indians would catch me watching Nina too. They'd smile at me through puffs of smoke. I'd shrug, order another cup of coffee, and sit at a picnic table so I could watch Nina come outdoors to serve them. It was worth any trouble for her quick glance, her smugly beautiful snub.

On lucky days, Nina would sit with the old Indians in the shade. I'd listen in, pretending I was reading the paper or checking texts. Nina sipped her coffee and reached for anyone's cigarette. She'd take a long pull, then blow a slow stream of smoke from her thin nose. She was sexy as hell but there was always a worried look on her face.

I overheard her say that her grandfather was getting worse. They'd all be in trouble if she couldn't get help. I gathered that he lived up Hell Roaring Creek, the last house before the road became a skinny ledge over the canyon. I knew the place.

"He's got some crazy shit going on up there," Nina said. "Anyone within a mile of his place is screwed." The Indians clucked their tongues. Nina gazed off toward the Mission Mountains that were as blue as a raven's heart above us.

Every once in a while, Johnny Sees Red Night would stop by and Nina would be out of the stand in a shot. There was a morose urgency to their chats. They'd head over to the scrub pines and talk in low voices. I'd catch a few lines here and there, enough to patch together there was trouble I couldn't comprehend. The other Indians would stop talking and glance over their shoulders at the two, swat at invisible flies, put their heads together, and whisper conspiratorially. Something bad was going down that apparently didn't concern my white ass.

By August, the wind woofed at the window screens and the double fans blew the smell of grease out to the highway. Tourists stopped by in their cutoffs and cover-ups, gulped iced tea and huckleberry shakes, and took off their reflector sunglasses to gawk at Flathead Lake shimmering just beyond the edge of the highway.

I'd been working up the courage to ask Nina out. I had a job at the Polson lumberyard and was finally making money. I put cash down on an El Camino, rented an apartment on the lake, and was ready to make my move. I planned to take Nina to Bigfork on a real date: after a meal at Showthyme, we'd go to the theater.

Summer unleashed the hottest spell on record. Heat sizzled the highway and glittered up from the shore. Squint became a dog on the prowl, a monster loosed on our tiny world. He slapped the asses of cocktail waitresses, leered at high-school girls, and spun nickels at them as he patrolled slowly past. Two teenagers from Browning got their skulls cracked and were left for dead but no one tattled. When old Bigshoe pissed behind the China Garden, Squint shattered every bone in his hands and still no one censured him, not even the whites. He whooped his siren without cause and gunned his car up on sidewalks to scare any Indian minding his own business. He turned his attention on Nina and pestered her relentlessly. He ignored the static of the dispatcher announcing disturbances—the damn Indians, always those damn Indians causing trouble for whites. Never the opposite, never whites like Squint causing Indians trouble. He let everyone know he was a big-shot son of a bitch who could shirk his duties to chase tail.

"Tell me where you live, baby girl," he said.

Nina tried to throw him off with kindness, play like she halfway cared, but that only made him more of a jackass.

"I'm going to find you," he said. "You know I have the means. I'll follow you home."

He wrapped his arms around her and gripped the back of her neck. "Please don't," I heard her say, and I stepped up. She swiped her hand at the window and cut me a pleading glance that said I'd only make matters worse. Whether for her or me, I couldn't tell. When Squint went to the head, Nina ducked outside and beelined for me. "You don't want to cause yourself trouble and please don't cause me any. But stay here," she said. "I have more I want to say to you."

I twisted a cigarette in my mouth and took a couple of drags. I thought she didn't want to be alone in the situation with Squint. She needed an ally, nothing more. We waited until Squint got into his cruiser and drove away. His heavy car humped up over the dirt road and as his front tires gripped the highway, his back tires spit gravel at a few customers lounging at the picnic tables. He was pissed.

Nina stood away from me to watch Squint leave. There was no glee in her watching. She waited until he was far down the road before she spoke: "He says he's going to come back for me." She rubbed her forehead and blinked away tears.

It was late. She closed up shop, slung her backpack over her shoulder, and headed toward the highway. "Don't follow me," she said. "I mean it."

But I did follow. I followed her on foot until she disappeared into the dark fields beyond the road. I called out but I'd lost her as if she'd vanished before my eyes. I'd become her second stalker. Lurking around. Chasing where I wasn't wanted.

I tried to conjure Nina's soothing voice telling me to calm down, tried to turn my thoughts from the Sig Sauer in my glove box. I didn't wish to cause Nina trouble. She needed this job and everyone knew it. It wouldn't do her any good if I was to pop a cap in his ass, but I had to make Squint back off. He was out of control.

I arrived at eight in the morning, the quiet time at Custer's. The regulars were drinking coffee and eating cinnamon rolls. It was already a scorcher, so hot my coffee didn't even steam the air. My stomach quivered. I had the peculiar feeling something was gaining on me. Squint wasn't going to give up his pursuit of Nina. There was no place to go but ugly from here.

Nina had just finished her prep work and was ready to

hear me out when I caught sight of an old pickup. I don't know what drew my attention, maybe a jagged flash of chrome. The pickup was miles away, just a speck on the horizon, but I swear I heard its engine. I wasn't the only one. As the vehicle covered ground we watched a bad-ass wind barrel round and round behind it, making its own crazy static.

Toolbox came out, whistled, then scurried back inside. I took off my shades. Man-sized tornadoes spun in the wake of the pickup, sparking tiny arrows of blue lightning. Wind rushed the fields and the muggy heat licked us like a pup.

Indian kids made for their cars. Old Indians limped away quick.

"If you know what's good for you," Angelina Thump Bird told me, "you'll skedaddle."

Nina raised the service screen and pushed herself halfway out the window to get a better look at the speeding truck. Her shirt hiked up to reveal the small of her back, the sensuous curve of her lean spine. "Shit," she said.

She swiped her forehead with the back of her hand and jumped down. She didn't take her eyes off the approaching truck. She reached over, switched off the coffee urn, and dumped the whole pot into the sink. Toolbox and Smug hid behind the ice-cream machine. Nina closed all the blinds and turned off the ever-blinking arrow sign. She slammed the window closed and flipped the sign on the door. *SHUT UP*, the sign read.

I stood beneath the arrow sign wondering what the hell was going on. I felt peculiarly alone. The only dumb-ass facing a churning funnel. A fierce wind roiled around me and I had to catch myself or fall. The wiry-haired Indian gunned his pickup and trundled toward the stand. The trash barrel tipped over and rolled toward the highway; napkins, paper cups, and greasy baskets flittered across the road and littered the fields. Hail pelted a twenty-foot circumference directly over Custer's. I tented my newspaper above my head and wondered if I was in my right mind. The sun shimmered down and cars kept passing, their drivers oblivious.

The Indian shunted his pickup around back of the stand and I heard the familiar slam of Custer's door. When Nina spotted me she gestured wildly, and before I could understand what she was trying to communicate, the old Indian was turning toward me.

In my nightmares, one bad dream plays over and over again: the hit-and-run. I hear ribs shatter, the snickering thunder of kneecaps striking earth, the hollow *ker-blonk* sound of a man's skull batting from grille to undercarriage. And now I smelled the acrid bloom of singed hair as the nightmare leaped from the Indian's palm.

I woke up in the bed of my El Camino—red as a red dog, my skin almost seared. I sat up and saw sparks of light. I couldn't tell how long I'd been out. What had happened to me?

The doctor took one look at the scattershot wounds that'd blown clean through my arms and legs and asked if I needed counseling. When I said no, he shook his head. "You don't like yourself," he said. I called in sick.

A little over a week later I limped my way back to Custer's and sat at the rickety picnic table. I didn't have enough energy to get a drink. The Indians kept their distance and I couldn't blame them. I looked worse for the wear—torn up. Nina came out with a cup of coffee, a weak offering. She sat across the table from me. "I should have warned you," she said. "But really, it's nothing you need to know. And nothing that can be any good for you."

I didn't understand but knew I wasn't meant to. "You mean, it's none of my business," I responded.

She patted her lips lightly. "That wouldn't be exactly right. I'm not trying to scold you." She touched my hand. "I'm trying to save you."

I didn't ask questions. I figured she'd tell me what she wanted to tell me, eventually. My ribs ached. Dry heat pulsed in my throat. I gulped my coffee.

"My grandfather didn't mean to hurt you," she said. A car passed by on Highway 93 and we heard the *tick tick tick* of studs. Nina was watchful but didn't look at me as she spoke. "Grandpa Magpie is scary crazy these days. He sees things other people don't. It's hard to explain. If it were only his dementia . . ." She shrugged. "If he doesn't like someone, well, that person kind of goes away." Her Salish accent gave the bad news a lilt.

The other Indians had gathered at the table behind her, listening to our conversation. "He got help, don't he?" Myra Little Bull asked. "Sure, he got that social worker. Snooping around. Shaking her big white finger. That's what those social workers do. Aye." The other Indians laughed and jostled each other.

Nina reached over for Joe Elder's cigarette. She pulled a long smoke then streamed it out her thin nose. "You guys didn't hear?" she said. "She disappeared about a week ago. They found her car straddling the road edge."

They quieted down. Angelina Thump Bird gazed at me. "Don't know what we're gonna do."

"All I need," Nina said, "is to have Squint follow me. Wouldn't that be great. I even told the tribal police not to go up there. To wait it out until I got some help."

Little Bull gripped her elbows and rocked back and forth. "We need a medicine doin's."

"Go home and heal up," Nina told me.

A car pulled up to the stand and a family threw open their doors but didn't move. They argued about the menu. "It's a joke," the woman said, applying her bright pink lipstick. "I sure as hell wouldn't eat here."

A fat boy struggled out of the backseat. "I want a JOE-RAN-imo," he announced.

Nina turned to me. "I gotta go, but come back when you're feeling better. I've got a surprise for you."

I'd had all the surprises I could take. I'd been off work for more than a week and I had some thinking to do. I told the boss I couldn't shake the flu and that I was giving notice. I hated to do it; I'd just been promoted to yard foreman and I liked my job.

I went home and slept. Out my door, Flathead Lake lapped the rocky shore. I drifted off and imagined I was swimming out to the deepest part of the water, out where the Flathead Lake Monster was hiding, and woke with the idea that there were things beyond my knowing in these mountains that only the Indians understood.

I thought about Nina working endlessly in Squint's hellish kitchen, how Custer's Last Stand really was a joke, another way for the white man to grind the Indians down and trivialize their victories. Can't beat 'em, make fun of 'em. Nina was between a rock and a hard place. I didn't understand what was going on with her grandfather, but knew it had something to do with dementia and his medicine powers run amuck, and deep down I was afraid. What if her grandfather did have the power to kill someone with his feelings? Or worse: what if he knew what I had done? I turned the idea over and over in my head until I was sick with it.

* * *

I was nursing a cup of coffee at the Polson Bakery. I didn't want to keep showing Nina how weak I'd become, how I'd got the stuffing knocked out of me, so I'd begun avoiding the stand. I was about ready to settle up when Squint came into the bakery and plopped down at a table not far from me. I'd lost so much weight I didn't think he'd recognize me. He slurped his soup and chomped his sandwich in three bites. His appetite sickened me. Squint surveyed the coffee shop, nodding at a few customers who shifted uneasily. He was about to leave when he took a hard look in my direction. I kept my head down as he sized me up.

He swaggered over to me and pushed back his hat. "I don't allow vagabonds in my town," he said. "And if I see you around here again, I'm going to haul you in." He stabbed his toothpick between his front teeth and smiled. "And if I catch you near that squaw again, it's not going to be pretty—*she's* not going to be pretty. Get my drift?" He gazed around the room to make sure he'd been heard.

My first thought was to be flattered, bowled over with giddiness, and that's when I knew I was in a world of shit. A man can get in trouble with the law; he can be obsessed with motorcycles and fast cars; he can drive himself to ruin with gambling and drink—but if a woman even shadows the frame of his life, if she begins to be his first thought in matters where he should be thinking, then he's already gone. I'd fallen in love with Nina Three Dresses, and Squint saw me as a threat. One big, glorious hallelujah!

I decided to keep my mouth shut and let it pass. I'd get even with the son of a bitch another way. But just as he turned to leave and his grubby mitt touched the door, I got a stab of inspiration.

"You don't have to worry no more," I called out.

Four old men who'd been gossiping stopped midsentence and glared at me, then at Squint.

"The two of us are heading south this evening. All she's gotta do is pack her bags and we're outta here. You get *my* drift?"

Squint gave me the kind of look that could fry eggs. He stopped picking his teeth and let the toothpick teeter in his mouth. "We'll see about that," he said. "We'll just see about that." I'd stepped into a scene from *High Noon*, an old-fashioned showdown between men where the woman would take the hurt.

My heart was a furiously ticking time bomb. I'd taken too big a risk. I should have headed over to the stand, talked to Nina, told her what I'd done. But I knew Squint would be on my tail. I'd counted on that, hadn't I? It was my ace in the hole. He'd follow me. Jesus, he'd follow me to hell.

I waited until Nina got off work and then I waited awhile more. The seconds ticked. Stink rolled down my rib cage in small rivulets and stars circled my head. I wondered if I'd ever feel right again. Yet that didn't matter. Nothing mattered but Nina, her future, and her happiness.

When the evening light rippled over the lake and the stars emerged, I got in the El Camino and headed slowly into town. I picked up a carton of cigarettes at the Town Pump. I checked my rearview mirror but saw no sign of Squint. I waited and then drove like a weary old man. I smoked three cigarettes while I searched. I canvassed the alleyways, the spaces behind the 4B's, and Walmart, but caught no sign of him. I blasted music. Bass thundered through the soles of my feet, edged up my spine, and flared out the windows like a flag, and still no sign of Squint. I rubbed my wet palms on my jeans and drove on, a man determined. I'd banked everything on an idea only a nutcase would believe.

I cracked a beer and took a long tug and headed up the east shore. I'd been up Hell Roaring many times and knew every sharp turn, every dry dip. As I followed the first curve up the road, dust sparkled in my headlamps like a sorcerer's mist. An electric charge hummed along the hood of the El Camino. Weird sparks lit the ends of my fingers. My funny bone was lit. Hell Roaring behind me, ahead of me, and still no sign of Squint. The thin moon smiled wickedly over the valley as I gunned the engine and headed up and up that dark road.

I came to the road chain and jumped out. I worked steadily, sawing through the link until it clanked off. I tossed the chain aside. The wind began to pick up, snarling through the trees and creating a bluish blister around me. I smelled the scent of freedom that is older than time, a scent immune to white civilization. For a reeling moment, the scars of my long-ago sadness disappeared. Then I heard a relentless chuffing, an engine grinding low. I cupped my ear to listen. Spinning tires huffed along the road below, growling, coming for me.

I continued onward, upward. The smell of elk piss wafted through my windows. The road was a thin gray tongue over hell's chasm. No road barriers. No fences. Nothing to save me but the thought of Nina. I spotted the white Buick half on, half off the road, straddled precariously over the darkness. One little push and it would clatter mercilessly off the cliff edge. One tire slip from me, and off it'd go. It had to be the social worker's car that Nina had spoken about, but I wouldn't risk edging past it.

I stopped dead center in the road and checked my glove box. No flashlight. I could smell the oily dust beneath the carriage of my car, the only thing that made the night seem real.

I'd driven a long way and had only a few more steps to go. The windows of the Buick glinted and flashed in the flimsy light of the moon, but just past the curve was Magpie's house—all its windows dark. An engine died behind me. I heard cussing. A thin light jittered up the road, then a tunnel of light roiled over the deep canyon, and I wanted to snicker with glee. My plan was working. The flashlight shot up past the line of trees and I skittered into the bushes.

Grandpa Magpie's shack sat perched above me. I'd seen this place way back when I was a teenager and had looked through the windows at the tidy kitchen, a few scrubbed pots hanging from the wall, a kettle boiling on the stove. I remembered I couldn't fathom how anyone could live up here, let alone survive the brutal winters.

I could make out a hundred tiny flags on the switchback path that led up to the house. I heard Squint's hard breath as he worked his way up the first step. Suddenly, an eerie light illuminated the darkness and for a second I was blind.

"Harold?" Nina's voice called. "Is that you?"

The thought crossed my mind that she was calling someone else. But Harold was my name.

"Stay where you are," she said. "Don't come any closer." She lifted the kerosene lantern and I saw Squint's oily eyes, his smug face haloed by darkness.

Nina gasped. "Officer Custer, don't. Please go away. You're in danger."

He chortled and quickened his stride. As he passed the first flag, a rattling gust blew so hard his hat flew off and tumbled down the road and off the embankment. He thrust his hands out to steady himself but continued onward, pitching unnaturally forward like a cartoon character. His clothing plastered his body and his coat flapped behind him. He was heading toward Nina but each time he passed a flag the wind would abruptly change and knock him backward and sideways. A shadow moved behind Nina and she retreated into the house.

"I warned you!" she shouted back. "I'm sorry!"

A sound careened from the old Indian's body, a warble that issued from his chest, a buzzy zing. Trees groaned and cracked around me. I felt jazzed, electrified. Squint's eyes flashed in terror. He was lit up, a gigantic neon-road-sign pig. His hair frazzled red like lit grass. I smelled burning fingernails, the old body scent of death. It came to me that I was only dreaming as I watched Squint sail through the night and wing out over the edge of the precipice to fall forever into the pitch darkness from where he'd come. The last thing I saw in the whistling night was the young man I had hit. He was smiling. He was alive.

The boss had left a message on my phone. My job was still waiting for me. I combed my hair and brushed my teeth. It was eight in the morning. I'd been asleep for three days. I got in my El Camino and was headed for the Polson Bakery when I changed my mind. I turned toward the mountains, toward Nina and Custer's Last Stand. I had a burning desire to see her.

I parked and watched her from my car. The windows of the stand gleamed as if someone had polished them to a squeak. I caught a whiff of fresh food—not fries or stale hamburgers, but good food. I smiled when Nina spotted me, smiled so wide my face hurt. I felt better than I had in years, better than I ever could or should. She took off her apron and unleashed her hair. Her beautiful hair tumbled down and the sun shone on her face.

"You would not believe what happened," she said. "Never in a million years." The concussive sound of wind drummed my ears. Her hair glittered with brilliant light. "He's gone. And even stranger . . ." She patted her chest and her eyes welled up. "His wife turned the place over to me. Just like that. Said she wanted none of it. I sign the papers this afternoon."

"Did it really happen?" I asked, dumbfounded at the larger question that loomed before us.

Nina didn't answer. She went back inside and poured me a large cup of coffee with real cream. All the stupid signs had been torn down. Now it was coffee, the best buffalo burger in the state of Montana. There were boxes of fresh vegetables on the counter. *Buy local. Buy organic. Buy Indian-made.*

She raised an eyebrow. "You're with me, aren't you?"

I looked off toward the blue Mission Mountains and understood their power was something akin to magic. "Yes," I said, "I'm with you."

RED SKIES OF MONTANA
BY KEIR GRAFF

Lolo

Sidd breathed hard as his shoes crunched the gravel. He thought: *You can't outrun smoke.*

He'd woken early to run his eight kilometers before the sun rose above the mountains and began to scorch the brown hills of the Bitterroot Valley. He loved the quietness, broken only by the *scree* of a cricket, the *twee twee* of a bird, the distant burr of an engine on the highway. After only two years in Montana, he was still unused to the exhilarating joy of being alone.

The cold nights, too, gave him a thrill, and it was a pleasure to be awake when the first rays of sunlight topped the mountains to warm his skin.

On a normal morning, the light would have had a lovely violet tint. Today it was just brown. Smoke from Idaho wildfires had been drifting east for more than a week, dimming the stars, blunting the sun, and, if the way he was gasping now was any indication, infiltrating his lungs.

Exercise in such foul air was probably worse than no exercise at all. He worked phlegm out of his throat and spat, laboring toward the Y in the road where he usually turned around.

He had grown up in heat and humidity, the air dense with smells of food, flowers, and garbage. He had come here to get away from all that. But he had not known about the fires.

Sidd had been told about the renewing qualities of fire,

how forests needed to burn so new growth could emerge. Some pine trees actually required the heat of a fire to release the seeds from their fallen cones. Old brush and dead trees became ash so green shoots could emerge on the forest floor.

He read about fires in Canada and Siberia that might not burn out until they had exhausted their tinder. He knew about rising temperatures, thawing permafrost, and melting ice caps. And Montana was so dry that the Forest Service fire-danger signs seemed permanently set at VERY HIGH and EXTREME. He wondered whether there came a time when the old rules ceased to apply.

Reaching the Y, he jogged a circle in the road, his trainers puffing dust as fine and arid as Martian soil, and turned back. Most of the road was monotonously straight, but a curve and a drop here, combined with the robust fringe of knapweed on the bank, made it a blind corner for cars coming up from behind.

Sidd heard gravel popping under the truck's tires before he heard its engine, a throaty V8. He stumbled into the weeds and pressed himself against the bank.

The black truck pulled up next to him, its window down. The driver leaned forward and shouted across a gray-bearded man in the passenger seat who was concentrating on something in his lap. "Wear some lighter clothes, asshole!" The man had mirrored, wraparound sunglasses resting on the bill of his baseball cap.

Sidd looked down at what he was wearing. Navy T-shirt, black shorts, blue running shoes. Should he apologize?

"I'm trying to save your goddamn life!" The man gunned the engine and the truck sprayed gravel and surged forward. A pebble stung Sidd's shin like a wasp.

It wasn't until the white GMC on the truck's tailgate had

disappeared around the bend that Sidd started running again, shakily, wondering whether the man would have said anything about his clothes if his skin hadn't been dark as well.

Poe pounded the wheel. "Swear to fucking God, you could pack into the Bob Marshall and some fucking jogger would still run through your camp in his underwear."

"That was stupid," said Mike, barely looking up from the glowing rectangle in the palm of his massive left hand.

"Woulda been more stupid if we came back with him stuck in the grille."

"Maybe better that way."

Thing was, Mike was right. It was stupid. Yell at some guy, he was that much more likely to remember seeing your truck. Poe had been trying not to lose his shit so easily lately, but no sooner had he promised himself he'd be Clint Eastwood–quiet than he was ragging on someone again.

Mike poked at the screen, calm as ever. Even when he said, *That was stupid*, it was like he was saying, *Pull over at the next gas station.* And if anyone had a right to be pissed at the world, it was Mike. Poor son of a bitch had only been out of Deer Lodge for a couple of months and it must have been like landing on an alien planet. He was so 1980s he still wore a fanny pack.

He'd also never seen a smartphone except on TV and now he couldn't stop playing the game Poe's daughter had downloaded for him. Poe had been around enough addicts not to fall for the free first taste, but Mike was hooked on Candy Crush crack.

Poe needed an extra set of hands and figured that Mike, who was still on parole, had plenty of incentive to keep his mouth shut about the job. That, and he was Poe's cousin's ex-husband and she'd been all over Poe to help Mike out. She needed money, so Mike needed money.

A low voice said, "Sweet!" as the big man took out a row of jellybeans or something.

"How's the game going?" Poe asked. "You win yet?"

"I think this is made for little kids' fingers," Mike said without looking up.

"Think you'll be able to take a break in a minute? We're almost there."

Mike nodded but kept playing. Good thing he wasn't behind the wheel. Poe was sure they didn't teach inmates about the dangers of distracted driving. He held the wheel carefully as the road went steadily up.

Poe wasn't a firebug by nature, but his first job, a foreclosed lumber warehouse, had been a career-maker. Though he'd torched a lot of things since then, this was his first ski resort. Well, it wasn't a ski resort yet, and if he did his job right, it wouldn't be.

The thing had been going on for years. Poe had seen headlines in the *Missoulian* a couple of times. Awhile back, Betty Jean Allaway, whose family had ranched the western half of the valley for almost 150 years, had surprised the shit out of everyone by marrying Bucky Severson, her ranch manager. Betty Jean was older than Bucky and didn't have any kids. When she died, Bucky inherited the whole spread and got it in his head that he was going to build a ski resort on the part that covered the north side of Lolo Peak—and not just any ski resort, but the biggest one in North America.

With the way society was going, you couldn't put up a fireworks tent without a shit ton of paperwork. Even Poe knew a ski resort was bound to be a ten-year project at least. But Bucky being Bucky, he went and bulldozed the ski runs anyway to get a jump-start. Maybe he figured that once people saw the potential, they'd say, *What the hell, you might as well finish.*

They didn't. Once the environmentalists got involved, the whole thing was doomed. Bucky didn't see it, so he lawyered up and got ready to fight to the bitter end. But apparently the developers he'd partnered with foresaw a different outcome. Because they were the ones who'd sent someone to find someone to burn the whole thing down a week before the Montana Supreme Court reached its bound-to-be-unfavorable decision.

Poe had no proof he was working for WashIdaMont Development Partners. As far as he knew, he was working for the guy who'd slipped him $2,500 in worn bills behind Lucky Lil's Casino. But there had to be insurance money, money that might not be on the table once the project was officially declared unviable. That's how things worked, right? What they were paying Poe—half down, half on completion—probably came out of the coffee fund. And Mike? Mike was more than happy to take home five hundred dollars for a morning's work. Given that his ex-wife had laid claim to the forty cents an hour he'd earned working in the prison bakery, it was the most money he'd seen at one time in twenty-seven years.

Reaching the first switchback, Poe turned the wheel and geared down. The truck climbed into the trees.

Siddharth Ghosh was an unlikely caretaker. But the world itself was unlikely—how else could he account for the fact that he was living in a trailer on a mountain in Montana, halfway around the world from where he'd grown up?

As a child, he'd felt perfectly at home in Mumbai. The heat, the rain, and the crowds were mundane obstacles his family navigated with good-humored exasperation. Even the city's uneasy relationship with the sea and the saltwater that flooded the sewers at high tide seemed part of a natural pattern of ebb and flow.

Then came July 26, 2005. When the skies opened, it felt as though there had been another ocean hiding in the clouds. Rain fell so hard and so fast that Sidd, watching schoolmates make desperate dashes to their waiting parents, imagined it might be possible to drown on two feet.

Twelve years old, Sidd himself remained stuck at school overnight, unable to go home once the trains stopped moving. In the dark, he sat with his English teacher and listened to the news reports on a battery-powered radio barely audible over the water battering the roof.

Sidd's father reached him late the following afternoon on an army truck with giant wheels. He brought bad news: Aunt Janani, his mother's beloved sister, had drowned in her car, unable to open her doors against the rising water.

His family mourned but seemed to recover. Sidd could not. From that day, he lived in Mumbai as if under siege. The jostling crowds frightened him. The sea became an enemy. Monsoon season brought with it unrelenting anxiety, the wet air and mold seeming to foretell a watery doom. A teenage recluse, Sidd paged obsessively through his late aunt's collection of *National Geographic*, an American magazine to which she had been peculiarly devoted. From the May 1976 issue, he cut out a picture of a snowcapped mountain in Montana. It seemed dry, cold, and tranquil—everything Mumbai was not.

In time, Sidd's older sister left Mumbai for the London School of Economics, and his brother was accepted to Stanford. Sidd, since the Maharashtra floods no more than a dutiful student, had fewer options. He earned his BS in chemistry at Mumbai University while plotting his escape to Montana.

Accepted to the graduate chemistry program at the University of Montana, he arrived on a hot and dry August day, emerging from Missoula International Airport like a grateful refugee. In his new school, he was surprised to find himself treated as an academic superstar—and to discover that India was not the only country struggling with the legacy of a caste system.

Most of his fellow students scrupulously avoided the subjects of race and skin color in his presence, while others went out of their way to remind him that they were color-blind. The wife of one professor rhapsodized about her months at an ashram in upstate New York, where she had temporarily taken the name Mavis Devi.

At the Oxford bar on Higgins Avenue, during a graduate-student pub crawl Sidd had endured as a forced march, two cigarette-voiced barflies had loudly debated whether he was a "feather Indian" or a "dot Indian" while everyone stared at their beers as if looking for signs. Sidd wondered if his color-blind new friends were color-deaf too.

By his second year, his grades were slipping. When his academic advisor suggested that maybe he needed a break, he grasped at her offhand advice like a lifeline and canceled his classes for spring semester. He lost his housing and his teaching stipend, but he didn't tell his parents. He didn't want to go home.

He found employment in a *Missoulian* help-wanted ad for a caretaker. The job paid poorly but included lodging and use of a vehicle. The interview, curiously, was held at the office of a local lawyer. A man named Buck Severson asked the questions while his lawyer keyed his laptop and frowned at the screen.

Very few of the questions had anything to do with his duties, which apparently involved looking after a large, rural property south of town. Severson wanted to know whether Sidd was an environmentalist (he didn't think so), whether he had voted in any local or state elections (as a citizen of India, he had not), and, puzzlingly, if he was a skiier (he wasn't; snow still made him feel like he was hallucinating, so he wasn't sure he could trust it to cushion his falls).

All his answers except the last one seemed to please Severson, who, after a whispered consultation with his attorney, offered him the job as caretaker of the Montana Gold Ski Resort.

Severson gave him a ride out that very afternoon, and it was only as they bumped up a road toward the site that Sidd realized the resort did not yet exist.

"But it will!" exclaimed Severson, a red-faced man whose arms were so small compared to his burly torso that they seemed like vestigial limbs. "Any great visionary has his doubters. When these suckers realize what it's going to do for the local economy, they're gonna build a statue of old Buck Severson."

Passing through a gate hung with signs that said, *NO TRESPASSING*, and, *FUTURE SITE OF THE LARGEST SKI RESORT IN NORTH AMERICA*, Severson shifted into four-wheel drive to give Sidd a tour of the property. Ski runs had been carved into the forest, leaving stumps and rocks behind.

As if making a pitch to a prospective investor, Severson pointed out the sites he had planned for the grand lodge with its roaring fireplace and Western bar, the condominium chalets, the pro shop, and several restaurants. Here would be the bunny slope, there would go the lifts, and right in front of them the buses bringing skiiers from the airport would drop off their cargo, turn around, and head out for more.

Severson was a good salesman. Sidd went from being skeptical that such a thing could be accomplished to vividly seeing it in his own mind. Instead of thinking of the job as a chance to regroup before resuming school, he imagined that if he worked hard enough, he might someday be managing Severson's ski resort. Perhaps he would even learn to ski.

After the tour, with Sidd feeling slightly seasick, Severson bumped over primitive roads to the only two structures that occupied the land so far: Severson's palatial log home and the dented trailer just down the road where Sidd would stay.

"I'm not here as much as I'd like," said Severson. "I still run the ranch, plus they got me flying all over the place pitching investors. It's a grind but it's gonna pay off."

"So I'm supposed to . . ."

"You're supposed to protect the investment. We need someone here basically 24-7. Look after my house and water the yard. Ride the property on a four-wheeler every day, check the fence, and make sure nobody's torn down a *No Trespassing* sign. Kill the gophers. Carry a shotgun in case any sandal-wearers hike through. You know how to shoot, don't you?"

Under Severson's brusque one-time tutelage, Sidd had learned to load and shoot the gun. Badly bruising his shoulder, he had pockmarked a tree stump, mutilated a plastic gasoline can, and murdered several other inanimate objects.

Mike opened the gate and waited for Poe to drive through so he could close it behind them. You could take the boy off the ranch and send him to prison for armed robbery, but he'd still remove his hat when a lady came into the room.

"Leave it open," called Poe. "We might need to leave quick."

Mike got back in, adjusted his fanny pack under his belly, and they rolled up the road. Poe hadn't scouted the site because he hadn't wanted to risk being spotted in the area. When he came to a fork in the road, he guessed and turned left, following a couple of tight switchbacks past an old trailer with a four-wheeler out front, before dead-ending at a varnished log palace with picture windows that must have given an IMAX view of the valley.

"Well, this ain't it," Poe grumbled, starting a three-point turn.

Mike unlocked the phone and started poking the screen again. Poe grabbed it out of his hands and dropped it into his own shirt pocket. Mike tensed, and Poe wondered if the guy was really as mellow as he seemed.

Poe nodded toward the windshield. "Look around. We're on the job. I'm not paying you to play video games."

Mike stared at his shirt pocket and for a long second Poe thought he was going to reach out and take the phone back. Poe looked away first and started driving back down the direction they'd come. Mike would not have gotten fucked with in the yard.

This time, they took the right-hand turn, which rose at a steady grade across the face of the hill. It was wider than the other one.

"This is the way," said Poe confidently. "They got this wide enough for two busses to pass on the corners and the drivers to high-five."

Then the road ended in a flat, open field of churned dirt, with weeds and pine seedlings poking through and ski runs carved out of the forest going up and out of sight. Poe put the transmission in park.

"No ski lodge, no lifts. What the hell are we supposed to burn?"

Mike dug in his beard like he was probing for ticks. "They didn't give you instructions?"

Poe remembered that fleeting moment in the parking lot of Lucky Lil's when he'd thought it was too easy, that the guy should have said something more. Or that he should have asked a follow-up question. But this was another problem he'd always struggled with: as much as he ran his mouth, he hated looking stupid, even when one simple question could save him a world of trouble.

"*Burn down the Montana Gold Ski Resort*, is what the man said," he told Mike. "That's it."

Mike leaned forward, putting his face right next to the windshield, so he could look up the mountain to where the stubbled ski runs disappeared into the haze. Dawn was breaking across the valley, making the air glow like a washed-out kitchen curtain.

"Maybe he meant to burn down *all* of this. Burn down the mountain."

Sidd pulled the gate closed behind him and looped the chain over the post. He always left it cracked when he went out for a run, but the breeze must have creaked it wide open. Not something he wanted Mr. Severson to see—the next time, he would shut it properly.

He went slowly up the road, barely faster than walking, the smoke getting thicker as he climbed higher. He thought he could taste dust, as if someone had just driven by. But Mr. Severson was still in Chicago, talking to potential investors.

Twelve thousand years ago, these valleys had been lakes filled with water backed up behind an icy dam. There was no evidence of that water now. Sidd had walked trails in the forest where the cracked dirt formed mosaics like a dry lake bed in a desert. The yellow grasses rustled and crunched like paper. Lightning strikes and stray sparks made fire a constant presence in summer, from the standing-next-to-a-campfire smell of smoke to the falling-ash smog of apocalypse. The first time he stood in the forest, it had been so quiet that he wondered whether anything survived here at all.

The water shortage did not bode well for Mr. Severson's dream. In his idle hours since taking the job, Sidd had read everything published online about the project and even some articles about the environmental forecast in Montana. To begin with, the lower ski runs were at too low an altitude, and snowfall would be uncertain each season, even more so as global warming wreaked havoc on weather patterns. The higher ski runs, which would have better snowpack, were not contiguous with the lower ones. Mr. Severson was counting on skiers' willingness to take shuttles between the two.

To Sidd's amazement, many modern ski resorts relied on huge machines that manufactured artificial snow. Water was required to make snow. Sidd saw now that Severson had counted on the goodwill and forbearance of so many people and government agencies that the project had almost certainly been doomed from the beginning. In years long past, the land owner could have played king, but Severson didn't even own the land now. He had signed over the deed to the Montana Gold Ski Corporation in exchange for a minority share of future profits.

The trailer almost in sight, Sidd slowed the four-wheeler. Again he tasted dust, and wondered whether it was carried on a hot wind. He knew that huge forest fires created their own chaotic climates, the oxygen-hungry blaze producing gusts that could howl like freight trains. But the fires in Idaho were nowhere near that close.

Even though he no longer believed the Montana Gold Ski Resort was viable, Sidd was still happy as its caretaker. He didn't fully understand his duties and sometimes felt he was cheating Buck out of his meager pay, but he loved the solitude and had come to love the land itself. The ski runs had scarred it and the persistent drought had choked it, but he knew now that he was wrong about its lifelessness. All he had to do was sit still. Large birds of prey wheeled on thermal currents, and deer came to lap the water that pooled around the sprinklers on the big house's green lawn. Sometimes it was so quiet he could hear beetles scratching in the dust.

Occasionally, at dawn or at twilight, he even glimpsed the gophers Mr. Severson so despised. Disobeying instructions, he hadn't shot at a single one.

He did his best with the other duties, though. He kept the four-wheeler fueled up and patrolled the land every day. And while the gopher invasion was real—the holes and mounds were proof of that—Sidd had yet to see a sandal-wearing conservationist, and the NO TRESPASSING signs had not been tampered with.

Winter was months away, but Sidd was anxious for his first one on the mountain. He was curious to see how deep the snow would fall. Buck had told him that riding a snowmobile was *more fun than bull-riding, not quite as fun as getting laid.*

Reaching the trailer's weedy yard, he stretched his hamstring and calf muscles, then worked the hand pump by the side of the trailer. He drank straight from the spout, the first mouthfuls of water lukewarm and tasting of iron. On a hot day, it was like drinking blood.

He worked the handle, letting water splash over the river stones that had been piled around the pipe to keep the yard from turning to mud. Then he drank again, gulping cooler water until his belly was full.

He walked to the edge of the yard and urinated into the trees, a genuine pleasure. It was in mundane moments like these that he knew he could never return to Mumbai. A man who belonged nowhere could live anywhere. This dry place would be his home.

Sidd liked to do his first patrol right after his run, before the sun grew too intense. It was best to change into jeans and a long-sleeve shirt to protect his arms and legs from the four-wheeler's hot metal and the rocks thrown by its knobby tires, but putting on clean clothes when he was sweaty was too unpleasant.

He climbed the railroad-tie steps, went into the dim trailer, and came out wearing the visored helmet and carrying the shotgun. He considered putting the shotgun back. He had already decided not to kill gophers, so logically it followed that he could not kill a human being. But nobody else knew he wasn't going to kill a human being, so he supposed the gun was at least good for show. If he did meet any of Buck's sandal-wearers, and if they refused to leave the property, he could always fire it into the air.

Sidd slung the gun over his shoulder, the thin membrane of his running shirt doing nothing to cushion the hard stock against his back. He tightened the helmet under his chin. Then he climbed on the four-wheeler and turned the key to start its engine.

The thing about arson was that it couldn't look like arson. Obviously. Insurance companies didn't pay out if they found a pile of melted gas cans at the place where the fire started. Poe did have two red five-gallon cans strapped in front of the wheel wells, but using an accelerant was an absolute last re-sort. Over his career Poe had figured out, usually by talking to contractors over cans of beer, a few simple ways of starting a fire and making it look like an accident.

"Why don't you just call him?" asked Mike.

Dumb shit had been in stir too long. He didn't even know why you didn't do business on a cell phone.

Poe put the truck in four-wheel drive and started easing up the slope. "Look, it makes sense. They got insurance for everything now. This place is insured as a ski resort. Scenery's part of the package. No one's gonna fly to Montana to vaca-tion in a moonscape."

They probably should have gotten out and hiked. The truck was lurching from side to side, and the undercarriage sounded like it was being swept with the wrong end of the broom. But he wanted to get this thing done.

At the top of the lowest ski run, there was a little bench and the ground leveled out into a meadow. Poe angled the truck toward a thicket of trees. "You think here?"

Mike didn't answer. He was tapping the screen again.

Unbelievable. Poe slapped the phone out of Mike's hands and it tumbled onto the floor mat. "Hey, Mike! You think this place is okay?"

Mike looked at him, and again Poe had the feeling that, if the sleepy man-mountain ever erupted, the crater would be deep and wide. But Mike glanced out the window and nod-ded. "Here's fine."

They climbed out of the truck, walked into the trees, and picked up rocks, which they arranged in a circle. Then they filled the circle with tinder-dry wood. The fake campfire sat right in the brittle yellow grass. Poe felt confident he'd be able to get the whole job done with one match.

"Good?" asked Mike, breaking a stick over his knee and leaning the pieces together like a teepee.

Poe thought, shook his head. "This looks like two guys drove up here to make a campfire. We need a stack of firewood next to it, logs to sit on, all that shit."

Mike rubbed his neck and then walked deeper into the trees. Poe heard him crunching around and wondered what went on in his head. Was he wishing he could get back to that video game? Missing his cage and his bunk?

Then Mike came back dragging a log so big Poe couldn't have managed it if there were two of him. He let it down with a grunt. "Bench."

They gathered more firewood and stacked it close to the fire ring. Poe pictured the campers as a couple of stoned college kids who don't know the first thing about fire safety.

"Needs trash," said Mike, and Poe was actually impressed.

"I got some beer cans. I'll wipe 'em down, but the fire'll burn off the prints anyways." Mike went back to the truck, knowing there would be empties rattling around in the bed. Yet when he came out of the trees, he stopped. The sun had cleared the bald hills to the east. The Bitterroot Valley was hidden by the flank of the mountain, but the Missoula Valley opened up below him to the north.

Brown smoke smothered the town like a winter air inversion, but above it, a steady wind had scoured the sky an aching, brilliant blue. It was like being in a plane above the clouds.

Then he heard a four-wheeler in the distance. It sounded like a VW Bus in reverse. He froze—no backup plan except to apologize, get the hell out of there, and try again in a few weeks. That's when he saw the rider. "What in Christ?"

"Oh boy." Mike was beside him.

It was the brown-skinned jogger from half an hour ago: same dark shirt and shorts. Only now he was wearing a helmet and had a shotgun strapped across his back.

Poe's first instinct was to open the cab and pull his Savage .270 out of the gun rack. But since it was fishing season, all he had to protect himself was the cheap Zebco rod he sometimes used to kill time. He never caught anything because he slept too late.

"You bring a gun?" asked Mike.

"Hell no, I didn't bring a gun. Nobody hired us to shoot anybody."

"I guess it's a good thing I did." Mike unzipped his fanny pack and took out a .38. It was small in his massive hand, and so old the bluing was wearing off. It looked like a $150 pawn-shop special.

Poe's stomach dropped. The big man really did want to go back to Deer Lodge.

Sidd's heart started hammering as soon as he came out of the trees and saw the men—real, live trespassers. It looked like one of them was holding a beer can, so hopefully they were just some "good old boys" enjoying a drink. But why had they driven so far up the mountain?

The whole thing was puzzling. Sidd braked the four-wheeler about fifty yards away. Buck had given him strict orders to show the shotgun and to fire a warning shot in the air if necessary, but he doubted it would come to that. "This is private property!" he shouted.

Then he saw the GMC on the side of the truck and realized that this was the one that had passed him while he was running, and the shorter man was the angry driver who'd yelled at him. Judging by the way he threw his beer can into the bed of the truck and spat on the ground, he was still angry.

Sidd suddenly had a powerful urge to fire the warning shot. As he pulled the shotgun over his head, the strap snagging on the back of his helmet, he saw the two men struggling over something. And then, as he raised the barrel of the shotgun in the air, the big man cuffed the smaller one, who staggered back. The big man leveled a small dark gun over the side of the truck.

Sidd didn't think. He dropped the barrel and squeezed the trigger. The big man ducked. The shotgun boomed and the recoil punched Sidd's shoulder, almost turning him sideways. The big man peered over the truck and shot twice. His breath loud in the helmet, feeling like a spaceman, Sidd peered down at his own body, checking for holes. Then he ejected the spent shotgun shell and fired again. The pellets ripped holes in the side of the truck, right above the gas-cap door.

The big man shot back again, and Sidd heard one of the bullets—he *heard* the bullet—whine past him.

Moving clumsily, as if a child were at the controls of his body, Sidd slung the gun around his neck and turned the four-wheeler down the slope, looking for cover. Swiveling his head, he saw the smaller man scramble into the cab. The truck started moving and the big man grabbed onto the tailgate, ran a few steps to keep pace, and pulled himself into the back, nearly getting thrown off as the truck lurched and bounced.

Sidd brought the four-wheeler around and braked. They were going up, toward what Mr. Severson had told him would be a black-diamond run.

He hesitated. Then he accelerated and went after them.

It was hard going up the slope in the four-wheeler—he had no idea how the truck was doing it. The white GMC on the tailgate blurred as the truck's tires chewed their way up the pockmarked slope. The man in the back rose up, aimed the gun, and lost his balance before he could shoot.

Sidd zigzagged back and forth, knowing it made no sense to follow but hating the intruders, wanting to chase them off Severson's land. *His* land.

The truck struggled as the pitch grew steeper. When the driver turned to take another diagonal line up the slope, Sidd half-expected the vehicle to roll over.

The underside of the four-wheeler struck a rock, so hard it almost jarred his palms loose from the handgrips. He smelled gas. He looked back and saw flames, little signal fires dotting the slope. *Sparks? A hot tailpipe?*

Then he looked forward and saw trails of fire behind the truck, moving unnaturally fast. At that moment he saw liquid sheeting out of the gap at the bottom of the tailgate. There was panic on the big man's face as he shouted to the driver and threw a large gas can, amber fuel draining from a dozen holes, beading and shining in the sunlight. Flame from the already-burning grass leaped up to meet it, ignited, and obscured the truck behind a sudden wall of flame.

Sidd stopped as another big red gas can arced through the air. He looked down the slope. The fire was spreading fast, the little islands joining together, the flames rising, smoke whipping. Once it spread from the grass to the trees it would explode. Men would climb the mountain to cut fire lines, and planes would drop orange plumes of retardant.

He turned the four-wheeler downhill, feeling a roller-coaster drop in his stomach, and aimed for a gap in the flames.

The heat from the rising sun was nothing compared to the heat from the fire. The sound, like ripping fabric, was louder than his engine. How could it spread so fast? He piloted the four-wheeler blind through a pocket of smoke, hitting a depression so hard his head almost banged the handlebars; he felt lost, felt fire singe his arms, panicked—and then he was through. Glancing up, he could just make out the truck fighting its way up the slope. He couldn't see the big man in the back.

Dawn was red. As smoke poured over the hills from the west, new smoke rose up from below. The hope of home was a dream for children. Sidd imagined the fire burning all the way to Idaho, through Washington, to the rising sea. Someday, someone would start a fire that would burn until all the fuel was gone.

ABOUT THE CONTRIBUTORS

Robyn Regan

DAVID ABRAMS is the author of the novels *Brave Deeds* and *Fobbit*. *Fobbit* was named a *New York Times* Notable Book of 2012, an Indie Next pick, a Barnes & Noble Discover Great New Writers selection, a Montana Honor Book, and a finalist for the *Los Angeles Times* Art Seidenbaum Award for First Fiction. His stories have appeared in *Esquire, Narrative, Glimmer Train,* and many other publications. He lives in Butte with his wife.

Richard Behan

JANET SKESLIEN CHARLES grew up in Shelby and attended the University of Montana. Her novel *Moonlight in Odessa*, which explores the business of e-mail-order brides, was translated into ten languages. She currently lives in Paris, France.

DEBRA MAGPIE EARLING is Bitterroot Salish and a member of the Flathead Nation. She is the author of the novels *Perma Red* and *The Lost Journals of Sacajewea*. She has been a recipient of an NEA grant, an American Book Award, and a Guggenheim Fellowship. She is currently the director of the creative writing program at the University of Montana.

Slikati Photography

GWEN FLORIO is an award-winning journalist who turned to fiction in 2013 with the publication of *Montana*, which won the Pinckley Prize for Debut Crime Fiction and a High Plains Book Award. *Disgraced* is the third novel in the Lola Wicks series, and two more are scheduled. Florio lives in Missoula.

Alan Alabastro

JAMIE FORD loves living in Great Falls, his home for seventeen years, though he occasionally calls it Adequate Falls. His debut novel, *Hotel on the Corner of Bitter and Sweet*, spent two years on the *New York Times* best-seller list and went on to win the 2010 Asian/Pacific American Award for Literature. His most recent novel, *Songs of Willow Frost*, was published in 2013. His work has been translated into thirty-four languages.

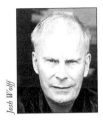

Josh Wolff

JAMES GRADY was born and raised in Shelby and graduated from the University of Montana. He was a research analyst for the state's 1972 Constitutional Convention and a legislative aide to Montana's US Senator Lee Metcalf during Watergate. Grady's first novel, *Six Days of the Condor*, became the iconic Robert Redford movie. He has published more than a dozen other novels, twice that many short stories, and worked as a national investigative reporter.

Zachary James Johnston

KEIR GRAFF was born and raised in Missoula, where he attended Hellgate High School and, briefly, the University of Montana. He is the author of four novels for adults (most recently *The Price of Liberty*), two novels for middle-graders, and many short stories. Graff now lives in Chicago, where he is the executive editor of *Booklist* and cohost of the popular Publishing Cocktails events. He returns to Montana every year.

Dagni Gleason

ERIC HEIDLE is a full-blooded Montanan-American working east of the divide as a creative director, writer, and photographer. In 2015 his story "At Jackson Creek" took first place in Montana Public Radio's fiftieth-anniversary short-fiction contest. Heidle's photography has appeared in *Montana Outdoors*, *Backpacker*, and other publications. When he's not at his desk, he is usually roaming the Rocky Mountain Front, paddling the Missouri, or failing to catch fish.

Alexis Daban

WALTER KIRN is the author of eight books and an e-book. His most recent is *Blood Will Out*, a memoir of his friendship with murderer Clark Rockefeller. His other books include *Up in the Air*, *Thumbsucker* (both of which have been made in to feature films), and *Mission to America*. A columnist for *Harper's*, he has also written for the *New Yorker*, the *New York Times Magazine*, the *New Republic*, *GQ*, *New York*, and *Esquire*. He lives much of the year in Livingston.

SIDNER LARSON is the former director of American Indian Studies at Iowa State University (2000–2015); an enrolled member of the Gros Ventre tribal community of Fort Belknap; and the author of *Catch Colt*, *Captured in the Middle*, and numerous academic articles and poems. He is currently teaching at the University of Arizona Law School and working on an indigenous peoples law book.

Dewey Vanderhoff

CARRIE LA SEUR is a Billings-based environmental lawyer whose debut novel, *The Home Place*, was on the Indie Next list, won a High Plains Book Award, and was a finalist for a Strand Critics' Circle Award. Her work has been published in the *Daily Beast, Grist*, the *Guardian*, the *Harvard Law and Policy Review, Huffington Post, Kenyon Review, Mother Jones, Oil, Gas and Energy Law, Salon*, and the *Yale Journal of International Law*.

Bruce Weber

THOMAS MCGUANE has written ten novels, beginning with *The Sporting Club* (1969), as well as three nonfiction essay collections and three short-story collections. His short fiction began regularly appearing in the *New Yorker* in 1994. McGuane's novel *Ninety-two in the Shade* was a finalist for the National Book Award, and other works have been included in *Best American Stories, Best American Essays, Best American Mystery Stories,* and *Best American Sporting Essays*. He lives near McLeod.

Phoebe Haefele

CAROLINE PATTERSON is the author of the story collection *Ballet at the Moose Lodge*. A former Stegner Fellow in fiction at Stanford University, she edited *Montana Women Writers: A Geography of the Heart* and published fiction in journals and magazines including *Alaska Quarterly Review, Big Sky Journal, Epoch, Southwest Review*, and *Seventeen*. She lives in Missoula, where she is the executive director for the Missoula Writing Collaborative.

Shawn Polen

YVONNE SENG has lived in Montana for most of the twenty-first century—in Missoula, Ovando, and Helena, where she was curator for the Holter Museum of Art—all after having worked extensively in the Middle East. Born in Australia, her first book was the nonfiction *Men in Black Dresses: A Quest for the Future Among Wisdom-Makers of the Middle East*. Her short fiction has appeared in the anthology *Explosions: Stories of Our Landmined World* and the literary journal *Gargoyle*.